The Timeless Apostle

by Kenneth Urbansky

SUTTON, ALASKA

Relevant Publishers LLC
P.O. Box 505
Sutton, AK 99674

www.relevantpublishers.com

Publisher's Cataloging-In-Publication Data

Names: Urbansky, Kenneth., author.
Title: The Timeless Apostle / written by Kenneth Urbansky

Identifiers: LCCN: 2023947155 | ISBN 978-1953263216 (paperback) | ISBN 978-1953263223 (ebook)

Printed in the United States of America

A Christian Inspirational Classic

For more great books, check out:

www.relevantpublishers.com

TABLE OF CONTENTS

CHAPTER 1
Tommy Evans

Knock, knock, knock.

"Tommy, it's time to get up, honey."

The pounding made sense, but the woman's voice didn't belong there.

Knock, knock, knock.

"Tommy?"

In my dream, I was back on the job site at Uncle Leon's construction company, where I'd spent the summer between high school and college.

Knock, knock, knock.

"Tommy? Are you alright?"

That was definitely my mother's voice, but why? Why is she at the construction site? She shouldn't be here.

The foreman was chewing out half a dozen grunts by the cement mixer, using words my mother probably never heard before. The crude joke one of the masons just told still had some of the guys laughing.

No, Mom, go away...please...go away!

"Thomas, let's go! Right now, son," My dad's shout from the hallway jolted me awake. "Breakfast will be on the table in a few minutes. The bathroom is free. Now, let's go! We leave for church in less than an hour."

I rubbed the sleep from my eyes. "Jesus! What time is it?"

"It's eight o'clock, and don't take the Lord's name in vain. I'll see you downstairs. Now get a move on. Put on something decent for a change."

"I'm not going to church."

The silence was exactly what I expected. I could almost see my father's six foot two inch, two hundred twenty pound frame standing in the hallway with fists clenched, jaw set, desperately trying to get his anger under control. I wasn't expecting my door to come flying open, slamming against the dresser, followed by his six-foot frame storming into my bedroom.

"Boy, as long as you sleep under my roof and eat at my table you'll do as I say! And that means going to church like everyone else in this house. And if you think you can come waltzing home at three in the morning and lay in bed all day, you've got another think coming. After church, we'll talk about what you're going to do with your life now that you've been kicked out of college."

The snort my dad made when he said, "what you're going to do with your life" told me everything I needed to know about what he thought of my chances of having a successful future. Of course, I'd known for a long time what he thought of me. In his eyes, I was a total failure, especially as a Christian.

"I'm not going to church, Dad. I'll be here when you get home. We can talk then."

When he took a step toward me, I thought he intended to drag me out of bed, but he stopped dead in his tracks when he heard my mother say something neither of us ever heard before.

"Tommy, please, it's important."

"What did you say, Mom?" I sat up as she stepped into my room. I couldn't believe she'd spoken up during one of my arguments with Dad. By the stunned look on his face, Dad couldn't believe it either.

"Would you please come to church with me this morning?" she asked. "I think the Lord has something special for you today. Please, Tommy, it's important to me, just this one last time. After today, I won't ask you again. I promise."

"If he is going to stay in this house—"

"Gene, could we please talk about that later?" She turned to me again, "Tommy, please." Her eyes pleading as much as the tone in her voice.

Outwardly, my mom always played the part of the quiet, submissive Christian wife. But I knew she possessed an inner strength which had single-handedly held our family together over the years. Despite rejecting her foolish religious beliefs, I still admired her sincerity and commitment to our family. And never once, no matter how much I put her through, did I ever doubt her love for me.

"Sure, Mom," I reached out and squeezed her hand. "I'll be ready in a minute. Why don't you wait for me downstairs?

I listened to my parent's fading footsteps as they receded down the carpeted hall. I knew exactly when they reached the top step of the wooden staircase by the squeaking sound it made when they stepped on it. I'd fallen victim to that step more than once, trying to sneak up to my room after being out too late with the guys or Becky. The thought of Becky made me smile. Then the pounding in my head reminded me I'd only gotten home about four hours ago from…ah, which one was it this time? Fort's Tavern, maybe? No, it was the Red Iron Saloon; Fort's had been on Friday night.

I shifted to the edge of the bed, holding my head until the room stopped spinning. Then, I carefully made my way to the shower using the wall as an anchor. Fifteen minutes later, I stood at the sink shaving, staring at my reflection in the mirror, and wondering how I'd gotten myself into such a mess. Going off to college was always more of an escape from the past than any initiative toward the future. But what else could I do? The distance between my parents and me had been growing for a long time. Their obsession with Christianity and Dad's insistence I comply with the "Principles of the Faith," as he put it, made my final years at home nearly unbearable.

His mantra, '*As long as you live under my roof and eat at my table, you will live by my rules*' grated on my nerves whenever we argued.

"Well, loser, here you are again. Back under his roof," I said to the face looking back at me. "I told you this was a bad idea."

Back in my room, I pulled on a pair of old cut-off jeans and my favorite Pink Floyd T-shirt, which was twice as old as me. I loved that shirt almost as much as I loved the times it came from. The seventies and eighties were the best! The bands, the movies, the clothes, the hair. Everything about those years radiated coolness. I'd spent a lot of time daydreaming I'd been born back then... Or in any time other than my own.

We arrived at Riverview Bible Church barely five minutes before service, much to my father's annoyance. My family had been members of RBC for as long as I could remember, sitting in the same pew each Sunday as if the Evans' family name was carved on it to reserve our spot. Taking my seat, the familiar routine brought back unwanted memories. Mostly of me squirming out of shear boredom and occasionally falling asleep...and later on the way home, Dad berating me for my failures. I couldn't remember a single day of my life when I hadn't felt like a disappointment to my father. Once, at the age of ten, I'd walked down the aisle to say the sinner's prayer to accept Christ and please my dad, but it didn't work.

I let out a deep sigh, *this was superstitious nonsense.*

Mom smiled and squeezed my hand, urging me to stand as the worship team took their places on stage and began the first song. I rose reluctantly. I knew the same boring routine by heart. Sing a song, then sit down for announcements. Then stand up again while the worship team led three more songs to get everybody hyped up for the message, which usually consisted of a solid thirty-five minutes of Bible-thumping by Pastor Nelson. I really wasn't looking forward to the next hour and sighed at the monotony of it all.

When Pastor Nelson began speaking, I leaned back in the seat and stretched out my legs. *Maybe I could grab a quick nap?*

"Does a single mistake define a person? How about a series of them? Should it follow them their entire life?" Pastor Nelson began. "Have you ever noticed how people put undeserved labels on each other?

Yes, I silently agreed, although I had to admit some of the labels were definitely earned. I checked my watch, thirty-three more minutes to go. The crowd around me nodded in agreement to the pastor.

"Take the apostle Thomas, for example. Can anyone here tell me what the apostle Thomas is most famous for?" the pastor asked.

A dozen people shouted at the same time.

"He was a doubter!"

"No faith!"

"He didn't believe in the resurrection."

"Doubting Thomas! Doubting Thomas!"

Pastor Nelson stepped out from behind the pulpit and walked to the front edge of the platform. "Well, well, ladies and gentlemen, I see there's a unanimous decision." He nodded at the control booth at the back of the church and a bible verse appeared on the giant screen behind him on the back wall:

But Thomas, one of the twelve,

called Didymus was not with them when Jesus came.

So the other disciples were saying to him, "We have seen the Lord!"

But he said to them, "Unless I see in His hands the imprint of the nails,

and put my hand into His side, I will not believe."

John 20:24-25

"I will NOT believe!" Pastor Nelson boomed. "It appears your label and judgment upon the disciple are well deserved."

The crowd nodded fervently in agreement. A few even called out, "Amen!"

I squirmed in my seat and wondered what label these hypocrites would put on me.

Loser! Failure! Worthless! I shifted in the seat uneasily at the thoughts.

Doubting Thomas! Yep, that's me. I'm a Doubting Thomas too. I silently agreed as the crowd quieted down around me.

The pastor's next question completely surprised me.

"Or is it?" his voice raised in challenge. He pointed to the control booth and a new bible verse appeared on the screen.

**Then said Thomas, which is called Didymus,
unto the other disciples,
"Let us also go [to Judea] that we may die with Him."
John 11:16**

"Let us also go and DIE WITH JESUS!" Pastor Nelson thundered. "Thomas voiced those words." He paused, "The Jews were seeking to kill Jesus when he decided to go up to Judea to raise Lazarus from the dead. Only Thomas said, 'LET US GO WITH HIM THAT WE MAY DIE!'" He let the thought linger then continued, "It wasn't John, the disciple whom Jesus loved, or John's brother James. It wasn't Peter, the Rock, or his brother, Andrew, either. Nor Nathaniel, in whom there was found no guile, or Simon, the Zealot, or Matthew, the tax collector. Oh no, my friends. None of those famous and honored apostles said, 'Let us go with Jesus that we may die.' Only Thomas."

The crowd stared attentively at Pastor Nelson. Intrigued by where this could be going, I sat up a little straighter.

Pointing to the screen Pastor Nelson reminded the congregation, "These words came from the very same man you condemned moments ago. These words came from the Doubter himself."

An uneasy conviction filled the church as Pastor Nelson paused to let the silence have its full effect. Then he began again, his tone strong and affirming, "Nowhere else in any of the gospels does any other disciple make such a profound confession of faith. Nowhere else in the gospels is there an affirmation of loyalty and devotion to the Lord stronger than Thomas' statement. Thomas followed Jesus to Lazarus' hometown knowing he could die at any minute if the Jewish leadership found out Jesus had arrived there." He took a deep breath and looked sternly over the crowd, "Now, I ask you, brothers and sisters—and let each of you answer in the privacy of your own hearts—why does the world remember Thomas for his one mistake and not for his courage and conviction? Or what Thomas did after Jesus strengthened his faith?"

Then Pastor Nelson closed his bible and walked toward the rear of the church. The keyboardist startled by the unexpected ending to the sermon stared after Nelson for a few moments. Then he began the closing hymn.

While overall the service followed the same routine as always, the sermon had taken a different twist. I couldn't remember Pastor Nelson ever leaving an open ended question or walking out so early. Usually, he asked rhetorical questions and answered every one. I found myself relating to Thomas. He'd been judged for his mistakes and failures with no one really remembering any of the good he'd done, just like me. I wondered if this was why my mom thought it important for me to come today. Did she know what Pastor Nelson would be preaching about?

"I always liked the apostle Peter better anyway," Dad began as he opened the grill and removed the burgers and hot dogs. "He was the strongest disciple. Oh, he had a few minor stumbles along the way like us all but it didn't stop him from becoming the Rock upon which the Lord built his church."

"Why am I not surprised you feel that way, Dad?" I took the plate with the burgers.

"What's that supposed to mean?" he asked, pointing the tongs at me like a scolding finger. "Ya know, if you took your faith a little more seriously and read the bible more often, son, you could be more like Peter and less like Doubting Thomas. And next week, I want you to be ready for church on time. I don't ever want to hear your mother beg you again."

"I won't be going to church next week, Dad."

"As long as you live under—"

"I won't be living under your roof," I interrupted. "I'm leaving in the morning."

My dad simply stared at me shaking his head. "Oh, please," he mocked. "Stop being so dramatic, Thomas. Where do you think you're going to go?" He waved the tongs for emphasis, causing me to take a step back. "They won't have you back at Ohio State, and your uncles sure as hel—are certainly not going to take you in. How will you get a place to live without a job and no money? And what kind of job do you think you'll get without a degree? After lunch, I'll call Uncle Leon and see if he'll take you back at the construction company."

"Don't bother, Dad. I'm not going back to Uncle Leon's," I set down the plate of burgers and hot dogs. I don't know where I'm going yet, but I made a mistake coming back home."

"Don't be foolish, boy. Just because I expect you to help out around here and go to church—"

"It's not the work, Dad. I don't mind helping out; you know that. I just don't believe in the stuff you do anymore. I don't think I ever have. It sounds like a bunch of fairy tales and fables. Most of those people we were with today don't act like Christians when they aren't in church. I used to hang out with their kids all the time, remember? They're hypocrites. I've seen how they act at home and how they talk when the pastor or anyone important from church isn't around. It's a total joke." Tears welled up in my eyes, and I didn't want him to see so I turned away. "I don't know what I believe anymore, Dad. Maybe I need to leave to figure it out. All I know is I can't be what you want me to be. I don't believe what you want me to believe. And I'm done trying."

Sometime in the middle of my confession, Mom must have walked into the backyard. I felt her place an arm around my shoulder.

"He says he's leaving in the morning, Clair," Dad scoffed, turning his back on me. "We'll see how that goes and what happens when his friends get tired of buying him supper every night. Or when he can't find a job and has nowhere to sleep? I'll tell you this, Clair, if he leaves now, he's not coming back here again. I mean it. He can—"

"I'm still standing right here, Dad."

"No, you're not." He grabbed the plate of burgers and hot dogs and walked to the table. He sat down with his back to me.

Mom stayed beside me as silent tears slid down my cheeks, confusing emotions ran through my mind. I swiped them away with the back of my hand. "Mom, I just need to...."

"I know, Tommy," she reassured. Taking my hands in hers, she looked me in the eyes, "Always remember who you are, honey. You're loyal and honest, and you're a good friend. The kind of friend someone can count on. Remember last summer when your buddy Ryan nearly died? The rest of the other kids ran off, but you stayed with him until the ambulance got there."

How could I forget? We'd spent the whole day drinking, and Ryan nearly choked to death on his own vomit. I had been the only one stupid enough to sit on the beach with him until the paramedics arrived. I didn't know if I was actually a good friend or just scared to go home to face my dad.

"Remember what Pastor Nelson preached this morning. Don't let your mistakes define who you are. Okay? No matter what happens, don't you ever forget that." She looked toward my dad and lowered her voice, "And I know you'll be there for him when the time comes."

Him? I glanced over at Dad's back. Turning back to meet Mom's gaze, I asked, "For who?" *Did she mean Dad or someone else?*

She kissed my cheek. "Just remember all of us." she encouraged before walking over and taking a seat next to my dad.

I stood there for a long time, trying to figure out what happened. Then I strode past them both and headed to my room to pack. Once finished, I placed my backpack and small duffel bag beside the bedroom door so I'd be ready to go in the morning. Then I wrote a brief note to Mom telling her not to worry, promising I'd text every day. I watched a couple of hours of TV before turning out the lights to get some sleep. As I lay in bed, my mind raced with possibilities and fears. I tossed and turned for several hours; I couldn't stop thinking about the church service. What Pastor Nelson said was true. Everybody labeled me by my mistakes and failures, just like they did Doubting Thomas. Everyone judged me by my weaknesses and shortcomings.

Maybe it was time I proved everybody wrong. Maybe I could make something of myself and rip those labels off. Yeah, maybe it was time.

I was sound asleep when Mom slipped silently into my room and placed an ancient object beneath the covers beside me.

The hand on my shoulder shook me hard. "Thomas, wake up! We have to go. Come on, why are you still sleeping?" I didn't recognize the man's voice, loud and harsh and strongly accented.

The bed beneath me felt like concrete. My body ached everywhere. "Jesus! What time is it?"

"Just before dawn, Thomas," another man replied with a laugh as I heard him walk by. "But Andrew is right. It is time to go; the crowd will be gathering soon." I felt an odd sensation wash over me. I tried to identify it but my mind focused on his words...*time to go.*

"Go? Go where?" I asked, sitting up and opening my eyes but the man was already gone. And so was my room, my house, everything! My mind tumbled in confusion, trying to make sense of what my eyes were seeing. There were no walls, no ceiling, and no bed. Instead, I was outside in an open field with a small fire burning a few yards away.

What's going on? Where am I?

I threw off a thin blanket and stood up. Feeling a breeze, I looked down to see myself wearing a long, dingy white, scratchy...something that reached well past my knees. Underneath...I was naked.

Where were my boxers? My T-shirt? Where was I? This is crazy! I thought.

Reaching my hand up to wipe my eyes, my fingers ran past a full beard. Impossible! I never had a beard in my life! I couldn't grow anything more than a patchy, ugly mess. A fact I tried to hide by shaving daily. At twenty years old, I couldn't grow a decent beard like my friends.

The man who woke me bent over and picked up what I'd originally thought was a blanket. He held it out to me, "Put on your robe, Thomas. Hurry! We must go."

Then another man stepped up beside him and stared down at me. A rough-looking man about my dad's age with a full beard and dark, weathered face asked, "Is Didymus with us or not, brother?"

"Yes, yes. Of course, he is. Go on, Peter. Go with Jesus. We'll be right behind you."

CHAPTER 2
A New Beginning

I jumped up, looking frantically in every direction. "Impossible!" the word slipped from my mouth, unintended.

I paced back and forth, taking in my surroundings, my feet desperately trying to keep up with my swiveling head. The trees, the fading fire, the filthy robe in my hand, and the man staring at me with a puzzled look on his face. None of it made any sense. Where was my bed? Where was my bedroom, for that matter? My house, my family?

Toto, I have a feeling this isn't Kansas or Ohio anymore.

But where in the world was I? The sun peeked over the horizon, revealing a patchwork of rocky ground with green and yellow fields beyond the trees.

One sun and a single moon. I chuckled to myself. *At least it appears I'm still on Earth.*

I knew immediately whatever was happening wasn't a dream. I'm a vivid dreamer and experienced some pretty fanciful emotions in my dreams. Fear, anxiety, anger, rage, lust, even love. But never pain. At least not pain like this. The ache in my back and shoulders felt genuine, and the stiff breeze blowing across the hilltop, stirring up sparks from the fire, raised goosebumps on my arms. Everything seemed like the real deal.

I crossed my arms across my chest as tight as I could and rubbed my shoulders trying to generate some heat. I needed a lot more than some thin knee-length T-shirt to keep me warm. I stared at the sun and felt the familiar ache in the back of my eyes. The pain certainly seemed real enough. Plus, the soles of my feet were screaming at me, making me painfully aware wherever my bedroom was, my socks and slippers were there too. Regardless of how crazy it seemed, everything I could see and feel told me this place was all too real.

"Thomas, what is wrong? Are you ill?" The man who awakened me asked.

I searched my mind for his name. Andrew, that was it. The man who had walked past us called him Andrew. He took the robe and threw it over my shoulders. I pulled it tight around my neck, grateful for the little comfort it provided.

"Yeah, Andrew, that must be it; I'm sick," I walked over to the fire and sat on one of the rocks. I found the neck hole in the robe and pulled it over my head. I needed some time to think about what was happening to me. I had to figure out where I was and how I'd gotten here.

Was I in danger? It didn't feel like it. The man stared at me. His rugged face appeared well-tanned or perhaps it was naturally caramel colored; I couldn't tell. His curly dark hair fell to just above his soft brown eyes and almost blended into his full beard along the sides of his face. He gazed down at me with compassion, not anger.

"I need sit for a few minutes, Andrew, and clear my head." I scoured the small encampment with my eyes, desperately searching for anything to give me a clue as to where I was. Unfortunately, nothing looked familiar. Most of the terrain surrounding the tiny camp appeared dry and rocky. A variety of crops I didn't recognize struggled to grow on the surrounding hillsides in a haphazard fashion. It looked nothing like the farms I'd seen in Ohio. Beyond the hills to my right rose a jagged mountain range, and on the left, a fertile green valley with a blueish-green snake of a river weaving its way from west to east.

As I surveyed the land, trying to make sense of what I saw, part of me still hoped to hear that squeaky floorboard near the top of the stairway signaling my mom or dad coming down the hall to roust me from bed and wake me from this strange dream. But deep down, I knew they weren't coming.

If this wasn't a dream, what was it? Could it be a practical joke hatched by some of my college buddies? No, that couldn't be it. Nothing even remotely similar to this kind of geography existed anywhere near my home in Springfield. Someone would have to transport me thousands of miles away to find an area similar to this. Arizona, maybe, or New Mexico. I couldn't possibly have slept through that. I knew I hadn't been drugged because my mind seemed clear, except for the shock of waking up in who knows where or...and...I had to at least consider the possibility of...when.

I looked at Andrew's clothes and the robe he handed me that I'd initially mistaken for a blanket. The man he'd called Peter wore something similar. Even the homeless in the cities near where I grew up wore better clothes than this. The only place I'd seen similar styles of clothes was in pictures or the movies. Movies from a time and place of long ago. Classic old movies my father considered "mandatory viewing" every Christmas and Easter. Another one of his "as long as you live in my house" rules that required my sister, Angela, and me to sit through hours and hours of religious propaganda served up by the cable company. *The Ten Commandments, The Greatest Story Ever Told, Ben-Hur, The Robe*. Now, as I stared at Andrew's garb, as totally impossible as it seemed, I had no choice but to accept the crazy notion this might be exactly as it appeared.

Everything in my mind screamed it couldn't be true, but everything my eyes saw and my gut felt told me I either awoke on the set of one of those old Hollywood movies, or somehow traveled back in time to where those movies took place, Israel. Back to the time of—if I heard Andrew correctly—Jesus Christ. I started to laugh as I thought about the words I saw only yesterday. The words of the apostle Thomas projected on the RBC screen next to a beautiful, shiny wooden cross: "Unless I see His hands and put my finger into the place of the nails and put my hand into His side, I will not believe."

"I'll believe it when I see it," I laughed again as I remembered the name the other man called me, Didymus. In a fantastical way, it all added up. The clothes, the name, the beard, the surroundings. Even the unexplainable emotion I felt and tried to ignore when that man had walked past me and spoke my name. I was running out of ways to deny what seemed abundantly clear. I was no longer in the twenty-first century, and my parents weren't downstairs waiting for me to show up for breakfast on time.

"We do not have time for joking." Andrew pleaded, "We must hurry. I want to hear what Jesus is going to say." Andrew picked up a pair of sandals and threw them at my feet. "Come on, Thomas, we must go now."

"You go, Andrew," I encouraged. "I'll catch up to you as soon as I can. I need to sit here for a little while longer until I feel better. Go on. I'll see you there soon."

"You speak strangely, Thomas." Andrew tilted his head and looked down at me.

I didn't know how long Andrew and I were supposed to have known each other. But it seemed apparent Andrew had already noticed differences between me and the Thomas he knew. I was about to get up and go with him when he suddenly nodded, turned, and started running.

I gathered a few branches from the nearby cluster of trees and threw them on the fire. I wasn't cold anymore but sought the comfort of something familiar. I glanced down at the sandals Andrew tossed at my feet. It took me a few minutes to figure out how to put them on. They were roughly foot-shaped pieces of leather with two long leather thongs attached to the front. I passed the thongs between my big toe and second toe, crisscrossed them across the top of my foot, and wrapped them several times around my ankle, tying them off above my calf. I could only hope it was close to the proper way.

Until I discovered what was really happening and why, it seemed smart to pay close attention to the new world around me. Even securing sandals to my feet incorrectly could draw attention I didn't need or want. Andrew acted like I looked like the Thomas he knew. But I needed to remember the beard, shoulder-length wavy hair, and face might make me look familiar to other people on the outside, but on the inside, I was a total stranger.

If I hoped to figure out what was happening to me and how to get back home, I needed to blend in as much as possible. Maybe then I could start getting some answers. I wasn't entirely unfamiliar with the time or the place I landed in. After all, I'd spent nearly every Sunday and Wednesday night of my young life in church. Some of that stuff had to stick with me even if I hadn't been paying too much attention. I ran my fingers through my beard and hair again. If the impossible had happened, and I occupied the body of one of Jesus's disciples in the first century, then I was a Jew. It also meant the Roman Empire occupied the entire area, and being Jewish in the first century had not turned out well for many. Surprisingly, none of those things troubled me much.

As I fed a few more branches into the fire, I tried to come to grips with what I was really feeling. Oddly, I felt happy. Really happy. Yeah, I was a little anxious about what might happen next. But mostly, I was feeling happy. It wasn't a feeling I was very familiar with, and it felt good. I no longer had to deal with my messed-up life back in Ohio. Today, I wouldn't be fighting with my father as we argued about me leaving home again and what I would do with my life. I wouldn't have to beg my friends for a place to stay or spend countless hours looking for a job I would probably hate anyway. If this were real, I would have a chance for a brand-new beginning. I rubbed the stiffness in my shoulders. I might even get used to sleeping on the ground. It didn't matter. It was what it was.

Through some strange twist of fate, a temporal vortex, a rift in the space-time continuum, or some other bizarre phenomenon I would never understand, I had been swept from my miserable life and carried away to here. For all I knew, the other Thomas sat on my bed right now, rubbing his face and wondering what happened to his whiskers. Man, I'd have given anything to have been there when he walked into the dining room and met my father for the first time.

"Have fun with that one, Dad," I said to the flames dancing before me.

Even though I never bought into the whole Jesus nonsense, I'd heard enough sermons and Bible stories, sat through enough Sunday school classes and youth group meetings, to know this story was not going to end well. Or at least it wouldn't if the story went the way I remembered it. If I was new to the group of disciples, then it had to be near the beginning of Jesus's ministry. That meant three years from now, Jesus was going to be betrayed by one of his closest friends. Later, he'd be crucified on a hill called Golgotha near Jerusalem, also known as Calvary. Some of his followers would claim he rose from the dead and would return to Earth again in the future. An entire religious system would grow around these ideas. But I never believed any of it to be true. It was just religious superstition. The opium of the masses. A windfall for savvy preachers who knew how to stir up the crowd and weasel money out of people. Nope, I simply didn't buy it.

Before this morning I hadn't even believed the man Jesus existed. Well, maybe he existed in some form, but he definitely wasn't who everyone claimed he was. It seems my current experience confirmed a man named Jesus did live long ago. I could adjust my thinking on his existence for now. But regardless, in three years, this Jesus was going to die, and the story would be over.

If I was still here then, what would I do? Would my part of the story be over too? Would I wake up back in my comfortable bed and discover this had been some crazy dream after all? Would I be stuck in ancient Israel to live out the rest of my life as a hated Jew in an occupied land? Maybe I'd be hunted down for being part of the troublemaker's inner circle? Perhaps my new life here in the past came with a few drawbacks. But it didn't matter. As impossible as it seemed I was where I was. And until I understood more, there was nothing I could do but make the most of it.

I couldn't escape the reality I was in a new world and a part of Jesus's posse. But who says the story can't be changed anyway? Surely it had already been changed with me being there, hadn't it? I decided it was best to blend in, keep my head down, my eyes and ears open, and try to figure out how to simply survive.

CHAPTER 3
Along the Way

I kicked some dirt onto the fire and headed south, the direction Andrew had gone earlier. It wasn't easy going. Once I left the gentle hills, the terrain quickly became rockier and steeper. Several paths circumvented the mountainside on my left, and I worked my way up to the closest one above me. I spied the long wide valley I'd seen from the camp to my right.

I must have walked nearly two miles and was about to abandon the idea of finding Andrew and the others when I noticed several people on the paths below me. Dozens more appeared over the next hour, heading for the ridge about half a mile farther south. I left the path and carefully made my way down to the trail below, where I met a man and a woman traveling with two small boys, about three and five years of age.

"May I walk with you?" I asked the man, who appeared to be well past fifty. He had a noticeable limp and leaned heavily on his thick walking stick, gripping it with both hands. The two boys moved to the other side of their mother, where they tried to sneak glances at me from behind her skirt. The older boy held her hand and put his arm around his younger brother, urging him to keep up. I had no idea what I looked like other than my beard and hair, and I wondered if my appearance somehow frightened the boys.

The man kept walking as though he hadn't heard me. After a few moments, he grunted, "Do as you wish."

"Where are you going?"

Again, he ignored me.

"We are going to see the Rabbi," the woman replied, keeping her head down.

The man stopped in his tracks, spun around, and raised his hand to strike her. Then he looked at me as if he'd forgotten I stood there. He lowered his hand and gave the woman an angry look. Then he limped to within a few inches of me. "Why do you trouble us? Leave us be."

He grabbed the woman's arm and dragged her and the two boys with him down the path.

Defiantly, the woman shouted over her shoulder, "He is angry with God. He believes God has abandoned us."

The man stopped and glared at his wife again.

"And he is dying," Her eyes, red and puffy, met mine for the first time. Then she turned back to her husband, wrapped her arms around his waist, and rested her head against his chest. The two boys reached their short arms as far as they could around both of their parents.

I watched the man's expression as the anger and hostility slowly drained out of him. That's when I noticed the blood streaking from his nose and through his beard. Both sleeves of his robe were stained with blood, where he had used them to wipe his face. He put his arm around his wife's shoulders, drawing her close, and tousled his sons' hair, one after the other, with his free hand. They began weeping now as they held one another.

"Now, see what you have done," he scolded, wiping the tears away with his bloody sleeve. He stared at me for a few more moments, then stretched out a hand toward me. "Come on, then. We will go together."

I stepped over to him. He handed me his stick and put his arm around my shoulder. We walked to the top of the ridge, me helping him on one side and his wife on the other. The boys trailed a few feet behind.

From the top of the ridge, I could see a large body of water on the right I assumed was the Sea of Galilee. The rocky ridge tapered off towards the sea until it melted into the valley floor below at the spot where the valley and the sea came together. Several small fishing villages dotted the western coastline. The mountains in front of us and to our left rose steadily until they became sheer rock cliffs. The bottom third of the mountain consisted of mostly gently rolling hills. People flooded the hills. My high school gym back home could seat nearly two thousand people for a varsity basketball game. I estimated there were at least that many people here, either sitting or milling about, shouting or arguing with one another with their hands and arms waving in the air.

We worked our way down the other side of the ridge, where we found a place to sit along the outer edge of the crowd near the top of one of the hills. I scanned the area but saw no sign of Andrew or Peter.

I turned to my new acquaintance and reached out my hand. "My name is Thomas. What's yours?"

"Micah." he responded, staring at my hand with a puzzled look.

"Well," I lowered my hand, "ah, why do you think God has abandoned you, Micah?"

Micah sat quietly, looking around at the crowd. His two boys sat in front of him, and he pulled the youngest into his arms with his back against his chest. Finally, he asked, "Where are you from, Thomas?"

The question took me by surprise. I hadn't even thought about having to answer questions about my life. If I was going to get along in this new world without drawing attention, I would need to get my story straight, but the only two Biblical locations I could think of at the moment were Bethlehem and Jerusalem, and neither seemed like the right answer. "A long way from here. To the south."

"A Judean then." Micah laughed with more contempt than humor in his tone. "God has turned his back on you as well then, Thomas the Judean. He leaves you to suffer alone under the godless pagan Pilate, who fills your purses with coins favoring his false gods of Rome. I warn you, Thomas, spend even one of those filthy coins, and you will be cursed forever." He made a motion like shaking a bag of money and laughed again, "Though we in Galilee fare no better under Herod Antipas. He taxes us, Rome taxes us, and the synagogue taxes us. Then when there is no coin left to take, they take our land and send us to break our backs, building their heathen cities. My father died building Tiberias"—he spat on the ground—"and I will die before Sepphoris is finished." He spat again, then looked around as if he were afraid someone heard him. Then he quietly whispered, "And if we complain, the soldiers come and take even more. I ask you, Thomas, where is he? Where is the God of Abraham and Jacob? Why is he silent when his people suffer like this? You ask why I think God has abandoned us?" Micah wiped his face with his blood-stained sleeve. "Just look at this!" he scoffed, waving a hand at the crowd on the hills around us. "Do you see all these people, Thomas? If God were with us, they would be peacefully at home with their families, not sitting on this worthless hillside looking for a miracle."

I looked out at the growing crowd and nodded.

Micah was visibly angry and broken. And like angry, broken people in any age, he unloaded on me, a complete stranger. As I studied the deep creases in Micah's face and his sad, lifeless eyes, I thought of my dad. *How different my life might have been if I could have talked to him like this. Someone I could unload on when I felt broken. Someone who would listen instead of lecture.* Thankfully, I could be here for Micah.

"Do you know why most of them are here, Thomas?"

I had no answer, so I remained silent and waited.

"Because they have nowhere else to go," he scorned. "They have no land, no jobs, no money, and no hope! They come from Capernaum and Cana, Nazareth and Bethsaida. Some, like you, all the way from Judea. They travel here because they pray maybe this time will be different. Maybe this prophet will finally be the one to deliver us. The one who will summon God's return to Israel." He pointed out at the crowd. "Many of these people grew up listening to stories about Hezekiah, the bandit, Simon of Peraea, Athronges the shepherd boy, or Judas the Galilean. Some of these men may have even been followers of one of those false messiahs who died at the hands of the Romans. But, as long as there is a new one to take the last one's place and preach a new message of deliverance, the people will come. Desperate people longing for even a glimmer of hope God will return and free us. So they come and listen. And if the crowds become too big, or the prophet's words become too loud or threatening, then Antipas or Pilate or Rome will send the soldiers, and another prophet's body will be left to rot in our streets."

I took in the enormous crowd with a new understanding.

"And do you see the ones out there with clean clothes and long robes, Thomas? They are not here to listen to this Nazarene. Oh no, my Judean friend, they come to judge him. If he speaks even one word against Herod or Pilate or the Emperor," Micah spat a third time, "or dares to even utter the word 'Messiah,' they will crawl back to their foreign masters and this Jesus will join the rest of the false prophets, losing his head or nailed to a cross." Micah's eyes filled with tears as he turned away from me.

I was about to say something when I looked up the mountainside and saw Andrew with a small group of men. The man who had walked past me this morning stood on a small rock outcropping, looking out over the crowd. I placed my hand on Micah's shoulder in a silent farewell, but before he could turn, I shot to my feet and raced up the hill.

CHAPTER 4
The Sermon on the Mount

When I reached them, Andrew pulled me into a hug and kissed my cheeks. Then he motioned for me to sit and be quiet. He pointed toward the man standing on the rocks a few feet away. "Glad, you made it on time. Jesus is just beginning."

"It is good if you realize how much you need God," Jesus began, "because when you realize how little you have of him and seek to know him, he will welcome you into his kingdom.

"If you anguish over how far you are from God, take heart; he is here to comfort you.

"You are wise if you do not take revenge on your oppressors. Rule over your anger, and someday the earth will be yours.

"Seek to do good and be good with the same persistence a starving man seeks bread and water, and you will always be filled.

"If you show forgiveness and compassion to others, God will show forgiveness and compassion to you. If you want to see God with your eyes, you must first see him with your heart. And to see him with your heart, you must desire to be as he is. God is good, just, loving and merciful. Be good, just, loving and merciful, and you will see God."

Jesus stretched out his arms. "Does the world you live in bring you peace?"

The crowd roared back, "No! There is no peace."

"Do you want to be called the children of God?" Jesus asked.

"Yes! Yes!" they chanted

"Then, do not wait for this world to bring you peace. Bring peace to this world. Bring peace to your homes and every place you go, and God will call you his children. You cannot expect this world to bring you peace.

"If you do as I tell you and choose goodness and justice and mercy and love above all else, even those you call friends will mistreat you. But, if you choose to do right even when they revile and accuse you, I promise you will be welcomed with honor into my father's kingdom. If you take my words to heart, people will hate you, and they will make up all manner of lies about you and call you shameful things. But you should be glad because my father will remember every evil word spoken against you and repay you with goodness in his kingdom, just as he has done for the men and women who came before you."

I looked out over the crowd and stole glimpses of the men sitting around me. The absurdity of the situation began to dawn on me. Was it really possible I was sitting on the side of a mountain in ancient Israel, next to the apostles Peter and Andrew, listening to Jesus Christ give the Sermon on the Mount? It was mind-blowing and confusing. I'd heard dozens of sermons about this event. But what I heard now was nothing like I imagined. Nor was it like anything I'd ever heard before. Of course, as I listened to Jesus now, I had to admit I never paid much attention to his words before either. I heard but never really listened to them. As much as I wanted to, I couldn't deny being moved by what I was hearing. Not only by his words but by the man who spoke them. A man I didn't even believe was real less than twenty-four hours ago.

I gazed out over the crowd, which had been loud and rowdy a short time ago. Now, they were sitting quietly on the hillside, as captivated by Jesus as I was. I leaned forward, trying to take in everything. Sometimes, Jesus's words were loud and harsh, like scolding an unruly child, and other times they were soft and gentle. But however he spoke, I felt his love. It was such a new experience I was entirely thrown off balance by it—almost angered by it. Jesus didn't even know me. How could he...I'd just got here. And yet, I felt love from him. Love was the emotion I felt back in camp when he first spoke my name. Somehow I hadn't recognized it before now.

"You have heard it said, 'love your neighbor and hate your enemy.'" Jesus continued. "But I have something new to teach you. Love your enemies and pray for those who hate you, even those who hurt you. Then you will be the sons and daughters of your father who is in heaven; who causes his sun to rise on the good and the bad alike. If you only love those who love you, how are you any different from the tax collectors? If you are kind to only your brothers and sisters, how are you different from others? Even those who do not know God can do that."

I noticed several of the men in the group of disciples sitting near me were whispering to one another and shaking their heads. One of them even spun around and turned his back to Jesus, his eyes burning with anger.

I scanned the crowd again, hoping to locate Micah, but the ever-increasing number of people swallowed him up. I had grown surprisingly attached to Micah in the short time I'd spent with him and wondered what he thought about this 'new prophet' as he called him. Would he like what he heard? Would he find any hope in it?

I laughed over my gullibility. Yesterday I thought people who believed in this fairytale Jesus were weak-minded and needed a crutch to make it through life. Today, after listening to Jesus for less than an hour, I wanted to run down the hill and tell Micah his prayers had been answered. I closed my eyes and tried to get a grip on myself. Things were moving too quickly. Caught in a whirlwind of emotions and confusion, my mind raced. I took a deep breath and tried to think about things more rationally. The one thing I had to face was I could no longer think of Jesus Christ as a make-believe storybook character. The man was, after all, standing less than twenty feet away from me. I bit down hard on the inside of my cheek and tasted blood. I couldn't escape it. This was real. The crowd, Jesus, his disciples, me. I needed to figure out what it meant.

"Thomas, come with us. We're leaving." Andrew shook me again.

I must have drifted off into another daydream. I looked toward the rock outcropping where Jesus stood moments ago, but he was gone.

"We need to help him get away." Andrew pulled me to my feet and pushed me farther up the hill to where Jesus stood with Peter and five other men. As we got closer, I could hear Peter speaking.

"…never seen a crowd this large before, Rabbi. They will crush you if you stay here any longer." He pointed in the direction of the camp. "If we stay up high, we can get ahead of them. Then we can—"

"Peter, Peter, Peter," Jesus put his hands on Peter's shoulder and looked him in the eyes. "We are not going back to camp. They are who I came for. They are why we are here. Now come, my friend, let us do some fishing." Jesus turned and walked past us, down the mountain, and straight into the heart of the crowd.

"Stay with him!" Peter screamed, his arms spread wide, trying to herd us down the hillside after Jesus. "Make a circle around him and give him as much room as possible. Go! Go! Go!"

I didn't know what else to do but follow Peter's instructions, so I rushed into the crowd with the others, hoping to do what I could. The next four hours were utter madness. We formed a circle around Jesus and tried to keep the crowd as far away from him as we could so he could breathe, but it was impossible. We were being pushed back against him by desperate people trying to reach him. Grown men and women crawled on the ground between our legs, hoping to simply touch him. Knocked to the ground a dozen times, I found myself staring into the hollow eyes of frantic people squirming to get over or around me. Three times, while on the ground struggling to get to my feet, Jesus fell beside me. I honestly thought Peter's words would come true, and we would be crushed to death. But somehow each time, someone managed to pull us back to our feet, and Jesus continued to pray for those he could reach.

The second time he fell, I caught his gaze and saw his weariness. I knew he couldn't go on much longer. He didn't even try to get back up the third time but remained on his knees, still reaching out to touch the people. He pressed their hands to his face, kissing their fingers. He touched their faces, often rubbing his spit on their eyes or ears or mouths. When he saw the weakest people failing to get through, he would point to them and speak silent words. I watched their faces change from fear and pain to calm and contentment as they turned and walked away, healed of whatever diseases ailed them moments before. Each time Jesus healed without touching them, it seemed to drain him even further.

Finally, the crowd thinned enough for us to begin moving Jesus toward the northern edge. I took hold of his left arm while a younger man took his right, and we started pulling him away from the crowd.

"Stop," he commanded gently but firmly.

We stopped and released his arms.

He placed a hand on one side of each of our faces. "John, Thomas, they have come a very long way to be here today. I will not leave until I have seen them all."

We helped him over to a large rock where he could sit. Andrew took my place, and he and John supported Jesus while the rest of us tried to manage the remaining crowd, letting them through one at a time.

I counted fifty or so people still waiting when I saw Micah and his family halfway back in the line. I ran to him and hugged him. Then I knelt and pulled both boys into a hug as I smiled up at his wife. "Did you hear him, Micah?" I stood. "Did you hear him? You see, God has not abandoned you, he—"

Micah spat on the ground. "How can he ask me to forgive the Romans? He has no idea what he is asking. My father died building Herod's filthy city. The Romans came for him every day from the time I was twelve. He taught me how to cut stone. As he lay dying, he begged me to forgive him for teaching me because he knew soon they would come for me too. If you can plane a timber or shape a stone, they come. Day after day, they come and take us to Sepphoris. They pay us less than enough to buy bread for our children. My wife must take our boys and go to the city to scrub the clothes of the rich so we do not starve. And now he says if they want one day from us, we should give them two. Forgive them, or God will not forgive us." He shook his head angrily. "I can forgive the scorpion that stings because it is all he knows, but these godless Romans and the Herodian scum they set over us? No, Thomas! Never! I will never forgive what they have done."

I thought about Micah's words as the line inched forward. "Then why do you wait in line to see him?"

Micah looked at his wife and started to say something; then he turned back to me. "Because she begs me and because I know him."

"How is that possible, Micah? How do you know him?"

"Like me, he is a craftsman."

We reached Peter and another one of Jesus's disciples, who stopped us. Peter put his hand on my shoulder. "Wait here, Thomas."

A few minutes later, they let us pass, and we walked up to Jesus. Micah stood in front of him with his two boys hiding behind his legs. Micah's wife fell at Jesus's feet and began to kiss them.

"Rabbi, please, my husband is dying," she pleaded. "I know you can make him well."

Jesus put his hand on her head and looked at me.

"This is Micah, Rabbi," I turned toward Micah. "He says he knows you."

Jesus turned weary eyes to Micah and smiled. "Do you still cut stone on the south side of the city?"

"When I can," Micah answered. "But many days, I cannot rise from my bed, so the soldiers don't bother with me. I am not worth the trouble of dragging into the city if I cannot work when I get there. Much of the work in Sepphoris is finished now, anyway." He knelt and put an arm around his wife's shoulders. "If it were not for Naomi, we would be beggars. It has been a long time since I have seen you and your brothers working in Sepphoris."

Jesus stood and helped Micah and his wife to their feet. "After we buried Joseph, we went to stay with my mother's sister in Capernaum. It has been nearly a year now. You should take your wife and sons and go there. I know many good fishermen in Capernaum. Ask for a man named Zebedee. He needs strong men who are willing to work hard. His two sons follow me now. He will be grateful for your help."

Micah started to laugh and then began coughing. He bent over as blood began flowing down his beard. "Rabbi, I do not think I will make it back to my village. I surely cannot make the journey to Capernaum."

Jesus took the corner of his shawl and wiped Micah's beard. Then he took the blood-stained sleeves of Micah's tunic and buried his face in them. He remained frozen for several minutes then lifted his head and put his hands on Micah's chest.

Immediately, Micah's strength began to return to his body. His back straightened, his shoulders lifted, his chest expanded.

Naomi clung to him, weeping as the children rushed to hug Jesus, who returned to his seat on the rock.

Micah bent on one knee and took Jesus's hand in his and kissed it. "Thank you, Lord," he repeated over and over.

"Do not return to your village, Micah," Jesus sighed. "You cannot go back to the quarries ever again. Go straight to Capernaum. Find Zebedee. He will have a place for you. Tell him we will be there soon."

"Yes, Lord, I will find him." Micah gathered his family and began to walk away. After a few steps, he turned and called, "Rabbi?"

"Yes, Micah."

"When you raise your army, I will be there. I will come and fight beside you."

Sadness washed over Jesus's face. Then, he nodded at Peter, who let the next person in line pass through.

CHAPTER 5
A Request

It was nearly dark when we arrived back at the camp where my day began. I spoke with John for a few moments along the way, but it became obvious he and everyone else was too exhausted to carry on much of a conversation. I finally drifted over to Andrew and walked quietly beside him, feeling some small comfort that at least I knew his name.

As we approached camp, I saw two fires burning about thirty feet apart and several women moving about. When they saw us entering camp, they greeted each of us by name. I tried to remember as many as possible. I already knew Peter, Andrew, and John. I assumed the man walking beside John with similar facial features was his brother, James. I also knew of Philip, Nathaniel, and Judas, pleased some of my Sunday School lessons were coming back to me.

A woman about my mother's age gave John and James an affectionate hug. Then she turned to me and smiled, "Peace be with you, Thomas. Come, warm yourselves by the fire. Mary is preparing bread and stew and will bring it as soon as it is ready. He was wonderful today, was he not?"

"Yes, he was Mother," John returned her hug. "Come sit with us. You have done enough for today."

"Soon, John, soon, now go on. I will see you and James in a little while." She pushed him toward the fire and stepped into the darkness.

I found a spot next to Andrew and was about to sit on the log when I noticed everyone else sitting on the ground leaning back against the log. I followed suit. There were so many little things to learn.

"He sounds less and less like the Baptizer every time he speaks," James shook his head. "Turn the other cheek, pray for your oppressors. The sun rises on the good and the evil equally. I know he wants to avoid drawing too much attention to himself, but a little fire from heaven would go a long way in drawing followers other than only the sick and the poor."

"James is right," Andrew agreed. "Did you see those fancy-dressed Pharisees and priests sitting among the crowd today? John would have called them out as soon as they showed their self-righteous faces." Andrew pulled his shawl over his head and started shaking his finger at the other men around the fire. "You brood of vipers!" he scolded in a loud, deep voice, drawing out each syllable. "Who warned you to flee from the wrath to come? What good does it do for you to claim Abraham as your father? I tell you this, from these stones, God is able to raise up children to Abraham."

Everyone roared with laughter at Andrew's impersonation. By the looks on their faces and the nodding heads, he'd pulled off a pretty good imitation of John the Baptist.

"John is beginning to doubt him," Philip stated.

The laughter died quickly like a fire doused with water. Everyone turned toward Philip.

"What do you mean, doubt him?" Peter asked angrily. "And how would you know that? John has been in prison for months now."

"Two of John's men came to see Jesus this morning. Nathaniel was with me." Philip gestured toward Nathaniel, who nodded.

"It is true, Peter. I heard them," Nathaniel confirmed.

"Who did you hear? What did they say?" Peter's anger rose.

"The one who spoke with Jesus said his name was Jacob. He gave his companion's name as Jonas."

"I know them both. They are good men who have been with John from the beginning. What did they say?"

"Nathaniel and I were the first to arrive with Jesus this morning," Philip began. "John's disciples were already waiting for us, as if they had spent the night there. Of course, many people looked like they spent—"

"What did Jacob say, Philip?" Peter snapped.

Philip looked around at the others, obviously regretting he'd said anything. Finally, he looked at Peter and whispered, "Jacob told Jesus that John sent them to ask him a question. I did not know they permitted

John to see his disciples while in prison, but they must have been able to—"

"Get to it, man!" Peter stood and put his hands on his hips. "What was John's question?"

Philip swallowed hard and spoke into the ground, "He asked, 'Are you the one who is to come, or shall we look for another?'"

A collective gasp rose from the group. Some were shaking their heads; others clasped their hands over their mouths like they were trying to hold in words they didn't dare speak. Peter saved them from having to say anything. He set his anger from a few moments ago aside. "John is a good man." He spoke softly, "A man sent from God, there is no doubt. My brother, Andrew, can bear witness. John himself pointed Andrew toward Jesus, and then Andrew brought me. He is a good man, to be sure, but only a man like us. He has been held captive in Herod's prison for a long time. Think how you would feel if you were in John's place." Peter walked around the fire, taking time to look at each of us. "Any one of us would have our doubts if we were rotting away in a godforsaken dungeon. Was it not moments ago, sitting here warm and free around this fire, you agreed with James some of the things Jesus says are hard to understand? You wanted Jesus to say things more in line with your own desires. 'Bring a little fire from heaven,' were your words, were they not James?" Peter's tone rose, "The Christ has not come to live up to our expectations, or the Baptizer's!" He kicked dirt onto the fire, sending sparks shooting into the air. Quietly, he added, "He has come to bring us the Kingdom of Heaven." He sat down again and turned towards Philip, "What was our Lord's answer?"

Philip took a moment to collect his thoughts, "I could tell Jesus felt troubled by what Jacob asked. How could he not be? Jesus and John have been friends since they were boys. After a long time, Jesus spoke directly to Jacob and Jonas, 'Go and tell John what you see and hear: tell him the blind receive their sight and the lame walk, the lepers are cleansed, the deaf hear, the dead are raised, and the poor have the gospel preached to them. And blessed is he who does not take offense at me.'"

Silence reigned for several minutes. I hadn't known these men long enough to tell what any of them were feeling. But, if I felt a mixture of anger, embarrassment, shame, and confusion, it was safe to assume they were likely experiencing similar emotions.

The sound of footsteps drawing near drew our attention. Jesus and two women stepped into the firelight.

The women were dressed very much like the rest of us. Each wore a light cotton or linen undergarment, like an extra-long T-shirt. It reached their ankles, whereas the same garment on the men stopped barely below the knees. On top of the undershirt was a heavier garment, probably wool, with a cloth belt tied around the waist. The women also wore their shawls differently, over the head, while the men wore them over one or both shoulders. The younger of the two women also wore a thin cap over her head and under the shawl. She looked to be in her early thirties; the second woman seemed only a few years older.

James and John jumped up to help them with the parcels they carried. James took a large clay pot from the younger woman, and John took a reed basket full of cups and bowls from the other. Jesus carried a basket of pita bread. The brothers set the pot and basket of bowls near the fire and passed out the cups. Their mother, who greeted us earlier, arrived with two skins of wine and began filling each man's cup.

When everyone was served, Jesus sat down with his basket of bread. The three women took spots around the fire as well. Jesus took a piece of pita bread, tore it in half, and passed one part to his left and one to his right. When everyone held a piece of bread, he set the basket aside and looked up, "Blessed are you, Lord, our God, who brings forth bread from the earth and creates the fruit of the vine."

Everyone raised their cups and drank.

John began dipping the bowls into the pot and passing them around. It consisted of some kind of fish stew with chickpeas and leeks, and it was delicious. I watched and learned how to create a scoop with the bread to use until all the pieces of fish were gone. After Jesus passed out a second piece of bread, I used it to soak up the broth. The meal was less than I usually ate around a typical American dinner table but by far the most satisfying meal I'd ever had.

There wasn't much conversation while we ate, but I learned John's and James's mother's name was Salome. She was also Jesus's aunt, his mother's sister. They lived together in Capernaum, where Salome's husband, Zebedee, operated a successful fishing business. He was the same Zebedee Jesus sent Micah to find.

As soon as Jesus finished his meal, he got up, put his cup and bowl in the basket, and walked away. I watched him disappear into the night, then gave Andrew a questioning look.

"He is going to pray," he told me. "It is the same each night. Sometimes he will return to the fire and speak with those still awake, but most likely, we will not see him again until morning." Andrew stood. "Rest well, Thomas."

I sat by the fire long after the other men fell asleep, listening as they filled the night with their snoring. Several of the men slipped out into the darkness, perhaps hoping to spare themselves the cacophony of guttural melodies percolating from the figures on the ground near the fire.

After Salome refilled my cup, she and the other women left, heading in the direction of the second fire. I could see several silhouettes moving in the firelight and guessed at least eight women were a part of Jesus's company. I remembered seeing Salome and the two other women moving among the crowd throughout the day as Jesus taught from his mountainside pulpit. If John had been correct when he spoke with his mother earlier, her day was even longer and more tiring than ours. It wasn't long before their fire began to dim and all movement stopped.

Rest well, ladies, I thought, repeating Andrew's last words, suspecting it was the first-century version of "good night."

I sat alone, trying to digest everything that had happened. It was hard to believe I'd been in this new world for less than a day. As I stared into the dying fire, it surprised me I actually missed my home and family. By this time in the evening, Dad would be sitting in his living room recliner, typing away on his laptop, with some mind-numbing sitcom playing unwatched on the TV. Mom would be reading the Bible, a commentary, or a devotional on her Kindle at the dining room table. Angela, my sister, would be upstairs with earbuds jammed tightly into her ears, hoping to conceal the "devil's music" she was listening to. I would have made my way to some bar or club by now, and the world around me would already be getting hazy from too many shots or beers, thanks to the fake ID I'd been using for the last year and a half. A few hours later, I'd stagger back to my dorm room. If I was at home, I'd either have Becky drop me off, or if I'd managed to borrow dad's car, hope I wouldn't get pulled over on the drive home.

As I reminisced about it, I realized how thoroughly miserable I had been. I guess I didn't miss my old world so much, after all. I hoped everyone at home was alright. Of course, being here with Jesus in the first century meant none of them would even be born for another 2000 years. For the first time in a very, very long time, I thought about saying a prayer. That's when the guy I was about to pray to walked into the firelight.

"Thomas, I am pleased to find you still awake." Jesus said, "May I join you?"

"Of course, Lord," I wondered if I was supposed to call him that. It must have been acceptable because he sat down beside me.

"Joanna must return to Tiberias for a few days. I would like you to accompany her?"

"Me?...Who?" I blurted without thinking as sweat began trickling down my back. *Why was he asking me? And who was Joanna? Where was Tiberias?* I couldn't recall ever hearing about a place called Tiberias. *Would this journey commit me to a day, a week, or a month?* My mind pondered a thousand questions, but instead of asking any of them, I heard myself say. "Yes, Lord, I'd be happy to. When is she leaving?"

"Tomorrow morning. She will meet you here at sunrise. You will not be more than four or five days. I plan on staying here tomorrow to let everyone rest. Then we will go to Nazareth and from Nazareth to Capernaum, with a short stop along the way in Magdala. Joanna will guide you to Salome's house if you arrive back in Capernaum before we do. Zebedee will find a place for you. Probably on his roof," Jesus chuckled, "and definitely on his boat. Thank you, Thomas. I will see you in a few days." Jesus got to his feet and started to walk away.

"Does Joanna have family in Tiberias, Lord?"

Jesus stopped and turned. "Yes, a husband and a son. She will be seeing them while she is there. But that is not the only reason she is going. She must take her place at Herod Antipas's court, and then the three of you will be attending his birthday party at the palace."

CHAPTER 6

Joanna

When I woke the next morning, the eastern sky was brightening and the men around me were still asleep. Yet, someone had already rekindled the fire. The remaining fish stew from last night sat on several large round stones, warming over the flames. Someone had already collected and cleaned the dirty cups and bowls and returned the reed basket to its place near the fire. It could only have been the women from the other camp.

How do they move around so quietly? I wondered.

They'd woken no one and left no trace of their presence except the clean dishes, food, and warm fire.

I stood, stretched, and barely pulled my outer robe over my head when I saw one of the women walking toward me. She held two cups of steaming liquid in her hands.

"Good morning, Thomas," she held out one of the cups. "Broth?"

"Yes, please," I replied, taking the cup. It reminded me of one of my pottery projects in elementary school. The broth smelled like some kind of vegetable concoction and not at all appealing first thing in the morning, but I doubted she would understand if I asked where I could get a good Starbucks's latte.

She reached into a pouch concealed in her robe and handed me a piece of bread similar to the bread we'd eaten last night, only it smelled sweeter and spicier. Then, she sat near the fire. "Please, Thomas, come and enjoy your broth. There is stew leftover from last night if you like. We do not need to hurry. We will be in Tiberias by midday. That will allow us the time needed to prepare for tonight's festivities."

This lady was the older of the two women from last night. I went over the names of those I could remember in my head. Peter and Andrew. James, John, and their mother, Salome. Philip and Nathaniel, who had brought the report about John the Baptist, Judas, and....Joanna. There were four other men I couldn't put names to yet or the younger woman with us last night.

Not bad, I congratulated myself.

Less than twenty-four hours and I could name over half of the men and two of the women.

"I am sorry to take you away from the others, Thomas, but Jesus believes it is best I continue to maintain my presence at court when I can. And I am also looking forward to seeing my son and husband."

"Hey, no problemo Joanna," I nodded. "Happy to oblige."

Joanna's eyebrows rose as she stared at me like I'd fallen from outer space. "You speak so strangely, Thomas. Your words are unlike any Galilean I have ever known. Does everyone from your village speak as you do?"

Once again, I was caught off guard by a question like with Micah. I needed to figure out how to fit in better. Joanna assumed I was from Galilee. I tried to remember how the map in my Sunday school room looked. I'd probably been in there over five hundred times, yet I could only vaguely remember some of the highlights. I remembered the two large lakes, one at the top of the map and one at the bottom, connected by the Jordan River. The smaller of the two, in the north, must be the Sea of Galilee. That's where we were now.

I knew Nazareth was in Galilee, as was Cana where the wedding took place when Jesus turned water into wine. But that was about all I could remember. Jesus told me he was going to Capernaum after Nazareth, which also must be in Galilee. I knew Judea was in the south, where Jerusalem was, with Samaria somewhere between.

Amazing, I thought. Five hundred times and that was the best I could do.

I simply hadn't paid close enough attention because it wasn't important to me back then. Of course, I never expected to be in the Holy Land in the twenty-first century, much less in the first century, and I doubted I would find a map store or library in downtown Tiberias. But somehow, I needed to figure it out before making a complete fool of myself.

I could only imagine what a disaster it would be if my new

companions discovered I didn't even know the town of my birth or where I grew up. Both Andrew and Joanna said my speech sounded strange. I heard everyone speaking English, yet wondered how that could be possible. *Was English even spoken anywhere in the world during the first century? Probably not.* Obviously, the people around me were hearing me in their native language, but I didn't even know what language it was. Rome ruled most of the world, and the people probably spoke dozens of languages. *But what would be the current language in Galilee that Jesus and his companions spoke?*

Man, how would I ever survive in this world if I didn't know the simplest things?

I wasn't stupid. I'd gotten through high school with B's and C's but never really applied myself or focused on the practical stuff. School was just what I had to do to get by. I'd only gone to college because my dad insisted on it and look how that turned out. I always thought sooner or later, I would end up working for Uncle Leon's construction company anyway. At least construction seemed like something I was good at. But now, the days spent daydreaming or staring off into space during class were coming back to haunt me. I mean, why would I ever need to know where Galilee was located or what language they spoke in the first century. Yeah, well, another big mistake for me. I wasn't even as bright as these fishermen, who'd never spent a day in a regular classroom.

I looked at Joanna, who was waiting for my reply. She studied me as though she thought the mystery might be hidden somewhere in my face. I was about to spill the beans and tell her the truth when a high-pitched voice cried out, "Joanna, Joanna!" The other woman from last night ran toward us. She threw her arms around Joanna's neck weeping.

Joanna held her patiently, like a child, while she cried. Something told me this wasn't the first time this had happened.

"Tell me what's wrong, Mary?" Joanna held the woman at arm's length now. "What has happened?"

"He is going to take me home. He wants me to go back with him to Magdala, Joanna. I cannot go back there. I cannot! Why would he do this?"

I stood up in awe. This had to be Mary Magdalene. Perhaps the most famous and heroic woman of this time period. Though at the moment, she seemed slightly less heroic.

Joanna pulled her back into her arms and held her until Mary stopped crying. Joanna looked at me over Mary's shoulder. "Thomas, there is a pot of broth staying warm at the women's camp. Would you fetch some for us, please?"

I ran as quickly as I could to the fire on the women's side of camp. I said hello to Salome, whose arms were full of laundry, and nodded at four other women I hadn't seen before. "Joanna asked me to bring her and Mary some broth," I blurted out.

Salome's eyes widened in surprise. "That is most kind of you, Thomas. Suzanna, would you help Thomas with the broth, please?"

A woman in her early thirties with a light-colored outer tunic and a brown and white striped shawl walked to the fire where a clay pot hung from an iron tripod. She dipped a small pitcher with a wooden handle into the pot and filled it. Then she wiped the pitcher with her tunic, put a lid on it, and handed it to me.

When I got back to the men's camp where I'd left Joanna and Mary, several men were stirring. Joanna and Mary had moved to a quiet place by some rocks about twenty feet away. I grabbed a cup from the basket by the fire and went to them and filled their cups from the pitcher. Then, I walked back to where I'd left my own and refilled it. I was about to rejoin Joanna and Mary when one of the men shouted. "You will make a fine wife someday, Thomas!"

When I turned, I saw them laughing and pointing at me. I resisted using a hand gesture they probably wouldn't recognize in this century. There were more important things to do, not the least of which was fulfilling Jesus's request to get Joanna to Tiberias.

As I approached Joanna and Mary again, I hesitated, wondering if I might be intruding on their private conversation. It still stung from being made the butt of a joke by the men, and I didn't want to have the same thing happen twice. But my desperate desire to start learning everything I could about my new situation pushed me forward. I took the chance.

"Do not let them trouble you, Thomas," Joanna said as I sat on a large rock next to her. "They are still having a hard time adjusting to the new kingdom Jesus is leading us to. If it were up to the men, we women would not be allowed to be here, much less help Jesus with his work. They claim to despise the teachings of the scribes and Pharisees, but they still cling to the old ways." She took a sip of her broth and peered at me over the rim of the cup. "But somehow, you seem different, Thomas. You no longer treat us the same way the rest of the men do. Has Jesus spoken to you directly? In private? Is that why you speak with such strange words?"

I had the feeling this might be one of those pivotal moments between Joanna and me that could make a big difference. I would be spending a lot of time with her over the next few days. If I said the right thing, maybe she would be more open to answering some of my nagging questions. I thought back to the botany class I'd taken in college, the only course able to keep my interest enough to get a B. I also recalled several sermons from Pastor Nelson.

"Trees," I began

"Trees? Thomas, I do not understand."

"Did you know there are male trees and female trees? And some trees are both."

Joanna thought about it for a moment. "I do not know if what you say is true, Thomas, but no one can tell the difference even if it is as you say. All trees look the same."

"That's right, Joanna. They do. You can only tell the difference if you know exactly what you're looking for."

Joanna and Mary exchanged a confused look.

"Yesterday, Jesus said we would know the difference between a good tree and a bad tree by its fruit, right?"

They both nodded.

"Jesus said we can't get grapes from a thorn bush or figs from thistles. He said good trees bear good fruit and bad trees bear bad fruit. You will know which one is which by what kind of fruit grows on it. He didn't say anything about male trees or female trees. He simply said trees. I think the only difference Jesus cares about is what kind of fruit grows on those trees: good fruit or bad fruit. It's the only difference he cares about with people too. Not whether we are men or women, but only if we are good or bad because he doesn't look at the other differences between us."

Mary stood. "You are wise, Thomas, I will think on your words, but it is your brothers who need to hear your lessons, not us." Turning to Joanna, "Thank you, Joanna. I will do as you say. And I pray you have a safe journey. If I am able, I will join you in Capernaum." She turned and walked away.

"Will Mary be alright?" I asked.

"Yes, I am sure she will be fine. Now come, we must be on our way."

CHAPTER 7
The Road to Tiberias

We walked in silence for the first hour. There was so much I wanted to ask, but I didn't have a clue where to begin. How long had Thomas been in the group? How much would I already be expected to know about Joanna, or any of the others for that matter? Would the wrong question make her suspicious? Would it blow my cover? Did I need a cover?

I concluded I'd seen way too many time travel movies. I was more concerned about causal loops and the grandfather paradox than learning how to live in the moment. After all, if I asked the wrong question, it wasn't as if the space-time continuum would suddenly unravel, and I'd find myself sitting in a DeLorean back in 1955. No, this wasn't a movie.

Considering where I was and who I was with, it was possible—and I couldn't believe I was even thinking this—the God I didn't believe in had brought me through space and time for a specific reason. But why me? Why now? I certainly never gave God any reason to choose me.

Joanna said Tiberias was about half a day away. If I was going to be ready to play my part, whatever that meant, I needed to start learning everything I could.

I might as well jump into the deep end, I thought.

"So, how did you meet Jesus, Joanna?

After a few moments, she answered, "My husband took me to see him."

"I thought your husband lived in Tiberias at the palace? I was under the impression he is also part of Herod's court."

"Yes, all true. He is Herod's chief steward. He manages all of Herod's holdings throughout Galilee."

"Then why did he take you to see Jesus? Is your husband a Christian?"

Joanna stopped and looked at me confused. "What is this word, 'Christian'?" she lowered her voice. "If you are talking about the messiah, you must know Jesus does not wish us to speak of it. It is not his time yet."

I couldn't believe I'd said the word "Christian." It wouldn't have made any more sense to her than if I'd asked her why we weren't taking a taxi to the Holiday Inn. I needed to start thinking carefully about my word choices before I used them.

"No, of course not, Joanna. You're right. It's just one of those strange words I've picked up along the way. Ah, forget I even mentioned it. I meant, if your husband took you to see Jesus, is he also one of his followers?"

She stared at me for a long time with her brow furrowed. I was afraid I'd given myself away again. Then she smiled and began walking down the path. "It happened about two years ago."

I jogged to catch up to her and listened to her story.

"My husband, Chuza, was traveling with Antipas to the Feast of Unleavened Bread in Jerusalem. While they were on their way, they heard people talking about a prophet named John baptizing and preaching at the Jordan. On the way back, they went to listen to him. Even though Antipas does not follow Moses or the Torah, he seemed very taken by John's preaching. Afterwards, whenever John baptized in Galilee or Antipas traveled to Judea, he would make time to go and listen to John.

"Then, about a year ago, John began telling his disciples another would come after him. Someone even greater than he was. Someone who would restore the Kingdom of God to the house of Israel. The news about this new teacher began spreading everywhere. The stories we heard in Tiberias claimed he was unlike anyone who had ever come before him. They reported he performed miracles and healings wherever he went. During the same time, our son's illness became worse than ever."

"Your son was sick?"

"Yes." She wiped tears from her face. "He had been a sickly boy from the day of his birth, and he kept getting weaker no matter what we did. Finally, he fell asleep with a terrible fever, and no one could wake him. All the physicians at the palace believed he would die, and they were trying to prepare us for his death. Chuza and I stayed with him day and night for weeks, giving him water and broth if he could swallow it, but he would not wake up.

Then, Antipas ordered my husband to go to Capernaum to settle some affairs at his estate there. Chuza pleaded with Antipas to let him stay with Samuel and me, but Antipas ordered him to go. He had no choice but to follow the king's orders. While Chuza was in Capernaum, he received word the new prophet had arrived in Cana. The messenger said he turned six pots of water into wine. Chuza rode for Cana that very hour. When he found Jesus on the road, he begged him to come to Tiberias and heal our son, but Jesus told him he would not go to Tiberias because the city was unclean. Then Jesus said to him, 'Your son lives.'"

Joanna wiped her eyes again. "I was holding Samuel the moment the fever left him, and he woke up. It was the very same hour Jesus said to Chuza, 'Your son lives.' Samuel is a strong, healthy boy now."

These were precisely the things I needed to learn. Now I'd confirmed Herod Antipas was, in fact, the ruler of this entire region, and the area was indeed called Galilee. It was very likely he was the same Herod who would be involved in Jesus's trial, coming up in about two and a half years. I also learned Antipas wasn't a religious Jew, but he either enjoyed going to the feasts in Jerusalem or went to keep up appearances as a way to gain support from his Jewish subjects. That must have been what he was doing when he went to see John the Baptist the first time and why he would be in Jerusalem for Jesus's trial during Passover. This was good. I was starting to get my bearings.

Wanting to hear more, I asked, "That's an amazing story, Joanna. When did Chuza take you to see Jesus?"

Joanna smiled. "Do you think you are about to die, Thomas? Perhaps before we arrive in Tiberias?"

"No, of course not. Why would you ask such a thing?"

"Because you are so impatient." She said then laughed. "You wish to hear the whole story before I have even finished the beginning."

Slowing down was one of the many things I would have to adjust to in this time period. Life here progressed slower, and the stories were much longer. The walk to Tiberias would take us the better part of the morning. The day before yesterday, I could have made it in fifteen minutes in my dad's Camry. Of course, paved roads didn't exist here yet. And by the looks of the rocky mountainous terrain, maybe never would.

Slow down and listen, I reminded myself. *Take your time and learn.*

"I'm sorry, Joanna," I tilted my head down in a humbling nod. "Please, go on. I promise I will be patient and listen."

Joanna nodded and continued down the narrowing trail, often leaving me behind her, straining to hear.

"When Chuza arrived home, it was one of the most wonderful days of our lives. One of the servants reported to Samuel and me that Chuza was in the palace. Samuel jumped up, ran out of our quarters, and disappeared down the hall." Tears flowed freely down her cheeks. "It was the first time I had ever seen him run. The very first time. When they returned to our rooms, Chuza carried Samuel on his shoulders. They sat on the bed with me, and the three of us stayed there the rest of the morning, laughing and telling stories. I think I fell in love with my husband on that day, Thomas. I feel I discovered what real love is like as we sat there together. All because of Jesus, and I had not even met him yet."

Joanna looked over at me when she noticed me wiping at the corner of my eyes. She must have also seen the unspoken questions on my face.

"I was born in Chorazin," she went on. "My father owns a vast estate west of the Jordan River on the Chorazin Plateau. The estate supplies much of the region, including most of Galilee, with wheat and barley, and I have also heard many say our vineyards produce the finest wine east of the Mediterranean Sea." A sparkle in her eyes told me she enjoyed this part of her story. "The Syrian kingdom and its army are only a few leagues to our north. So, to ensure my father's loyalty and keep the supplies flowing south from the plateau, King Herod the Great assigned a garrison of soldiers to protect our land. Then he summoned my father to Jerusalem, where he became a member of Herod's court.

"When Herod the Great died, Rome sent his son, Antipas, to Galilee, and Antipas retained my father and took him with him to Tiberias. Once my parents were settled, my father arranged my marriage with Chuza. I was fifteen and Chuza thirty-five. It was not a bad marriage. Chuza has always been kind and caring from the very beginning, but I did not love him. Nor do I think he loved me. Our marriage worked well for everyone. Antipas was content because it further sealed my father's obligation to the Roman province and kept the grain and other supplies flowing south uninterrupted. My father was happy because it secured his family's station in the royal court for generations to come. And Chuza was pleased because he found a suitable Jewish wife."

"Suitable Jewish wife?" I questioned.

"Chuza is Nabataean. He grew up in the Arabian court of King Aretas in Petra. He was a childhood friend of Phasaelis, who became Antipas's first wife. Shortly after Phasaelis and Antipas wed, she used her influence to bring Chuza to Tiberias, where he continued in his role as Master of Servants. As he moved up to more prestigious positions in Antipas's household and finally became Chief Steward, he needed to convert to Judaism, at least outwardly. A Jewish wife would prove to the religious leaders he was a true proselyte.

"My father arranged the marriage and brought me to the palace for the wedding. I met Chuza the day we were married. I always expected my father to choose my husband, but I found it difficult at first. Life in Tiberias differs greatly from growing up on the plateau. My father is very wealthy, and I grew up wanting nothing. But, even so, being among the nobles and aristocrats terrified me. I lived in constant fear I would do or say something to humiliate my husband, and we would be expelled from the court or worse. After only one month at court, I saw one of the servants flogged to death for spilling wine on a linen table covering. I believe living with constant fear is what caused me to bring the greatest shame of all on my husband."

Joanna walked silently for the next few minutes, trying to pull herself together.

"I was unable to bear him children," she said finally. "For four years, I was barren. Every day I was afraid Chuza would be forced to put me away and choose another wife, and I would be sent back to Chorazin in disgrace. Then in the fourth year, I conceived, but Samuel and I both nearly died on the day he was born. It was dreadful, Thomas. I suffered for almost two days without being any closer to delivery. Finally, when it became clear we were both going to die, the midwife saved us by turning my son in my womb so he could be born. It was a risky thing to do, but it spared both our lives."

I found myself leaning closer, hanging onto Joanna's every word. What an incredible story of love and survival!

"I was crippled for the next eight years."

I stopped dead in my tracks. I couldn't help glancing down at her legs, covered by her long tunic. My mouth moved, but no words came. Finally, I pointed at her feet and managed a weak, "But how?"

"Jesus, of course." She smiled, then continued down the path. "We were deeply grateful to Abigail, but whatever she did to save Samuel's life left me unable to walk. Because I had servants to help me, I was able to take care of Samuel, but my life at the palace became very different. Strangely, even though I had to be carried everywhere, I lost my fear of the other noblewomen and aristocrats. I began taking my responsibilities in Antipas's household more seriously and applied myself to my role as the Chief Steward's wife. I even began meeting with prominent Jewish women throughout Galilee and Perea as a representative of Herod's court. I became a highly valued member of the household, just as my father was appointed overseer of the entire Chorazin Plateau."

"I might still be there today, being carried about on my litter, my life wasting away, had my husband not sought out Jesus on the road from Cana. I dare say, Thomas, few in Antipas's household, including Antipas himself, were not affected by Samuel's healing. Word traveled quickly through the palace, and as Chuza, Samuel, and I were rejoicing together that first day, one of the palace guards knocked on our door. 'Lord Chuza. The Tetrarch requires your presence in the audience chamber,' he announced.

"'Of course,' Chuza shouted back. 'On my way.'

"Then the guard added, 'He would have you bring the boy.'"

CHAPTER 8
Antipas

Joanna continued her story, "As soon as he heard the summons, Chuza sent for my bearers. He lifted me onto the litter, and we hurried down the long corridor to Antipas's receiving room, where he met with visiting royals and nobles. Even without seeing his face, I knew Chuza beamed with pride as he and his son ran together for the first time. Usually, Samuel rode on the litter with me, or one of my bearers carried him. Then, Chuza would instruct Samuel to wait outside the door while we were with the king. It had been years since Antipas invited Samuel to join us. Antipas is squeamish about being around anyone who is sick or infirmed.

"When we arrived, the guard opened the door and ushered Chuza and me into the chamber. Chuza led the way down the long aisle and knelt on one knee before Antipas. My bearers carried me in, set me down behind and to the left of Chuza, and quickly departed. I bowed as deeply as I could. When I lifted my head, I was surprised to see Antipas standing.

"'Send in the boy at once!' he shouted. 'I will see this wonder for myself.'

"The door opened and the guard led Samuel into the chamber. He ran directly to his father and wrapped his arms tightly around his neck, burying his face in Chuza's shoulder. Chuza whispered something into Samuel's ear, and Samuel stood up straight, turned to face Antipas, and gave a surprisingly proper bow.

"'Come,' Antipas said as he sat down. 'Come here, boy, let me take a look at you.'

"Samuel glanced at Chuza, who gave him a quick nod, and then Samuel stepped toward the dais. He walked steadily up the three steps and stood in front of Antipas, who looked Samuel over from top to bottom. He put his hand against Samuel's shoulder and gave him several shoves, trying to knock him off balance. He looked in Samuel's mouth and nose as if he were the garrison captain buying a new horse.

Then he pulled Samuel into his lap and hugged him close to his chest. Antipas looked at Chuza, 'This is the work of the Nazarene?'

"'It is, my lord,' Chuza replied, rising.

"'You have seen him?'

"'I have, my lord. I found him on the road between Capernaum and Cana. I begged him to come here and heal Samuel, but he refused. Then he said to me, 'Your son lives,' and when I arrived back at the palace this morning, I found Samuel as he is now.'

"Antipas looked at Samuel shaking his head. Then he whispered barely loud enough for me to hear, the words he must have heard from the Baptist, 'One whose sandals I am not worthy to untie.' He sat there holding Samuel for a long time, then looked up and spoke to Chuza, 'What was he like, Steward? Does he speak like John? Does he condemn me as John does? How many follow him? Do you intend to go after him now, as well? Will you take up this man's cause because he saved your son, Nabatean?'

"I could tell Chuza was giving careful thought to each of Antipas's questions. The wrong answers could cost him his life, perhaps mine and Samuel's as well. After only a moment Chuza addressed the king.

"'My lord, during the day I spent with him, I heard the Nazarene teach the people that no man can serve two masters. I believe he speaks the truth. I will forever be grateful to him for what he has done for my son, but I have sworn my allegiance to you and your house alone. I will not forsake that pledge. If you will pardon me for leaving my post in Capernaum, I will continue to serve you. As for the Nazarene, he draws large crowds, but his words are hard to accept. His ways are difficult. His followers sleep in open fields or caves. They depend on the benevolence of others to sustain themselves. Only a few travel with him wherever he goes, mostly fishermen and day laborers. Though he speaks of a kingdom, he claims it is not of this earth. As such, he poses no threat to your rule in Galilee or Pilate's in Judea, my lord. He makes his case only against Israel's religious leaders, not against Rome or you. He is nothing like John. He speaks with a gentle voice. He seeks to shepherd the people, not rule over them, or turn them from you.'

"'Where is he now?'

"'When I left him, he and about twenty others were on their way to Magdala.'

"Antipas allowed Samuel to slip off his lap and rejoin me on my litter."

"'I would very much like to meet this Nazarene who has mended your son,' Antipas gazed past us at something only he could see. 'Now that John is here in the palace, he refuses to speak with me, other than rail against my new wife. Your former monarch, Aretas, wants to go to war because he claims I dishonored his daughter. Perhaps I should have heeded the Baptizer, after all, Chuza. These women may yet be my ruin.' He stood and turned his back on Chuza, clasping his hands behind him. 'Regardless of what you say, these prophets can be a troublesome lot. They have more power than you think. The people love them. And love is always stronger than fear, Steward. Nonetheless, if this Nazarene speaks somewhere locally where I can listen to him without being seen, report to me at once.'

"'Perhaps I could learn of his plans, my lord. I could—'

"'So, you do intend to see this prophet again, after all?' Antipas spun quickly toward us as he spoke.

"Chuza bowed his head low, 'With your permission, my lord, I wish to take my wife to see him. I believe he could do for her what he has done for Samuel. Then, I will immediately return to your service.'

"I have no idea what went through Antipas's mind over the next few moments. He returned to his throne and sat quietly, looking between Chuza, Samuel, and me. Occasionally he looked down as though he could see John in one of the dungeons below. Finally, Antipas rose and walked toward the back of the chamber. He stopped at the door and without turning around and said, 'You go alone, Steward. No servants, no guards. Just the two of you. You may take one horse. Samuel stays here.' Then he left the room without looking back."

CHAPTER 9
Two Healings

After finishing the story, Joanna pointed to a tree shading the side of the road and suggested we stop for a bite to eat. She handed me something that looked like a brownie but tasted similar to a Fig Newton.

"Is that when you went to see Jesus?" I asked, accepting a wineskin Joanna pulled from beneath her robe.

"Yes. We made arrangements for Samuel to stay with one of my servants and left that very afternoon. It was a short but challenging journey. I had not been on a horse since Samuel's birth, and because my legs were so weak, I was not much help to Chuza. By the time we reached Magdala, he was exhausted from keeping me on the horse. We stayed the evening with an official from the court who lived nearby and rose early the following day to find the entire village gathering on the seashore. Jesus had arrived.

"Chuza picked me up like a child, and we joined the crowd. When we reached the shore, hundreds of people were already there listening to Jesus. He stood in a boat several paces off the shoreline. 'A farmer went out to plant his seed,' Jesus began. 'As he went, some seed fell alongside the path, and the birds flew down and ate it up. Other seeds fell on rocky places where there was not much soil. The seed sprouted quickly. But when the sun came up, the young plants were scorched, and since their roots were not very deep, they dried up. Other seeds fell among thorns, and when the plants grew up, the thorns choked them. But other seeds fell onto rich soil and produced grain. Some thirty, sixty, or a hundred times as much as had been sown. If you can hear, then listen to my words.'

"Chuza began making his way through the crowd, moving us closer to Jesus. That's when we heard a horrific scream behind us. A woman came running from among several tall towers standing against the sea. She weaved her way between dozens of fishing boats moored on the beach. Three men were chasing her. Several women followed behind them. The screaming woman was Mary whom you met this morning back at the camp."

"Ah, Mary Magdalene," I nodded in understanding.

Joanna gave me a puzzled look again. A look I was growing far too familiar with.

"We call her Mary of the Tower, but Mary Magdalene sounds perfect, Thomas. I think she will like that name much better. Mary of the Tower reminds her too much of her former life and family."

"The family Jesus intends to return her to. That's why she was so upset this morning, right?"

"Yes," Joanna answered sadly. "The men chasing her were her two younger brothers and her father. She nearly reached the shoreline when her brothers caught her and began dragging her back toward the towers. They tore her tunic badly during the struggle but did not seem to care they'd exposed their sister to the crowd. Chuza set me down and turned to help just as Jesus commanded the brothers to stop. He left the boat and waded ashore, reaching Mary at the same time her father did. I remember how Mary's father pointed his finger at Jesus accusingly.

"'Go back to your boat, Rabbi. This has nothing to do with you.' He waved his hand at the crowd which parted to let Jesus pass. 'They are who you came to see. These fools are waiting for you to touch them and cast your spell, but leave us be. My daughter is of no concern to you.'

"'All of my father's children are my concern, Benjamin,' Jesus replied.

"'Mary broke free from her brothers and let out a crazy laugh. Then she crawled across the sand to wrap her arms around Jesus's legs. She began screaming, 'Benjamin, Benjamin, Benjamin,' shouting louder each time she said her father's name.

"Jesus knelt beside her, and she went silent as he tied her torn tunic together at her shoulder.

"'Is it not true your family owns the salting towers and the docks, Benjamin?' Jesus asked, rising to face Mary's father.

"'I am the firstborn. It came to me, yes. Someday it will be his." Benjamin pointed to one of the boys. 'My three brothers and their wives work here, along with their sons and daughters. Half of Magdala profits from our work. Fishermen and fisheries throughout the whole empire depend on our salt.'

"'The whole empire,' Jesus repeated with a touch of sarcasm. 'Yet one of your own is lost.' He placed his hand on Mary's head. 'What do you think?' he raised his voice so the crowd could hear him but continued looking straight at Benjamin. 'If a man has a hundred sheep, and one of them has gone astray, does he not leave the ninety-nine on the mountainside and go and search for the one astray? If it turns out he finds the lamb, without a doubt, I say to you, he rejoices over it more than the ninety-nine that have not gone astray. Let me assure you. It is not the will of your father who is in Heaven that even one of these little ones perish. You provide well for your sons, Benjamin, for your brothers, your nephews, their families, half of Magdala, even the whole empire, yet you could not save this one.'

"'She is a thief and a liar,' one of Mary's brothers shouted. 'She steals from the till and spends it foolishly. She lies about—'

"'What she has taken, Asher is easily replaced,' Jesus interrupted, turning to look at him. 'They are nothing more than pieces of metal dug from the ground. But what you and Ephraim have taken from your sister, neither of you has the power to return. Without a doubt, I say to you she will be made whole again this very day. Now tell us, Ephraim, what other sins has she committed against you? Or shall we ask Mary to speak?'

"Jesus maintained eye contact with Mary's brothers until they both hung their heads in shame and walked away. He looked at Mary's father, then at her mother and sister, who had come to stand beside Benjamin. Each one, in turn, lowered their eyes in shame. Then Jesus knelt on the sand next to Mary. He placed both hands on her head and prayed. He did the same for her ears, eyes, mouth, heart, stomach, and feet, casting out seven demons from her. He sat with Mary until she finally looked up at him with clear eyes. The woman who had come screaming across the beach only a short time earlier was gone, and Mary of the Tower—Mary Magdalene—was born.

"Jesus rose, helped her to her feet, and led her to her mother. Her mother and sister wrapped her in their arms and began walking her back toward the tower. Jesus looked at Benjamin until he also turned and walked away. Mary spent that night with her family, but she left before daybreak the next morning. She found Jesus in Capernaum a few days later and has been with him every day since. That was over a month ago."

Tears streamed down my cheeks hearing Joanna's version of Mary's story and healing. If only I'd arrived a month earlier, I might have witnessed it myself. I was blown away with emotions I'd never encountered before. Joy for Mary, rage toward her family, especially her brothers who had obviously done something horrible to their sister. I was especially grateful I was now a part of this wonderful story. Then it dawned on me. "You came all the way to see Jesus, but it was Mary who got healed and not you."

Joanna took the wineskin from my hand, and it disappeared under her tunic. She stood and resumed the walk toward Tiberias. When I caught up with her, she smiled, "Just a bit more patience, Thomas. My story is nearly over.

"When Jesus turned back toward the crowd and saw Chuza standing there with me sitting beside him, he came directly to us. 'Your son is well,' he stated. It was not a question."

"'Yes, Lord,' Chuza answered. 'He runs and jumps like any boy his age. I wish he were here to thank you himself. I can never repay you for what you did.'

"'I believe you can, Chuza. If I could ask it of you?'

"'Of course, Lord, anything.'

"'Please, sit with me.' Jesus took a place on my left so the three of us could sit together. 'I have much to do in Galilee, and my time has not yet come. I must be able to finish my work and move about freely for a short time longer. Galilee, Samaria, Judea, and Peraea need to hear the words of my father's kingdom and see his works. If that fox who sits in his palace in Tiberias believes I am a threat to him, he may move against me before it is my time. Tell me, Chuza, is what you have seen here today a challenge to his power? Does your son's healing threaten him or Rome?'

"'No, of course not, Lord.'

"'Then that is what you must report. Tell him what you see and hear. The blind receive sight and the lame walk; lepers are cleansed and the deaf hear.'

"'I have already spoken these very same words to him, Rabbi. And I will speak them again. He listens to every report coming to the palace about you. He very much wants to see you.'

"Jesus lowered his head. 'I know,' he responded quietly. 'Tell him the day will come soon enough. When the time is right, I will be brought to him. Tell him, I will not finish my work without coming before him.' Then Jesus turned and looked at me, 'Why are you here, daughter?'

"'To see the one who is the Promise of Israel and behold his kingdom,' I answered.

"'And to walk again?'

"'Yes, Lord, if it pleases you.'

"Jesus turned to Chuza, 'If she walks again, her legs will carry her away from you for a time. I have already asked much of you. Can you give still more?'

"Chuza took Jesus's hand and kissed it. 'Yes, Lord. Even though I have pledged myself to Herod Antipas, I will do anything for you that does not require me to betray my oath.'

"'Your presence in Herod's house will serve me and my father well, Chuza. But take care; Antipas does not love you. He will turn on you the moment he senses your loyalties are divided.'

"Then Jesus asked me. 'Will you follow me, daughter? The journey will require much of you as well. Remain as you are, and you can return safely to the palace and your son. If you follow me, there will be many tears and lonesome nights. You will miss watching your son grow up.'

"When I told him I would follow him wherever his path took him, he put his hands on me, and the strength in my legs returned immediately. He and Chuza helped me stand for the first time in eight years. Then Jesus walked back into the crowd and began to heal those who had come to him. He remained with the people throughout the day, healing and teaching them about the Kingdom of God. Chuza left for home in the evening without me. I have been with Jesus and the others since that day."

"Over a month has passed since you have seen Samuel and Chuza?" I asked.

"Yes, Thomas, but the wait is over. Tiberias is beyond that hill." She pointed.

CHAPTER 10
The Palace

When we reached the top of the next hill, I could see Tiberias in the valley below, snug up against the western shore of the Sea of Galilee. The contrast of the fertile green valley on the right, the blue-green sea on the left, and the busy city in between created a stunning sight. Tiberias was smaller than I expected but not lacking in imperialistic grandeur. The royal palace stood on a man-made hill in the center of the city close to the sea, giving the whole area an ominous, almost foreboding feeling. From our perspective high above, the city looked like someone had taken hundreds of cardboard boxes of different shapes and sizes, painted them a brilliant white, and laid them out in a crisscross pattern. Narrow paths between the buildings allowed foot traffic within the city, while several larger main roads led straight out from the palace like spokes on a wagon wheel.

I stood there amazed, my eyes moving slowly over the scene, trying to take in as much as possible.

"The city was built and founded by Herod Antipas ten years ago," Joanna said. "Much of it is still under construction." I followed the line of her finger as she pointed to an area south of the city. "There, among those tall shrubs, are the hot springs of King Solomon. Antipas moved his capital from Sepphoris to Tiberias to be closer to the hot springs. He believes the waters have healing power and often goes there to bathe. One of the reasons he is so curious about Jesus is because he lives in constant fear of becoming sick and dying. Having a healer in his debt is a cunning plan and typical of the way Antipas thinks and schemes."

"In his debt?" I asked.

"Antipas does nothing without a plan. And you can be sure whatever he does will benefit him and his rule somehow." She sounded like someone with personal experience. "There is no other explanation for why he has allowed me to leave my place at court and travel openly with a band of vagabonds and commoners who follow a religious leader who could easily become a threat to his rule. Antipas has already come under sharp criticism from the royal families and aristocrats here and in

Jerusalem for allowing me to tarnish the court's reputation. He knows Chuza and I intend to use our wealth to support Jesus and the others. He would have delivered me back to the palace in irons by now if he did not believe he had something to gain in all of this. And Jesus is right at the center of it. I fear one day Antipas will use his benevolence as leverage for his own gain. There is much to learn over the next few days, Thomas, if we keep our eyes and ears open. Now, come. We must hurry. Many things need doing before we make our submission before the king." Joanna started making her way down the steep slope.

"We? Oh no! No way, Joanna! My job was to get you here safely. Jesus didn't say anything about me meeting with a king. Look at my clothes! Look at me! He'll take me for one of those... vagabonds."

Joanna couldn't help but laugh at my discomfort. "Do not be dull, Thomas. You are one of Jesus's closest disciples. Antipas will insist on seeing you and speaking with you. He already knows you are with me."

"He does?"

"Of course, he does. You have not seen them, but his men have been watching us since we stopped to eat."

I looked around me suddenly, searching for any sign of spies but saw nothing.

"But do not worry, Thomas. Antipas rarely has anyone executed the first day." She laughed openly again. "Though I would suggest you refrain from using so many of your strange words when he calls you before him. He may think you are a spy and have your head removed."

Joanna didn't turn around, but I could sense the smile still on her face as she taunted me. I wasn't amused. This was serious. What did I know about meeting with a king? And she was right. I might be able to fool her and the others into believing I was the genuine disciple Thomas, but Antipas would see right through me. I really could lose my head if I weren't careful. This little trip back in time had just taken on a whole new dimension.

"Chuza will have the appropriate clothing for you," she shouted over her shoulder. "You will need them for the king's party tonight anyway."

Thirty minutes later, we reached the outermost edge of Tiberias.

Joanna weaved her way through the narrow, crowded streets as if she'd grown up in the neighborhood. The buildings were single-story dwellings or shops, maybe ten to twelve feet high, made of large limestone blocks and covered with a stucco-style finish. Some had small courtyards in the front with reeds or large wool blankets over the doors and windows. Many had stone steps at the front or side leading up to a flat roof.

As we drew closer to the palace, the buildings became larger. Here, the shops had two stories, with different purposes for each floor. The further into the city we went, the more extravagant the buildings became. Wooden doors and shutters replaced the reeds and blankets.

While entire blocks around the city's perimeter were single structures divided by walls or stairs, near the palace, many of the homes were not only larger and more opulent but stood alone as separate buildings divided by tall, freestanding stone walls or iron fences. It seemed the opposite of the American cities I had visited, where the innermost parts were the poorest, and the outer suburbs were where the wealthy built on spacious lots of land.

We stepped out of a small alleyway between two large fenced-in homes and found ourselves directly in front of the palace. A courtyard about half the size of a football field occupied the area immediately in front of the palace steps. Dozens of pushcarts or small makeshift structures filled the square. Vendors sold everything from fish and bread to bolts of cloth or leather belts to scarves and jewelry.

"This way, Thomas!" Joanna called, pulling the hood of her cloak over her head. She led me to the right, down the outer edge of the courtyard, and past several of the most prominent buildings facing the palace. The two dozen soldiers guarding the steps paid us little mind, caring more about controlling the vendors and the crowd. Joanna led us back into the poorer section of the city for several blocks, then behind four wooden buildings which smelled like horse manure. I guessed these must have been the stables.

Once past the stables, we left the city behind and walked down a long hill to the edge of the Sea of Galilee. We blended with a large group of fishermen tending to their boats, mending nets, or cleaning fish. Other workers loaded mule-drawn wagons or handcarts with today's catch and drove or pulled them up the hill toward the large courtyard or south along the shoreline where another group of boats and fishermen were waiting.

I glanced at the palace, now about a hundred yards away. "What are we doing here, Joanna?"

"There's someone I need to see," she said, "and I cannot get to him by going through the front. There's an entrance to the palace in the back for the laundry. We can use it without anyone alerting Antipas."

"Won't there be guards at the back door? And what about the men who are watching us?"

"They left us when we entered the city. And no one bothers guarding the servants who scrub the pots and wash the bedding. There will be guards above the washer room, but we don't need to go that way. There will only be one guard on this side of the dungeon, and if God grants us favor, it will be one I know."

"Dungeon?"

"Yes. We are going to see the Baptizer."

I followed Joanna along the shoreline, hurrying to keep up with her.

"The palace is three stories tall, and the only access to the top-level is from the front," she explained, pointing to the back of the palace.

I looked carefully and noticed the top-level rose at least thirty feet above the bottom level. No doors or windows were visible on any level of the rear wall except the single door at ground level, which appeared to be our destination.

"You saw the soldiers at the foot of the steps out front," Joanna continued. "If you get past them and go up the sixteen steps to the portico, you would encounter the rest of the garrison before reaching the front doors. The royal bedchambers for Antipas, his new wife, Herodias, and her daughter, Salome, are on the top level, as well as the royal meeting rooms. The rest of the court resides on the middle level, which can only be accessed by a single stairwell near the center of the palace. The kitchens, laundry, servants' quarters, and dungeons are located on the bottom level...Thomas, are you listening to me? You will need to know this if we get separated."

I shook myself to focus on her words again. "Yes, yes, the dungeon is on the bottom level." But honestly, I hardly heard a word after she said the name "Salome." Why hadn't I seen it before? It was so obvious. The men discussed John's arrest last night around the fire. We were here so Joanna could take her place at court, but more importantly, so she could attend Antipas's birthday party. Herodias and Salome would be there. And Salome would... dance...which meant John the Baptist was going to die in only a few hours.

Joanna's pounding on the door brought my attention back to the present again. When no response came, she stooped down, picked up a rock, and used it to knock again.

"Coming, coming, coming!" a man shouted from inside. "The king will have your head if you damage that door! Now step back, you swineherd. Step back!"

We did as we were told, and not a moment too soon. The huge wood and brass door swung out toward us. "What could be so da—"

The old man who'd nearly knocked us over was bent sharply at the waist. His wrinkled hands looked like they spent more time underwater than in the dry air. What little hair he had left on his head grew long, white, and stringy. I guessed it hadn't seen a comb or brush in years. Unlike his hands, it didn't appear his face had felt the touch of water since he was a boy. I watched as his dark, weathered complexion turned a ghostly white and his mouth dropped open, revealing toothless gums.

"Lady Joanna!" he squeaked, falling to his knees and bowing his head. He reached out blindly, trying to find Joanna's hand. When he found it, he kissed it over and over, weeping. "Forgive this old fool—my lady. I thought you were one of those godless Peraeans from upstairs with more linen for washin'. Forgive—" he stopped again, toothless mouth hanging open, rheumy eyes staring at Joanna. "Praise be to the Highest! How is this possible, my lady? You walk!"

"A story that will have to wait for another time, Simeon," Joanna said, freeing her hand from his grip and walking into the laundry room to look around. "Where is Abigail?"

"Upstairs, my lady. Delivering the king's garments for tonight's banquet. Shall I send—"

"No, no, Simeon. You can take care of what I need. But we must hurry. How many prisoners does our good Tetrarch have in his dungeon today?"

"Six, my lady. Not including the prophet."

"Good. Then I shall need a small basket of bread; three loaves should be enough, and a pitcher of clean water and eight cups."

"Of course, my lady. It will take no time at all, not at all." The old man scurried out of the room through a side door.

I followed Joanna to the other side of the room where she inspected several wooden tables covered with stacks of carefully folded sheets and blankets. "What are you looking for?" I asked.

"This," she held up a rectangular piece of cloth about the size of a dishtowel. A beautifully embroidered profile of a man within a circle about the size of a fifty-cent piece decorated both ends.

"What is it?"

She folded the cloth in half longways and draped it across her left arm. "It's a mappa. A Roman custom. The servants will be wearing them like this tonight as they move among the guests during supper." She raised her arm slightly. "They will have a small bowl of water in their right hands and the mappa over their left arms. The guests will dip their fingers in the water and then dry them on the mappa. I first saw them when my mother and father entertained Roman dignitaries at our villa in Chorazin." She took the mappa off her arm and held it up for me to see. "And today, God is with us, Thomas. This one has the royal signet embroidered on it."

I was about to ask her what she meant when Simeon returned carrying the basket and pitcher.

"Thank you, Simeon." Joanna took the basket from him and handed it to me. She made slight adjustments to the bread and cups, then unfolded the mappa and placed it over the contents.

"I may not need this, but if I do, I will only have it for a short time, Simeon. I will return it with the basket when we are finished."

"Of course, my lady."

"Who is the guard on this side of the dungeon today?"

"Markus, my lady."

"Then, God truly is with us. Come, Thomas. Bring the basket. The hour is getting late."

Joanna led me through several storage rooms containing tables filled with bedding and regal garments. The rooms were spotless, well-lit with sconces every few feet, and had several narrow openings near the tops of the walls to let in natural light.

As we continued down the narrowing hall, the smooth, clean floors and walls gave way to rough-cut limestone blocks and loose gravel underfoot. I drew my cloak closer as the cold, damp air began to seep into my bones. The hall became so narrow Joanna and I could no longer walk side by side. When Simeon mentioned only one guard on this side of the dungeons, I wondered why the security was so light. Now, seeing how tight and dim the passage was, I understood how one well-trained soldier could easily defend it.

Joanna led the way until the hall made a sharp turn to the right. I could see over her shoulder where the hall widened again about thirty feet ahead. Several wall torches lit an iron gate and firelight glinted off the armor of a Roman soldier.

"Stop where you are and state your name and your purpose!" he shouted, drawing his short blade.

"Markus, it's Joanna. Lord Chuza's wife."

"Lady Joanna? Why are you here, and who is that with you?"

"We come on behalf of His Highness. She looked up at me and smiled. We have bread and fresh water for the prisoners and for you as well."

"Who do you have with you?" he demanded.

"His name is Thomas. He is my escort. May we approach, please?

"Come."

I followed Joanna until the passage widened and I could walk on her left. When we reached the guard, he rested the tip of his sword against my chest but never took his eyes from Joanna.

"So the rumors are true, my lady," he said, looking Joanna over from head to toe. "You walk. And now I hear you abandoned your senses and follow this healer." He turned to me, sliding the tip of the sword up my chest until it reached the hollow of my neck. "And you, Thomas the escort, do you follow this Nazarene as well?"

Joanna opened her mouth, but the guard's hand shot up to silence her. "Speak up, Galilean, or I will make your silence permanent."

As the tip of the guard's sword dug deeper into my throat, I became intensely aware of how very different life really was here. In my entire life as Tom Evans, I'd never known a single moment when my life was in grave danger. I never knew fear for myself or anyone else like I experienced in this moment. In the few short hours I'd spent with Joanna, I'd come to care for her deeply. How I answered this soldier's question could not only cost me my life but hers as well.

Do you follow the Nazarene? Less than three days ago, I would've had no problem answering that question.

I thought back to my last night at home. At 2:30 am, Becky and I were leaving Fort's Tavern on Saturday night. "Let's head over to the Red Iron," I suggested, putting an arm across Becky's shoulders to steady myself. "They always stay open past closing."

"Don't you have to be up for church in a few hours?" Becky asked. "Your dad—"

"My dad doesn't run my life or tell me what to believe anymore, Beck!" I shouted with a slur. "I'm sick of pretending I believe in a God who doesn't exist. It's time I followed my own path, not some make-believe Jesus who never existed."

The warm trickle of blood running down my chest brought me back to reality.

Do you follow the Nazarene? Do you follow Jesus Christ?

Well, there it was....the million dollar question. Do you follow the Nazarene? I couldn't very well deny I knew him. I walked with him, talked with him, and listened to him preach. I came here to this miserable prison because he asked me to escort Joanna. And I agreed. But why? Why had I been so willing to say yes? Who was the Nazarene really? A man? God's son? A savior? An impostor? I couldn't answer any of those questions. All I knew for sure, whoever this Jesus was, he had changed me. In one incredible day, he changed me. The only important question of the moment was the one being asked by the man with his sword to my throat.

Do you follow the Nazarene?

"I do," I answered in as steady a voice as I could muster, preparing to accept the consequences of my answer.

"Markus, enough," Joanna whispered.

Markus removed the sword from my throat and slid it back into the sheath at his waist. Then he went to one knee and bowed his head to Joanna, "Forgive me, my lady. I regret it was necessary. I had to be sure. If Antipas discovers believers among his guard, he will have us flayed and given to the dogs. Then he would send word back to Rome, and our families would be slaughtered."

"I know, Markus, I know." Joanna placed a hand on the guard's breastplate. "It is alright. Thomas understands."

I wasn't sure I understood at all, but at the moment, I was simply relieved to still have a head on my shoulders.

Markus stood and held out a hand to me. I reached out my hand to take his, but he reached past it and grabbed my forearm tightly. I copied his move, and we stood there, gripping arms and staring into each other's eyes. A first-century Roman soldier and a twenty-first-century college dropout whose lives would never be the same because they had both chosen to follow the Nazarene.

"We need to see the Baptizer, Markus. When did the day guards make their last round?"

"Less than an hour ago. You should be fine if you do not stay too long. If any of them do come in, tell them I—"

"No need, my dear brother. I will simply show them this." Joanna lifted the basket covered with the mappa bearing the king's signet. "It seems Antipas is feeling unusually benevolent on his birthday."

Markus smiled wide as he pulled the large set of keys from his belt.

CHAPTER 11
John

I picked up the basket of bread and grabbed one of the torches from the wall while Markus unlocked the heavy wooden door.

"Be careful, my lady. These are dangerous men."

"I will, Markus. We will not be long."

Joanna stopped at every cell and gave each prisoner a piece of bread and a cup of water. The men were more grateful than threatening and accepted Joanna's gifts with thanks. Two of them cowered in the back of dark cells, unwilling to come close to the bars and the bright light of the torch. Joanna left their bread and water on the floor inside the bars. After we passed, I heard them scurrying across the floor to retrieve their prizes. We finally arrived at the last cell on the left.

"John?" she called.

No reply.

"John, my name is Joanna. I am the wife of Chuza, the steward of Herod's household. I have food and water and a message for you from Jesus."

We stood in silence for several minutes before we heard movement from a dark corner of the cell. Naked except for a filthy cloth around his waist, a man stepped into the light. His hair and beard were long and dirty, and his bottom ribs poked through his skin like two old washboards. When he reached us, he grabbed the bars of the cell to steady himself and keep his hands from shaking.

He stared at Joanna for a long time, struggling to get words out of his trembling lips. Finally, he whispered, "The blind see, the lame walk, the deaf..." his right hand released the bar, and he waved in the air as though trying to remember the rest of it.

"The deaf hear, the dead are raised, and the good news is preached to the poor," Joanna finished.

John stood, hands gripping the bars, and studied Joanna, nodding his head but saying nothing more.

Joanna retrieved the last tin cup from the basket, filled it with water, and handed it to John.

He gulped it down, water trickling from the corners of his mouth into his beard. With a gasp for air, he held out the cup for more.

Joanna refilled it.

He drank slower this time, guarding every drop. When he finished, he returned the cup and spoke with a stronger voice, "You have shown me a great kindness, Joanna, wife of Chuza. What message do you bring from my cousin?"

Joanna put the cup back in the basket, got the last small loaf of bread, and handed it to John.

He held it like a piece of gold but made no move to eat it.

Joanna stepped back and raised the hem of her tunic enough to reveal the tops of her sandaled feet. "For eight years, John, since the day I gave birth, I could not walk. In a single moment, Jesus made me whole when he touched me. Before that, from leagues away, he brought my son back from the edge of death. Throughout Galilee, thousands come to him wherever he goes, and he heals them all. Every ounce of strength he has, he gives to them. Some of the leaders of our people follow him now, John. Not openly yet, but they will in time. Even the demons obey him, freeing many people who have been bound for years. The Kingdom of God has come to Israel as the Scriptures promised. He is the one. You were correct, Baptizer. You were correct from the beginning."

I felt as if I watched these strange events unfolding on some magical big screen TV. I looked at John. He stood shivering, clutching his last meal to his chest. I watched Joanna as she lowered her skirt to cover her feet, thinking what a loving, bold move she made to bring a moment of comfort to a man she had never met. I thought about Markus risking his life to let us into this horrible place. I couldn't help but be in awe of their courage. As I took it all in, I acknowledged this would always be the moment I would look back on and say, "In that hour, I was born again." And it wasn't only because I'd met Jesus. It was meeting the others as well. Disciples like Markus, Joanna, and John the Baptist. Each person had given so much to do their part—some risking their lives and families too. I felt entirely unworthy among these amazing people who made such enormous sacrifices and took dire risks to follow Jesus. I laughed to myself, thinking Jesus wasn't even famous yet. The stories hadn't been lived out yet, much less recorded for humanity.

The Bible wouldn't exist for another three or four hundred years, yet here I was, watching the gospels being written right in front of me. I wanted to slink away and let these noble heroes carry on without this Doubting Thomas, who just a few nights before called Jesus a make-believe god. In the light and warmth John and Joanna were bringing to this cold dark prison, the words Jesus spoke yesterday on the mountainside rushed back to me. As they rang in my mind, I touched the collar of my robe, and for the first time in my entire life, I knew exactly who I was and precisely what I was supposed to do.

I put the basket on the ground and handed the torch to Joanna. Then, I pulled my cloak off my shoulders and pushed it through the bars to John.

He looked at it but didn't take it. Then he turned and moved toward the back of the dark cell.

"I was with him yesterday, John."

John stopped but didn't turn around.

"You should have seen him. He stood on this big rock on the side of a mountain with a thousand people below. It was marvelous. He was marvelous. His words filled the whole mountainside. 'For this reason, I say to you, do not be worried about your life, what you will eat or what you will drink, or what clothes you wear. Is not life more than food and the body more than clothing? Look at the birds of the air; they do not sow, nor reap, nor gather into barns, and yet your heavenly father feeds them. Are you not worth much more than they?'"

John returned to the front of the cell; my arm still stretched through the bars, offering my cloak.

I nodded at him and continued, "See how the lilies of the field grow. They do not toil nor do they spin, yet I say to you not even Solomon in all his glory was clothed like one of these. But if God clothes the grass of the field, which is alive today and tomorrow is thrown into the furnace, will he not much more clothe you? For your heavenly father knows you need all these things. But seek first his kingdom and his righteousness, and all these things will be added to you."

John's eyes grew sad as he listened to the words of Jesus. Tears flowed down his cheeks, leaving crooked trails on his dirty face.

"You are far more precious to him than the birds of the air and the lilies of the field, John. So today, he has fed you and given you drink." I nodded at the bread he still clutched to his chest and pointed at the tin cup in the basket.

"And clothed you," Joanna assured, reaching through the bars to hold my cloak with me.

John said nothing for a long time. Then he met my eyes, tears still streaming down his face. "Will it be soon?"

I knew what John meant. Did I dare say anything in front of Joanna? My heart broke for this pitiable man who, until today, had been nothing more to me than an imaginary character in a mythical tale. "Tonight, John," I whispered before realizing I decided to tell him. "Now, take my cloak and be warm until then. And enjoy your bread. For your heavenly Father knows you need all these things. He remembers you, always."

After a moment, John nodded, "Good." He took my cloak, threw it over his shoulders, and looked down at the basket.

Joanna filled John's cup again and handed it to him through the bars.

"I will not forget your kindness." He disappeared into the dark cell.

CHAPTER 12
An Audience

We followed the same narrow hallway on our way out. We said goodbye to Markus and Simeon along the way. Joanna and I didn't speak until we were crossing the courtyard, weaving between the vendors.

"What is going to happen tonight?" Joanna asked.

And there it was. I hoped my strange words hadn't made sense to her, but she noticed. I needed to answer her, but how?

In my life as Tom Evans, I was a proficient and accomplished liar. Whether I shifted the blame to Angela for the trouble we got into as children, or concocting excuses for not turning in school assignments, or covering my disloyalty to Becky, I could lie with the best of them and never blink an eye or feel a second of remorse.

Now, the thought of being untruthful felt like an insult to the one who brought me to this time and place. But how could I tell the truth without revealing who I really was and from where and when I came? If God had anything to do with bringing me here and wanted the others to know who I was, he could have made it evident from the beginning.

No, it was beginning to sink in, not only was it possible God orchestrated me being here, but he also had a part for me to play in his plan. Was it the same part the original Thomas played or was he weaving new things into the story? Was I simply following the same path from long ago, or was this timeline different? Was I free to rewrite events happening around me? Even the events recorded in the Bible? I knew I wouldn't intentionally say or do anything to change or jeopardize Jesus's mission, but absolutely nothing even hinted I wasn't free to say and do whatever I chose. A tremendous weight of responsibility descended upon me. Could I accidentally mess up this timeline? Could I mess it up by doing the wrong thing or by not doing the right thing at the right time? How could I guard history as I knew it and yet honor the freedom God gave me to be me?

"John is going to die tonight," I wondered how I would explain it even as I said the words.

Joanna stared at me curiously, "How could you possibly know that, Thomas?"

"I, uh...heard the Word of God."

"God has revealed John's death to you?"

"Something like that. I mean, yes! I have heard the Word of God since I was a boy, Joanna. I know it will happen." I continued walking toward the palace, congratulating myself for finding a way to tell the truth and not expose myself.

Joanna hurried after me. "John seemed to take comfort in your words, Thomas. I hope you are right, and his suffering will be over. You are a good man."

"Lady Joanna, your return has been highly anticipated," the soldier stood in our path. "Lord Chuza will be pleased." He looked at her legs. "We were informed you would not require your litter. You appear to be quite fit... for a cripple. The work of the Nazarene, they say."

The unique crest on his helmet and the ornaments on his breastplate hinted he was probably the one in charge. It took me less than five seconds to determine I didn't like him or his tone. But I could also tell not to cross him either.

"Thank you, Gaius. That is quite true. Please inform Lord Chuza of our arrival. We will wait for him in the atrium." Joanna stepped past the guard.

When I attempted to follow, he put his hand on my chest and stopped me. "I have not been made aware of this one's permission to enter the palace." He looked me over disapprovingly. "He will wait here with me until I hear differently."

Joanna looked at me and nodded, then continued on her way into the palace.

An hour later, a well-dressed man, woman, and young boy emerged from the palace and descended the steps. They were halfway to the bottom before I realized the woman was Joanna. Her plain linen tunic and robe were replaced by a light olive, long-sleeved silky gown with a white, lacy shawl around her head and shoulders. The shawl covered rich auburn hair pinned up by silver chains and broaches. The man accompanying her wore a white knee-length tunic beneath a beautifully embroidered, blue sleeveless vest that equaled his tunic in length. He approached the guard and gave a slight bow.

"Your diligence protecting the palace and his lordship is duly noted, Centurion Gaius. I trust Thomas caused no trouble while in your custody."

"None, Lord Chuza. I merely—"

"Yes, of course, duly noted, Centurion. Now, if I may take the prisoner off your hands, we must arrange to get him into proper dress before his audience with Antipas. You know how the Tetrarch gets when he is kept waiting."

I watched the guard's face pale as Chuza grabbed my arm and pulled me toward the steps, Joanna and her son trailing behind. As we ascended the sixteen steps, the portico guards separated, letting us pass.

We made a sharp right turn inside the palace and followed a narrow hallway between the palace's outer wall and the spacious atrium wall. When we reached the end of the hallway where it made a sharp left turn, a man in a simple white tunic stood waiting.

"Get him washed and dressed," Chuza instructed the man. "Antipas wants to see him before the banquet."

The man made a deep bow to Chuza, turned like a soldier, and hurried down the hallway without a word.

Chuza gave me a shove in his direction. "Go with him, now. If you go before the king smelling like that, he will most certainly send you to the dungeons. Now go!"

I followed the man through several more twists and turns, down a steep flight of stairs to a room with a shallow swimming pool. The pool filled almost the entire space leaving only a narrow mosaic tile walkway between the pool and the walls. Two very large, naked men stood on either side of the doorway. There was no escape. Stripped, they led me down the steps into surprisingly warm water, and scrubbed me from head to foot with natural sponges, which felt more like coarse steel wool. Once they were satisfied I could pass the king's sensitive smell test, they dressed me in a white tunic, and long dark blue vest similar in style to the one Chuza wore, minus the embroidery.

Again without speaking, the man led me out of the bath, up the same flight of stairs, and through several chambers where cloth banners and paintings depicting soldiers at war hung on the walls. The last door opened to reveal Chuza and Joanna.

Joanna smiled and raised her eyebrows. "You look quite presentable, Thomas. You may live through this after all."

Chuza smiled and sniffed the air. "Yes, a notable improvement."

Before I could respond, Chuza knocked lightly on one of the large double doors to my left. A guard opened the door, and Chuza announced, "He is ready."

"What am I—"

"The guard will escort you to the foot of the dais. When you get there, go to one knee and bow your head. Do not say or do anything until you are told."

"But I—"

"Go on. Be careful, but answer his questions. We will remain here until you return." Chuza took my arm and nudged me through the door.

"If you return," Joanna added quietly.

When I looked at her, she had her hand over her mouth, trying to conceal her laughter. Oddly, it made me feel a little better.

Chuza pushed me the rest of the way into the large chamber. I stumbled in and straightened up to stand next to the guard. The square room was made entirely of stone with the only wood an ornately carved throne where Herod Antipas sat about thirty feet in front of me and three steps up on a platform that filled the entire front of the chamber. Four cylindrical marble pillars extending from floor to ceiling on the left and right created a walkway to the throne. Between the pillars and the outer walls were stone benches that I guessed could seat about twenty royal court members on each side.

The guard put the back of his hand on my chest and whispered, "Walk when I walk. Stop when I stop. Match my steps exactly. Understand?"

I nodded.

"When I stop, go to your knee as Chuza told you."

I nodded again.

The guard stepped forward with his left foot. I copied his movements until he stopped about five feet before the dais. I lowered to one knee and bowed my head. I watched the guard's feet turn and disappear. A moment later, the door slammed shut, and I stood alone with the most powerful man in Galilee. I remained still and silent for what seemed like an eternity.

"You are Thomas. Also called Didymus, the twin. You are among the Nazarene's closest companions. You have been with him since he moved from Nazareth to Capernaum, being from nearby Bethsaida. Is that correct?"

He wasn't asking because he didn't know the answers. Clearly, he knew a great deal more about me than I knew about myself, or the Thomas in whose body I now resided. Could Joanna or one of Jesus's other followers be feeding him information? I needed to keep my wits about me if I was going to get through this.

"You are correct, my lord," I kept my eyes on the floor.

"Stand, Thomas of Bethsaida. You are safe here. You do not need to be afraid."

"Thank you, my lord." I stood to look Antipas in the eyes. He looked younger than I had expected, with a closely cut black beard and wavy black hair that almost reached his shoulders. He wore a gray military-style jacket over a red tunic and a simple gold band on his head.

"I have sent word to this teacher of yours that I wish to see him. To hear his words. Why does he continue to refuse me?"

I searched my memory. I hoped I paid close enough attention to Joanna's story to get it right.

"He cannot, my lord. The city is unclean to him."

Antipas's hand came crashing down on the arm of the throne. "That cursed graveyard again." He sighed bitterly. "Will the Jews never forgive me for building this city over their precious cemetery? It is the finest city in all Galilee, and I must fill it with gentiles and foreigners because of these absurd religious superstitions." He sat quietly. "Well, there is nothing to be done for it now. Perhaps I will have to go to him, this great healer you follow. Or meet in Jerusalem. He attends Passover, does he not?"

It sounded like Antipas was talking more to himself than to me, but I answered anyway, "Yes, my lord. He will attend the feast." I knew Jesus and Antipas would, in fact, meet in Jerusalem, but it wouldn't be this year.

After another long silence, he asked in a whisper, "Does John live?"

"My lord?"

"The Baptizer. Surely you visited him in my dungeon earlier. Did you find him well? Did you talk to him? Does he still speak ill of me?"

I was stunned Antipas knew and terrified if I gave the wrong answer it would go badly for me as well as Joanna. Maybe even Chuza and the boy. I remembered Markus saying Antipas would have him flayed and given to the dogs and his family slaughtered if he knew he deceived him. Could the wrong answer expose everyone to danger? Cost them all their lives? My old instincts were screaming at me to lie my way out of this jam. But that Tommy died this afternoon in the dungeon. I touched the spot on my neck where Markus laid the tip of his sword only a few hours ago.

Do you follow the Nazarene?

It became clear answering questions in this time period could be a lot more hazardous than in the world I came from.

"He lives, my lord. He is a man accustomed to great hardship. It seems unlikely your dungeon will kill him. He was grateful for the bread you sent."

"Bread?"

"Joanna said the bread and water we took to the prisoners was a largesse from the king on his birthday."

Antipas laughed long and hard. "Yes, yes. Without question Joanna would say so—always prepared with a wise answer, that one. I cannot imagine how my household functions without her here." Then he sobered and leaned forward, rubbing his chin. "You follow this Jesus of Nazareth. Tell me, Thomas of Bethsaida, how much longer before the people grow weary of this champion and move on to the next one?"

I wanted to tell him that two thousand years after his mighty Roman Empire had fallen and been relegated to the pages of history, Jesus would still be changing the world. Instead, I said, "The crowds continue to grow. People from all walks of life follow him. He is not like the others, my lord. I believe he may continue to grow more popular for some time to come."

"Does he call himself a king?"

"No, I have never heard it from him, my lord. He refers to himself as the 'Son of Man.' A humble title, Lord Antipas."

"Yet, I have been told he preaches about a kingdom."

Antipas was no fool. He would catch me if I weren't entirely truthful. "He does, my lord. I've heard him speak of this kingdom many times. He compares it to a farmer who plants seeds in his field. Or a woman who bakes bread with yeast. Or a vineyard owner deciding what to pay his workers. Hardly a threat to a kingdom as mighty and enduring as Rome, my lord." I paused, then added with a chuckle. "Unless, of course, you are a corrupt landowner trying to cheat his workers, or a poor cook, or a worthless farmer. But certainly, his kingdom is no threat to your rule here in Galilee, my lord."

Antipas smiled again. "You speak oddly, Thomas of Bethsaida, but you speak plainly and with an honest heart. I will permit you and your master to continue on your way for now. But warn him not to disrupt the peace or welcome armed men into his group."

"Yes, my lord. I will tell him."

"And Thomas?"

"Yes, my lord?"

"Tell the Nazarene he is welcome here whenever he is near. I can arrange for him to get in and out of the city without being seen if he chooses. I am eager to meet this one who is not, as you say, like the others. Now, let us end this. I have a banquet to attend."

Antipas left through a door behind his throne, and the soldier returned to escort me out.

CHAPTER 13
The Party

Joanna and Chuza were waiting as they promised.

"My apologies, Thomas," Joanna offered. "There was no time for introductions before. This is my husband, Chuza. Chuza, this is Thomas."

I waited to see what sort of greeting Chuza would offer before I stuck out my hand only to have it ignored again. When Chuza offered a slight bow, I returned it in kind.

"Yes," Chuza replied. "We've met."

I must have had a puzzled look on my face, so Chuza explained.

"The day I found Jesus on the road from Cana, the day Samuel was healed, we spoke for a few moments."

"We did?" I tried to make it sound more like a statement than a question. If I remembered Joanna's story correctly, it would have been over a month ago. I would have been in the final days of flunking out of college, and Chuza would have met the real apostle Thomas. I decided again, truth was my best option. "My mind must have been somewhere else, my lord. I don't remember our conversation."

"No doubt." Chuza laughed, ushering me with a hand on my back toward a hallway to our right. "I believe your mind was on a family-owned vineyard north of Bethsaida, where the young woman you promised to marry waited for you. You were considering leaving the group altogether and going back home to wed her when last we spoke. It appears you changed your mind again, Thomas." Chuza's smile faded as he looked over his shoulder at his wife, who followed a few steps behind. "I only hope you two have made the right decisions for all of our sakes."

I didn't pay much attention to anything Chuza said after the word "marry." It had never occurred to me that Thomas, like the others following Jesus, had a real life. They had real stories, much like the one

Joanna told as we traveled to Tiberias. Stories about mothers, fathers, families, and jobs and—as I learned—wives or fiancées. I chuckled to myself and corrected my own words.

Betrothed, I believe would be the correct term.

Chuza's words were disturbingly informative. He confirmed Antipas's claim I originated from Bethsaida near Capernaum, wherever that was. Apparently, I was one of the first to follow Jesus and left work in a vineyard, either my family's or my fiancée's. At least once, I must have doubted my decision and thought about returning home but ultimately stayed with Jesus. And somewhere, right now, a woman who loved me wondered why I had left her and if I would ever come home.

During my musings, we arrived at the banquet hall. Another guard greeted us, "Lord Chuza, Lady Joanna, you and your guest are at the first station on the left."

I followed Chuza and Joanna into a room similar to the audience chamber where I spoke with Antipas. The left wall in this room was an outside wall with a long row of rectangular windows about six feet high and two feet wide with rounded tops, spaced about a foot apart. Through those windows, I could see soldiers silently patrolling the enclosed courtyard. The stone benches in this room were only about ten inches tall, with various shaped pillows in a variety of colors surrounding them. A beautifully carved walnut table sat on the dais with three oversized chairs behind it. Antipas sat in the middle with a woman in her late thirties to his right and a young girl of about fifteen on his left. Herodias and Salome.

Chuza led us between the pillars to the front of the room and the first bench on the left. Servants greeted us immediately with red or white wine served in crystal glasses, while others—as Joanna described to me earlier—roamed the room with small bowls of water and a mappa across their left arms. We stood, sipping our wine while royal court members and guests filled the room. The sun had started setting, so another group of servants scurried around the room, lighting sconces on the walls and pillars. As soon as they were finished, a trumpet sounded from the back, and a man walked down the center of the room to stand at attention near the foot of the steps. Antipas, Herodias, and Salome rose.

"Hail Lord Herod Antipas, son of King Herod the Great, Tetrarch of Galilee and Peraea," he shouted. He turned slightly to his left, "Hail Lady Herodias." Then to his right, "Hail Lady Salome." Then again to Antipas, "Lord Herod Antipas, your royal court is assembled to celebrate your fiftieth birthday. A thunderous roar erupted from everyone in the room. I thought it would be wise to join in, so I did. The clapping and shouting went on for at least five minutes while Antipas looked around the room, raising his glass to various courtiers and guests.

Finally, the room fell quiet enough for the herald to continue, "Lord Antipas, your royal court is here to celebrate your fiftieth birthday. With your permission, your loyal subjects come with a toast."

Antipas raised his glass again, gesturing at the whole room. Then he, Herodias, and Salome sat.

For the next hour, every man in the room offered a toast to Antipas. Some extolled his accomplishments, especially for the building of Tiberias, while others called on one god or another to grant him strength, power, or long life. I recognized several men in robes like those I had seen on the mountainside a few days ago. Pharisees. They gave rambling oratories in defense of the One true God of Israel and praised Antipas for his Jewish ancestry. It began to sound more like a religious debate than a birthday celebration.

I glanced at Antipas. His droopy eyes and slouched posture told me he had lost interest long ago and was nearly asleep at his table. I couldn't help being thankful for his disinterest when it came my turn to toast. I did the best I could, borrowing lines from a few others and remembering lines from weddings I attended over the years.

Chuza spoke last, and he was mercifully short-winded.

When he finished, the trumpet sounded, waking Antipas and signaling the guests to sit down on their pillows.

Antipas clapped twice and servants rushed into the room, refilling glasses and bringing baskets of food.

It was fully dark outside by the time the meal ended. Three musicians playing stringed instruments, none of which I recognized, replaced the trumpeter. As the evening wore on, the feeling in the banquet chamber became more and more surreal. It reminded me of the hazy fog of college parties after too much alcohol or drugs. At least here in the palace, the guests were better behaved. Religious and social stations provided a curb to their alcohol-fueled emotions, and well-fed stomachs contributed to a sense of drowsiness. While the political guests conversed or laughed in various groups, the religious guests maintained a physical and emotional distance, looking on silently with cursory glances of contempt crossing their judgmental faces. Apprehension grew rapidly, causing my heart to pound and my stomach to feel queasy. John's death drew ever closer, and I could do nothing about it. Or prepare for it.

All of my previous experiences with death were from the news on TV, video games I played, or the sterilized environment of a funeral home. Joanna, sensing my discomfort, gently squeezed my arm. I glanced at her and caught the question in her eyes, *How soon?*

I shrugged and squeezed my eyes shut, breathing deeply and slowly calming myself. I looked around, hoping to regain my composure.

When I looked at Antipas, the wine appeared to be taking its toll. His customary air of dignity and command was unraveling. I could see the boredom in his body language and the annoyance in his eyes. Protocol and tradition were forcing him to play a role at his own party to satisfy expectations, making him restless to get it over.

I stole another quick glance at Herodias. She had been carefully observing Antipas the whole evening, just as I had been intently watching her. She subtly plied him with more wine than the other guests and had his plate removed as soon as he had lost interest in it. Her aristocratic coldness allowed her to converse and smile with a politician's polished practice while hiding her true feelings and objectives. I knew she was the stage master soon to raise the curtain on the final act of the Baptist's life.

"What do you know of the queen?" I asked Joanna quietly.

"Very little," Joanna answered with a slight shake of her head. "I rarely see her, and Chuza seldom speaks of her. After John's criticism, I think we have seen even less of her. She stays behind the scenes, but everyone in the palace suspects she is the one pulling the strings."

The deadly finale commenced when Herodias slowly turned to look at one of the musicians behind her. She caught his eye, then moved her gaze to her daughter Salome and nodded slightly. The musician acknowledged her with a nod.

Salome continued staring straight ahead, silent and expressionless, unaware of the communication between her mother and the musician.

While she appeared in her mid-teens, it was hard to determine her exact age. Salome was exceptionally pretty, having a softer version of her mother's high cheekbones and angular face. Unfortunately, she also had Herodias's cold, hard eyes and worked hard to maintain control over her facial expression. I could only imagine the political forces controlling her life, jerking her from her father's home and dragging her to wherever Antipas delighted. She may have been a princess, but a patriarchal system with a royal twist called the shots in her young life. Still, knowing what was about to happen didn't generate much sympathy from me for her.

"My dear esteemed guests," Herodias rose. "We are honored you have come to celebrate with us." She gestured toward Antipas, smiling and curtsying elegantly.

He returned the smile with some effort, an odd expression on his face as if the wine's effect and her sudden outburst had caught him off guard.

I glanced at Chuza, who looked concerned and unprepared. I clenched my teeth, suspecting the only people in the room who knew what was coming next were the queen, her daughter, me, and Joanna.

"A special event has been prepared," Herodias bowed toward Antipas, "from the hearts of those who love you, my lord." She smiled and nodded, then looked directly at her daughter.

Salome stood and walked down the steps of the dais to an open area. At her mother's signal, Salome threw her arms upward, flinging off her embroidered robe to reveal the exotic, translucent gown beneath. Her arms were bare, and parts of her legs and back were visible through the fabric.

The audience began to murmur. I heard several quiet gasps behind me. From the knitted brows of the religious leaders, they obviously disapproved.

With another nod from Herodias, the musicians began to play, and

Salome started her dance. Salome followed the steadily rising rhythm of a tambourine-like instrument as she moved across the open space. Even though she still had a teenager's body, shy of the fullness of womanhood, she made the most of what she possessed. She swayed to the music, moving her arms in a hypnotic serpentine pattern as she swirled gracefully and skillfully around the room, weaving between the guests. From the mixed reactions, I suspected her dancing bordered somewhere between cautiously acceptable and scandalous. She mimicked the blossoming of flowers, birds in flight, and the slithering of serpents with an artistic sensuality that captivated the room.

Antipas stared glassy-eyed, following her every movement, his mouth agape with lust, his brow covered with sweat. The second song began with a slower, more earthy pulse. Salome glided up the steps to Antipas, straddled his legs, took his chin in her left hand, and traced the contours of his face with the fingers of her right, without losing the sensual rhythm of the song. Antipas seemed utterly enraptured. I saw the devious smile on Herodias's face as she watched her husband and daughter act out the roles of the drama she had so meticulously planned. She gave the final cue to the musicians, and the music began its slow ascension to its final crescendo. As the music reached its climax, Salome whirled away from Antipas, spinning wildly, her gown and veils whooshing past his face tauntingly until, at the final note, she dropped nimbly to the floor clutching his feet.

Many of the guests jumped to their feet, shouting and clapping with enthusiastic approval, while others stood obligingly, clapping softly. There was no sign of the Jewish leaders. Antipas stood, swaying under the effect of the wine.

"Bravo, bravo, beloved daughter!" he slurred, clapping clumsily.

"Like an angel," someone shouted.

"Like a demon," I heard a whisper behind me.

"Again! Again!" cheered many men.

Herodias stepped to Antipas's side, steadying him. "My dear husband, does she not deserve something special from her king?"

He blinked, gathering his thoughts. "Yes, yes! Of course. Something special!" He shouted, reaching for Salome.

Salome skillfully avoided the king's grasp, staying slightly beyond his reach, breathless but still remarkably stone-faced.

"Make her Prior of the city Garrison. She could bring your troublemakers under control with her dancing," someone laughed.

This seemed to register with Antipas, who suddenly blurted out, "Yes! Name whatever you want, daughter. Whatever you may wish for is yours," He paused, "up to half of my kingdom."

A stunned silence filled the room until someone chuckled, "I think perhaps my lord has over- reached a bit."

The tension eased with awkward laughs. If the offer of half the kingdom was a joke or a careless faux pas, no one knew. Perhaps Antipas didn't know either, but he laughed anyway.

Salome stared at him for a moment, then walked over to her mother and whispered in her ear. I could feel the cold knot tightening in my stomach. Herodias smiled slowly, staring at Antipas with narrow, glittering eyes. She whispered to Salome, who walked boldly to Antipas and spoke loudly, "If not half your kingdom, then I want the head of the Baptizer."

Once again, the room fell awkwardly silent. I could hear the muffled whispers of the soldiers outside in the courtyard.

Antipas's bloodshot eyes tried to focus on Salome. He seemed to be coming out of his fog, realizing what Salome had asked for. "W-what?"

"The head of the Baptizer," Salome repeated. "On a dinner platter. If you please, my lord."

The king looked around as if he were searching for someone, anyone, who could undo what had just happened. Joanna gripped my arm. I turned to see her face pale and troubled, her eyes brimming.

"He has become a torment to you, my lord," Herodias urged quietly, breaking the silence.

"She speaks the truth, my lord," a man standing near the front agreed. "It would end any doubt about how far these rabble-rousers are allowed to push the tolerance of Rome, my lord."

"Give it to her!" shouted a woman from the back of the room.

"On a platter, if you please, my lord." Salome repeated softly.

"His head and another dance!" A man shouted, bringing a round of laughter and shouts of agreement.

"His head! His head! His head!" The guests chanted wildly.

Antipas looked around desperately for help. Nothing. No one. Everyone chanted except Joanna, Chuza, and me.

"His head milord, his head milord, his head milord…"

After what felt like an eternity, Antipas raised his arms, silencing the crowd. His frantic eyes continued to search the room until all hope faded. Finally, he gestured to one of the guards.

The guard acknowledged with a nod and left to a volley of cheers.

"My lord…" Chuza started, but a piercing look from Herodias silenced him.

I grabbed Chuza's arm, pulling him back down to keep him from stepping over the dangerous precipice he stood on.

People slowly began to talk among themselves.

Herodias spoke over the crowd, "He never supported your rule, my lord. He turned his back on you when you went to him. You gave him every chance. This is his own doing." Her voice pleaded, edifying Antipas's pride as if she were coming to his rescue.

He looked at her suspiciously as if he were trying to decide whether she had betrayed or saved him.

Then came footsteps from the hall. The massive doors swung open, and a soldier strode in, holding a serving platter that held the severed head of John the Baptist, blood sloshing and spilling onto the floor.

The man I met a few hours ago is gone, I thought to myself.

I heard Joanna's breath catch beside me as she tried to control herself. Chuza had his arms wrapped around her to comfort her.

Antipas stared at the head, not daring to come closer. John's lifeless eyes stared back at him. Suddenly, Antipas whirled, his fierce eyes darting from one person to another. "Out!" he hollered hoarsely.

Everyone stood there in shock.

"Out!" he roared again. "Get out! Get out! Every one of you! Leave me! Leave me this instant, or your head will be next!"

Panic and confusion took over as the guests scrambled to empty the room, Herodias and Salome among them.

Chuza and Joanna grabbed my arms and rushed me toward the exit. My heart and legs felt like lead as they dragged me out of the room and down the hallway.

CHAPTER 14
A Sabbath to Remember

Joanna spent the next few days with her son and husband while I wandered the city, trying to make sense of what had happened.

After the midday meal on our fifth day in Tiberias, Simeon returned my clothes, washed and pressed. One of the guards escorted me out of the palace, and I met Joanna on the front steps. She was also dressed in her traveling clothes.

We spent much of the walk back to camp in painful silence. Both of us were trying to deal with the events of the last few days in our own way. If I was having a hard time coping with my problems, I knew Joanna fared far worse. Not only had she witnessed the gruesome murder of John the Baptist, but she had been required to attend court proceedings the following day and conduct herself as if nothing genuinely monstrous happened. It was one thing for Antipas to allow her the freedom to roam the countryside with the charismatic new prophet and his vagabond followers because he was curious about Jesus's healing gifts. But Joanna's independence would quickly come to an end if she attended the royal proceedings still mourning the death of Herodias's victim from the night before or in any way conveyed disapproval of Antipas's actions. So for nearly six hours, she maintained her genteel veneer and performed her duties with charm and dignity. Today, the look on her face and the slump in her shoulders told me the pretense had taken its toll. Along with the grief of being separated once again from her son and husband, she fell into a silent and lonely dungeon, not unlike the one we visited a few days ago.

As for me, the reality of my new life became chillingly clear. In the last forty-eight hours, I encountered two Roman soldiers, one of whom had held a sword to my throat and another who would have gladly added me to the dungeon population had Chuza not intervened. I spoke with a ruthless wannabe king who had the power to take my life simply for the fun of it. I'd been forced to stand and applaud when the severed head of a good and decent man was paraded around the room dripping blood. No, this was nothing like my college dorm or comfortable home back in Midwest America anymore. Death loomed everywhere. Fairness existed only in the hands of the powerful. There were no constitutional protections. No court system to find justice unless you were a Roman citizen. No ACLU or Amnesty International. No Nolan Center or American Center for Law and Justice. The things I took for granted my entire life were now gone. They wouldn't even exist for another two thousand years. The very notion humans had rights and rulers can't simply take everything you have, including your life, was not even on the radar in the first-century Roman Empire.

Before the last few days, I couldn't remember a single morning when I woke up with the fear I had at the palace in Tiberias. There hadn't been a military draft in America since before my father was born. Wars were fought in obscure places like Iraq or Afghanistan by volunteers who liked those sorts of things. I couldn't recall ever discussing those places in high school or college. Most could travel almost anywhere in America without fear. Even my friends with high-performance motorcycles could show off without getting noticed by the police. None of those realities existed here. I was entirely unprepared to deal with first-century Palestine and its concealed dangers. The only time I had felt a sense of peace was the day spent with Jesus. I could hardly wait to see him again and forget about the strange, troubling mission he sent me on.

"Peace to you, Thomas. Greetings, Joanna." Jesus and about thirty other men and women stood in the middle of the path.

Mary Magdalene pushed between Andrew and Peter and rushed into Joanna's arms. "I missed you so much," she whispered. "I am glad you arrived in time to go with me."

Jesus approached and kissed me on both cheeks. Many of the men reached out to squeeze my arm or pat my shoulder.

"Welcome back, Thomas."

"Good to see you, Thomas."

"Missed you, friend."

It was a wonderful moment. However, my bliss quickly faded when I heard Joanna say, "Lord, John is dead." Then she burst into tears and the suffering of the last few days poured out of her. Salome joined Mary

Magdalene to embrace Joanna.

Jesus put his arms around the three women as they wept. "I know." For a long time, he held them and waited for Joanna to quiet. Then he stepped back and spoke, "What did you go out into the wilderness to see? A reed shaken by the wind? Let me ask you again. What did you go out to see? A prophet? Yes, I tell you, one who was more than a prophet. He was the one about whom it is written, 'Behold, I am sending my messenger ahead of you, who will prepare your way before you.'" Jesus paused. "John's work is finished now. Mine is just beginning. Yours is yet to come." He turned and addressed the men. "James, take ten men and spread the word as far as you can. I will be in Magdala tomorrow after midday. The rest of you go back to camp and wait. I must spend some time with my father and grieve the loss of my cousin. I will meet you in the morning, and we will go on to Magdala together." He nodded at Mary and then walked east toward the sea.

The camp was about a mile away and set up much like the night I first met everyone. The women separated to their own camp about thirty yards away while the men sat around the fire and began to pass a couple of wineskins among themselves, talking in small groups.

Andrew touched my shoulder and passed me a wineskin. "He was nearly killed in Nazareth, Thomas. The crowd turned on him so fast, we barely got him out alive. I still do not know how we managed to escape." He gazed into the distance as if trying to piece together the scenes of a fading dream. "I honestly thought it was going to end before it even got started. That everything we believed about Jesus would be proven wrong. I thought what we had given up so much for was falling apart right before our eyes. And then, just like that, he... well, I do not think you will believe me. I am still not sure I believe it myself."

"Tell me what happened, Andrew."

Andrew stared at the darkening sky for a long time. "We stayed at the camp for the rest of the day after you and Joanna left. The next morning, Jesus called me, Peter, John, James, and Philip and asked us to travel with him to Nazareth. He told us it would be his first time back home since his family moved to Capernaum. He did not expect it to go well. 'A prophet is welcome everywhere but his hometown,' he warned us.

"We got to Nazareth before sundown, and Jesus led us to the house of his uncle and aunt, Clopas and Mary. We arrived as they were beginning Sabbath. They were not expecting us, but they divided the small pot of lentil stew Mary prepared, and we shared our wine and bread with them. It was a fine evening, Thomas. We reclined around their table long after the meal and spent a good part of the evening listening to stories about Jesus's childhood in Nazareth. Mary kept us laughing for hours with tales of Jesus and his brothers getting into trouble or chasing after one adventure or another. We laughed when Jesus told us Jude was the worst. He told us a story about climbing rocks around Sepphoris one afternoon and seeing some Roman soldiers marching out of the city. Jude dared James to find out what the soldiers wore under their leather skirts. The Romans chased them halfway back to Nazareth when they caught James trying to sneak up on them. Jesus said Joseph lined up all five boys behind the house with a switch in his hand, and Jude still tried to convince him it was James's idea."

Andrew smiled. "We were still laughing at the story when Clopas added, 'Jude was not the only one of the boys to get into a little mischief, though. Your teacher gave his parents a few difficult moments as well.' We were eager to hear more, but Mary took over the story.

"'Jesus recently turned twelve,' she said. 'And we traveled to Jerusalem for Passover as we did every year. Joseph and Mary, Salome and Zebedee, Clopas and me, our children over the age of twelve, and several other families from Nazareth. Most of the other boys had to be herded like sheep to the slaughter. But not Jesus. He loved it. He loved the temple, the priests, the animals, the sanctuary where only the High Priest could enter. Oh, he loved that best of all. He stood there staring at the temple door until he was forced to move along. We stayed the required two days, made our offerings, and on the morning of the third day, we started back toward Nazareth. I was making bread when Mary rushed into our camp.

"'Is Jesus with you?' she demanded.

I'd never seen her so upset.

"'No,' I told her. 'I haven't seen him since last night. I thought he was with you and Joseph.'

"'No, he is not. I have searched for him everywhere. No one has seen him.' She began to cry. 'We must have left him in the city. He will be terrified by now. Will you go back to Jerusalem with me?'

"The next morning, we sent the others on to Nazareth with Salome and Zebedee while Mary and I returned to Jerusalem with our husbands. We searched all night and the next day, but found no sign of Jesus anywhere. Mary was beside herself.

"'The Lord entrusted him to my care,' she said, 'and I have failed him.'

"That night, she lay curled up in my lap like a little child. She would sleep for a short time and then wake crying out. 'I have failed him. I have failed him. Surely I have lost favor with the Most High. I have failed to keep his son safe.'

"The next day, she refused to eat and went straight to the temple. The temple guards nearly arrested her for trying to get past them into the area restricted to men. She cried and paced until Joseph and Clopas returned, shaking their heads. Finally, the third time we passed by the twelve steps of the temple terrace, we saw a large crowd gathered at the top.

"Mary stopped. 'He is there!' she whispered almost too quietly to be heard, and then she started up the steps.

"When the four of us reached the terrace, we found Jesus sitting with a group of scholars discussing the Scriptures like it was the most natural thing. Mary pushed her way between the crowd and cried out, 'Son, why have you treated us like this? Your father and I have been frantic looking for you!'

"Jesus looked up at his mother and said, 'Mother, why would you need to look for me? Did you not know I would be in my father's house?'

Andrew paused for a moment and smiled as he remembered Mary's telling. "For this last line of her story, Mary straightened her shoulders and lowered her voice to speak with a tone of authority, 'Did you not know I would be in my father's house?' We broke out laughing at that statement. We laughed and laughed until we noticed Jesus was not laughing with us. He was weeping.

"'It was thoughtless of me,' he said to Mary and Clopas. 'I caused you and my parents a great deal of pain.'

"Mary nodded and placed her hand on Jesus's arm. 'Yes,' she said with a warm smile. 'But you were different after that. I do not believe you caused your mother or Joseph or any of us any sorrow after that day.'

"Jesus sat quietly for a long time, then rose and moved toward the door. We heard him whisper, 'Until now,' as he stepped out into the night. The evening came to a close, and Clopas found us places to bed down. When we rose the next morning, he and Mary had prepared a breakfast of barley cakes with figs and honey. We ate a hurried breakfast and then walked to the synagogue at the top of the hill, where we found Jesus standing out front with nearly all of Nazareth gathered around him."

CHAPTER 15
Scripture Fulfilled

Andrew continued his story, "We rushed up the hill expecting trouble, but there was none. It seemed like the village welcomed him as they did everywhere. Those who knew him greeted him warmly. Others were murmuring among themselves.

"They brought a young lame boy to him. Jesus sat on the ground and held him, praying. After a long time, Jesus got up and sent the boy back to his mother. The boy's leg appeared to be better. They led an old man to Jesus who had lost his sight. He was healed after Jesus prayed for him over and over and rubbed the man's eyes with his spit. He kept asking the man. 'What do you see?' until finally, the man said he could see clearly.

"Others were waiting to be touched by him, but Jesus turned from them and entered the synagogue. I could see by the sag in his shoulders and his hollow eyes, he was already weary from the few he had healed. The synagogue was overflowing when the leader called for order and instructed the attendant to give a scroll to one of the village elders. The elder stood and read from the third book of the Torah, 'Then the Lord spoke to Moses at Mount Sinai, saying, 'When you come into the land which I shall give you, six years you shall sow your field, and six years you shall prune your vineyard, but during the seventh year the land shall have a sabbath rest. You are also to count off seven Sabbaths, namely, forty-nine years. It shall be a jubilee for you.'

"The elder returned the scroll, sat in the seat of Moses, and began to teach everyone the meaning of what he had just read. We were nearly asleep by the time he finished and returned to his seat. But it had given Jesus a chance to rest, and when time came for the next reading, he was ready. He stood, and the attendant handed him the scroll containing the book of Isaiah. Every eye was fixed on him. No one was sleeping now. He opened the scroll, found the place he wanted, and began to read, 'The Spirit of the Lord is upon me because he has anointed me to preach the gospel to the poor. He has sent me to proclaim release to the captives and recovery of sight to the blind. To set free those who are oppressed and to proclaim the favorable year of the Lord.'

"He handed the scroll back to the attendant and sat on the seat of Moses.

"'Today, this scripture has been fulfilled in your hearing,' he said. 'But when the Son of Man comes, will he find faith on the earth?'

Almost as if they had been waiting for it, the entire synagogue went into an uproar. Everyone began to argue with one another and started shouting questions at Jesus.

"'Who is this Son of Man?' one man cried out.

"'Who do you claim to be?' shouted another. 'Are you him? Are you this, Son of Man?'

"'He speaks with wisdom and authority. Perhaps he is a prophet,' another said.

"'No prophet comes from Nazareth!'

"'He's the carpenter's son. He grew up here.'

"'Who do you claim to be, Son of Man? Are you the Messiah? What do you say to that? Are you the Messiah? Are you the one we are waiting for?'

"When Jesus heard the word Messiah, he got up to leave, but a man near the door climbed onto one of the stone benches, pointed at Jesus and shouted, 'I saw you in Capernaum, Son of Man. You healed everyone who came to you. Heal the people of your own hometown, and we will believe!'

"'He is no healer. This is Joseph's son. He is a carpenter, not a healer.'

"The man standing on the bench got down and took a cup of water from the stone jar near the door. He stood in front of Jesus. 'We heard about your trick in Cana. Turn this water into wine if you are the Promised One. Do that, and I will follow you myself.' He held out the cup to Jesus, but Jesus simply stood there. Peter and James were on either side of Jesus, trying to move him past the man, but others were crowding in so tightly getting out of the synagogue was impossible.

"I knew things were getting out of control when a wineskin sailed over my head and landed at Jesus's feet. 'That is good wine, carpenter's son or son of Joseph or Son of Man or whatever you call yourself. Maybe it will be easier for you to change wine into water.'

"Everyone began to laugh, and if Jesus had any supporters left in the room other than the five of us, they were deserting him quickly.

"'Silence, all of you!' commanded the elder. 'Men of Nazareth, this man will bring nothing but trouble to our village. Whether he can do the things he claims or not, it does not matter. If he is a prophet or a healer or the so-called Messiah, we must let God decide. But he has already drawn too much attention from our leaders in Jerusalem and the Romans in Tiberias. If he is allowed to stay here, he will bring the wrath of the Tetrarch down upon us. Even now, the disciples of the Baptizer hide in villages throughout Galilee and Judea, and when Herod's soldiers find them do you think they will leave that village in peace?'

"The men looked at each other and began nodding in agreement. I caught Peter's eye and could see even he started to doubt we could get Jesus out of there safely."

"'We must protect our village!' shouted the man who had thrown the wineskin. 'Think about your families! Cast this troublemaker out of Nazareth before he puts us all in danger!'

"'How Jacob? How do we protect Nazareth? What shall we do?'

"'Take him outside the village and drive him away, along with these men who follow him.'

"'He has family here,' the elder said. 'He will only return and bring more trouble with him. We should be rid of him and make certain he does not return.'

"'Take him to the cliff!' someone suggested.

"'Let God save him if he is a prophet!' another shouted.

"'Toss him off the cliff! Off the cliff!' everyone began to chant.

"The mob moved toward the door pushing Jesus along with them. Peter and James were dragged away and knocked to the ground. When I reached them, they had both been beaten badly by the men who now had Jesus and were dragging him up the hill. By the time I got Peter to his feet again, he was desperate.

"'Get Philip!' he shouted. 'Go that way. See if you can work your way around the crowd. I will take James and John and try to get around them on the other side. Go! Go! Hurry!'

"We were too late. The crowd had reached the edge of the cliff, and the ground dropped off too sharply on the left for us to get around them. We ran back to Peter, who tried to force his way past the men at the rear of the crowd. Several of them turned and attacked James and Peter again. We were just reaching them when the men in the front of the crowd began waving their fists and shouting, 'Save yourself, Son of Man! Save yourself'

"Peter had one of the men who attacked him on the ground and was about to strike when John grabbed Peter and pulled him away. Peter struggled to get out of John's grip until John got right up in Peter's face and screamed, 'Stop!' The attackers turned back to join the frantic crowd. 'Stop, Peter, look!' John screamed again and pointed.

"The four of us turned and about halfway down the hill, maybe fifty paces or so away, Jesus walked with Clopas and Mary toward the northern edge of the village. It was as if they had finished breakfast together and were out enjoying a morning stroll! We caught up with them as Clopas and Mary were saying goodbye. They turned back toward the village, and we traveled on with Jesus to camp. Clearly, he was in no mood to talk, so we walked quietly beside him back here where we met the others."

"Then today," Andrew concluded his tale, "without a word, he gets up after our meal and comes to meet you and Joanna. I think he knew about John even before Joanna told him. Tonight was the first time he spoke since we left Nazareth."

I could tell the experience Andrew described left him shaken. No doubt the other four men were dealing with their own anger and fear. I wondered if Jesus had known the trouble he would face in Nazareth. Was that why he had not taken the others, especially the women? Whatever the reason, he would be back in the morning, and we would be traveling to Magdala. Another place where he would not be welcome. We all needed to be more aware of the dangers if we intended to see Jesus survive to accomplish his mission.

"We need to be more careful in the future, Andrew," I said. "We can't let him get swallowed up by any more crowds like what happened in Nazareth."

"I agree, Thomas, never again."

"Never again," I repeated, even though I knew full well it was a promise I would never be able to keep.

CHAPTER 16
Parable of the Talents

The following morning, I woke to the buzz of quiet voices. Jesus, Joanna, and Mary sat together near the fire. The men around me were beginning to stir, wiping sleep from their eyes and stashing their few belongings in the folds and pockets of their tunics. Chuza had retrieved my cloak from John's cell, and I threw it over my shoulders and moved closer to the fire. The night had been cold, and I was still unaccustomed to sleeping on the ground, but that was not the reason for my restless night. Everyone in camp had either been in Nazareth or heard the story. Tension and worry hung in the air like a dense fog.

After everyone gathered around the fire, and cups of honeyed water and dried dates were passed around, Jesus began teaching.

"You must not be afraid. My father's kingdom is like a certain man who went on a journey. But before he left, he called his trusted servants together and gave them each some of his money to invest. He gave one of the men five bags of gold, and that man made some trades and did some business and gained five more. The one who received two bags also doubled his money, but the one who received only one bag went away and dug a hole in the ground and hid the money. After a long time, the man returned home and settled accounts with his servants. The man was very pleased with the two who had invested well and said, 'Well done, good and faithful servants. You were faithful with a few things; in the future, I will trust you with much, much more. Rejoice, for you shall remain a part of my household.'

"Then the one who had received only one bag of gold said to him, 'Sir, I knew you to be a hard man. I was afraid and hid your money. But see, you have back what is yours' and handed him the bag of gold he'd retrieved from the hole.

"When he heard this, the man became furious and deeply disappointed. 'You wicked, lazy servant. You should have at least put my money in the bank so I would have received it back with interest.' Then he took the bag of gold from him and gave it to the others. Then he had the weeping servant thrown off his land."

Jesus looked at each of us in turn, "You must not be afraid. Fear is like a thief who steals and destroys, and it will prevent you from doing the things my father desires of you. I will only be with you for a short time; then I will go to him who sent me. Therefore, you must take the gifts my father has given each of you and be like the servants who were bold and did well with what their master entrusted to them. Not like the anxious servant whose fear kept him from doing good and was cast out." Jesus stood. "Now, let us go. We must be in Magdala by midday."

When we reached the bluff overlooking Magdala and the Sea of Galilee, Jesus stopped for a brief rest. Salome distributed leftover bread, and after eating, most of the men found a cool spot to take a short nap before Jesus returned from his prayers.

I found Joanna, Suzanna, and Mary sitting together outside the camp. I approached but stopped a few yards away, waiting to be invited.

Joanna waved me over.

I was about to sit when Mary spoke in a disgusted voice, "Are you sure you wish to sit with us, Thomas? Do you not fear what your brothers will say when they see you sitting with women? Are you not afraid they will mock you again?"

Her bitterness shocked me. After my conversation with her and Joanna before the trip to Tiberias, I hoped she and I could be friends. But, perhaps I had expected too much. Regardless, I'd spent too many years sparring with my father and sister to let her hurtful words pass without taking a shot back.

"I think my brothers mock me because they are ignorant and haven't accepted some of the things Jesus teaches. What I fear more than them, Mary, is being mocked by someone who knows better and understands how much it can hurt." I folded my arms across my chest and looked down at her feeling pretty proud of myself. I held my own on that exchange and was about to point it out when she burst into tears and buried her head in Joanna's lap. Instantly, I knelt beside her and put my hand on her shoulder. "I'm sorry, Mary. I didn't—" The shock on Joanna's and Suzanna's faces told me I too had a lot to learn before I started sticking out my chest and acting like a know it all. I pulled my hand away from Mary's shoulder like it was a hot stove. "Sorry, Mary. I guess I should know better too."

Joanna smiled at me. "It is alright, Thomas. Mary has not known many men like you in her life. Perhaps, we all need to learn more about Jesus's ways before we start judging one another."

Mary nodded under Joanna's arms.

Joanna motioned for me to sit. "She is very frightened about returning to Magdala and seeing her family today. She still does not know why Jesus is taking her back."

"I'm sure it's nothing to worry about, Mary. I can tell you for sure, you will be with Jesus for as long as he is here on earth."

Mary lifted her head to give me a puzzled look. She was about to say something when I heard a voice from behind us.

"Do you number yourself among the prophets now, Thomas?" Jesus asked.

If I could have found a rock to crawl under, I would have. "Lord, I..."

"Would you please have everyone gather here, Thomas?" Jesus asked. "When you have everyone together, follow me into Magdala." I heard him ask Mary to walk with him as I ran to tell the others.

Jesus and Mary walked about fifty yards ahead of the rest of us for the thirty-minute walk to Magdala. I could see Mary wasn't saying much, merely nodding and looking up at Jesus as they walked. When we entered the outskirts of the village, we were met by dozens of people who were waiting to see Jesus. He passed through them, explaining as he went he would be speaking to them later. Hundreds more were waiting for him near the center of Magdala in the exact spot Joanna described to me as the place where she and Mary had been healed. James, John, and the others had done a good job spreading the news of Jesus's arrival.

Jesus and Mary made their way through the crowd and stood in front of the tall salting towers owned by Mary's father. They waited as the crowd fell silent. I worked my way through the crowd with the rest of the men, trying to get as close to Jesus as we could. We were very much aware of what had happened in Nazareth a few days before, and I could see the nervous looks on many faces as the disciples tried to sense the mood of the crowd. So far, everything seemed peaceful and calm. When I finally reached the front of the crowd, I could see Jesus and Mary about ten yards away. The difference in Mary's appearance shocked me. The anger and fear in her eyes were gone and a look of peace had taken their place.

The crowd remained quiet in anticipation. After a few minutes, the massive wooden doors of the salt tower crashed open. A short, barrel-chested man a little older than my father emerged followed by two men in their late twenties. An older woman with her head and much of her face covered by a hooded cloak came next. After her, a woman who looked like a younger version of Mary stepped out. They were followed by about twenty men and women in aprons or clothes covered with wet stains. The older man approached Mary and Jesus, the two younger men to his left and the women to his right. No one spoke. Jesus turned to Mary and nodded. And the born-again Mary of Magdala stepped forward.

CHAPTER 17
Magdala

"Tired of her so soon, Rabbi?" The barrel-chested man sneered then began to laugh. "That's not to say I do not sympathize with your dilemma. Crazy Mary can wear you out with her hysterics and tantrums; that'd be the plain truth of it. If she was not the best fishmonger in Magdala, maybe all of Galilee, I would tell you to keep her." He laughed hard again. "But keeping up with orders has lagged since she ran off with you and your little flock." He turned away from Jesus and spoke to Mary. "Get inside, girl," he ordered, hiking a thumb toward the fishery door. "You will be working two shifts every day until you make up for what you owe me."

"She will not be staying with you, Benjamin," Jesus said quietly. "She travels with those who seek the Kingdom of God now."

Benjamin took a step toward Jesus and put his hands on his hips. "You would take a child from her home, Nazarene? From those who love her? From the place where she was raised? From her mother and sister and brothers? Did not Moses himself teach that a child should honor her father and mother? You have no right—"

"You are correct," Jesus interrupted. "That is what Moses said. But the prophet Micah also prophesied a man's enemies would be the members of his own household. Now hear me, Benjamin." Jesus raised his voice and turned so everyone in the village square could hear. "He who loves father or mother more than me is not worthy of me, and he who loves son or daughter more than me is not worthy of me. And he who does not take up his cross and follow after me is not worthy of me. He who has found his life will lose it, and he who has lost his life for my sake will find it." He turned back to Benjamin. "The men and women who travel with me have chosen to take up their cross and follow. They have chosen to lose their life so that they may find it. Your daughter has made a choice, Benjamin, which is far better than the choices you forced her to make. When we leave Magdala, she will leave with us, and she will not return. But this I offer you, Benjamin, son of Benjamin. Repent and believe the good news. You, your wife, your sons and daughter, your entire family, even those who labor for you," Jesus looked past Benjamin and motioned toward the group of workers. "The Kingdom of God draws close to you this very day, Benjamin. Your time has come. If you wish to be whole, go and sell all you possess, give to the poor, and you will have treasure in heaven, and come follow me."

I watched Benjamin's face as he considered Jesus's words. For the tiniest moment, I thought I saw it soften, but it passed too quickly to be sure. Whatever had been there was replaced almost instantly by anger and then rage. He stepped up to Jesus and gritted his teeth. "Do what you have come here to do, Nazarene. Beguile these people with your fancy words and your tricks and snares, just as you have my daughter and these other fools who follow you." Spit flew from Benjamin's mouth, but Jesus made no move to wipe it away. "But I warn you, if you are still here in the morning, I will send word to Tiberias you are disrupting my salting business. I pay too much in taxes for Antipas to ignore your interference with the commerce of Galilee." Benjamin stepped back and several of the men behind him approached and patted him on the back, making comments in his ear. I assumed they were congratulating him for putting the troublesome preacher in his place.

"How sad it will be for you, Magdala," Jesus spoke loudly again. "For if the miracles performed in you had been performed in Tyre and Sidon, they would have repented long ago in sackcloth and ashes." Then, quietly to Benjamin, he added, "How sad it will be for you, Benjamin! For you know the truth, yet you hide it from the people around you. You will not accept it for yourself, and you prevent others from having a chance to believe it as well."

Jesus turned to Mary again. "Do what you came to do, daughter."

I could see Mary struggling to regain the courage she had before coming face to face with her family. The resolve to do what she had come to do was slipping away like sand through her fingers. When I thought she would turn and run away, her whole demeanor changed. She stepped forward to stand directly in front of her mother.

"I forgive you, Mother," her voice trembled. She paused for a long time before continuing, eyes never leaving her mother's. "Your silence was the loudest voice in all of Magdala. Every evil thing done to me sought permission from you, and you silently gave it."

Mary's mother opened her mouth, then closed it again, a single tear falling from her eye before she lowered her head and turned her back on her daughter. I couldn't tell whether it was anger or shame. Mary didn't seem to care. She looked at her mother's back while her lips moved silently, then she shifted to face her two brothers.

"I forgive you, Asher," her voice grew stronger now. "I forgive you, Ephraim. My fear of both of you made me your prisoner. I gave you the key you used to keep me chained and under your control. But I am free now, from Father and from you. You can never hurt me again or take away what is mine and what has been restored to me. You can choose to repent and come with us if you wish." She looked at Jesus, who nodded. "You do not need Father's permission to do what is right. You can be free, as I am free."

I watched Mary's brothers, looking for even a hint of remorse, but there was none. Their faces remained hard and defiant. Mary reached up and touched each of them gently on the cheek before moving on to stand in front of her father.

"I forgive y—"

"Keep your forgiveness, child. I have no need of it." Benjamin snarled, waving his hand. "If anyone has been wronged here, it is me. Return to your work, and I will forgive you."

Mary's shoulders rose and fell as if Benjamin's words were physical blows. The conflict within her radiated such deep pain I thought for sure everyone could feel it. Finally, she nodded sadly, took two steps back, removed the shawl from her shoulders, and let it drop to the ground. Then she pulled the linen skull cap from her head, freeing her shoulder-length dark hair. She reached behind her head, grabbed the back of her outer tunic, and pulled it over her head, dropping it to the ground.

When she reached for the back of her linen undergarment, her father finally spoke, "Stop! Enough, girl. What is it you want?" His voice had lost its edge. He sounded defeated. Fearful, even.

I leaned over to Joanna and whispered, "What's happening? I don't understand."

"Her father has beaten her since she was a child. She bears the scars he inflicted with his strap from her knees to her shoulders. She is about to reveal her father's sins to everyone in Magdala. He is afraid if the word spreads, it will hurt his business. A father can get away with much, but I have seen her back. You can be sure he does not wish anyone else to see it."

"My wages," Mary said.

"What?!"

"I want my wages, father. Twenty-one years. I believe that comes to—"

"This is madness! You are a woman," he shouted, spit flying from his mouth again. "You have no right to wages. I gave you a roof over your head. Clothes on your back. A place at my table. Those are your wages. If you were a normal woman, you would have been married fifteen years ago, and I would have received a proper dowry. I am the one who has been wronged, not you. And now you come back here with this rabble and bring shame on your mother and brothers and expect me...."

Mary grabbed the back of her garment again.

"Alright, alright! Stop! If it will put an end to this nonsense, alright." He leaned closer to Mary and spoke quietly, "You will leave and never return?"

Mary stared at her father, tears flowing down her face. She nodded once.

Benjamin turned and stormed toward the door of the tower, pushing other family members and workers out of his way. Before he reached the tower, he turned and shouted, "Now put your clothes on, woman, you look like a whore!"

Mary stood like a statue waiting for her father to return. The crowd began to whisper to one another. I wondered if they were deciding which side they were on. Most likely, the residents of Magdala depended on the fishery for their existence. If Benjamin's business suffered, so would they. It's probably why the good people of Magdala had turned a blind eye to Mary's suffering for so long. I looked into the faces of the other young women in the crowd and wondered how many of them had similar stories. How many were nothing more than slaves and a potential dowry in this male-dominated world?

Then, I remembered Joanna's words: They are still having a difficult time accepting the new kingdom Jesus is leading us into. If it were up to the men, we would not be allowed to be here at all, much less help him with his work. They claim to despise the teachings of the scribes and Pharisees, but they still cling to the old ways.

Anger washed over me as I watched Mary trembling in her undergarment, waiting for her father to return. I was angry at her brothers, still defiant in their denial and at her mother, who lacked the courage, even now, to turn and look at the daughter she failed to protect for thirty years. I was also angry with Andrew and Peter and James and John and all the other men who followed Jesus. Jesus was trying to lead them into a new kingdom. A kingdom where everyone would be treated with respect. Where men and women could serve equally, and where women were not the property of their husbands or fathers but coworkers in this new adventure he called the Kingdom of God.

Nice try, Jesus, I thought. *Even you couldn't change human nature that much.*

It would be more than nineteen centuries before any significant changes took place. Even then, in the twenty-first century, women still struggled to be treated equally. And no one was more notorious than the leaders of churches in keeping women "in their proper place." The church bore great guilt in oppressing women, denying them the privilege of becoming priests or pastors or serving in leadership roles. How had the example set by Jesus become ignored so quickly and easily? How could they have missed what he was trying to show them?

Again, I searched the faces of the women in the crowd as they stood quietly beside their husbands or fathers, wondering if they could even begin to comprehend the significance of what was happening right before their eyes. History would remember this brave woman as one of the most mysterious yet significant of all of Jesus's disciples. She had been with him from the beginning of his ministry and would watch the gospel unfold decades before Matthew, Mark, Luke, or John put it to paper. Or papyrus, I guess. Mary stood at the foot of his cross at his death and was the first to claim she had seen him resurrected. Her example would become an inspiration to women for the next two thousand years. I had an overwhelming desire to go to her, wrap my cloak around her, and comfort her, but I knew she had to finish this alone.

The door of the salt tower slammed open again. Benjamin stormed out, pushing his way through his workers and family. He threw a sack of coins the size of a softball at his daughter's feet. By the gasps and murmurs from the people, it must have been a sizable amount of money.

"That's all you get, girl. I kept back the cost of feeding you and housing you. It is more than you deserve. Now leave me and do not trouble your mother or me again. If these were the days of Moses and Joshua, you would be stoned where you stand instead of robbing us."

Mary picked up the bag of money and handed it to Judas. Then she retrieved her robe and shawl and stepped to within a few inches of her father. "If we were in the days of David, Father, he would say to you, 'The Lord is my light and my salvation, whom shall I fear? Though my father and mother forsake me, the Lord will receive me." Then she returned to Jesus's side.

Jesus walked to the other side of the plaza. The crowd made a path for him. He found a cart and climbed into it. "If you can hear," Jesus said to the crowd, "listen to me. Suppose one of you wants to build a tower." Many people turned to look at the salt tower looming behind us. "Will you not first sit down and give some thought to how much it will cost to build and see if you have enough money to complete the task? For if you lay the foundation and cannot finish, everyone who sees it will ridicule you, saying, 'This person began to build and was not able to finish.' Or suppose there is a king who is about to go to war against another king. Will he not first sit down and consider whether he can defeat him? If he decides he is not strong enough, he will send a delegation while the other king's army is still a long way off and ask for terms of peace. In the same way, those of you who do not give up everything you have cannot be my disciples. You must decide if you truly wish to follow." Jesus looked at the tower. "Salt is good," he continued, "but if it loses its saltiness, how can it be made salty again? It is no longer fit for salting fish or the manure pile, but is thrown out. If you can hear me, then listen to me."

When we reached the beach, Jesus climbed down from the cart and began to walk among the people, healing and teaching them with stories as he went. It was well past dark by the time he finished. Dozens of fires were burning all over the beach as the visitors to Magdala prepared their evening meals.

When the last person had been prayed for, Andrew, Peter, and I helped guide Jesus farther down the shoreline to the camp the women had prepared with a couple of fires and a meal of fish and bread. As he always did, Jesus rose immediately after he ate to go off alone and pray. Just before stepping into the darkness, he turned and pointed at Mary, who was refilling our cups of wine.

"If you do not forgive, you cannot be forgiven," he said. "What Mary did today was not an easy thing to do. But she is free now. Free to follow me and be numbered among my disciples. Follow her example. If you have broken relationships with people in your life as Mary did, you should leave in the morning and do as she did. The rest of us will leave for Capernaum at sunrise. You can rejoin us there."

Peter grunted and began to mumble to himself.

"Peter? Do you disagree with my words?" Jesus asked.

"How many times, Lord?" his tone grew angry. "What if someone sins against me seven times? Must I forgive him for the same sin seven times?"

I noticed the slightest smile on Jesus's face as he stepped back into the firelight and knelt in front of Peter. "No, my dear Peter. Not seven times. Seventy times seven times."

It was a shocking moment for the several dozen men and women around the fire. I had heard this passage of scripture taught in my church since childhood. It was another one of many lessons I took for granted or dismissed as foolishness. I'd never given a moment of thought to how ridiculous it must have sounded the first time the disciples heard it. Seven times seemed beyond reasonable to Peter. Now the number became incomprehensible. It was a number so large it meant my brother could offend me as often as he wanted to, and my commitment to Jesus Christ meant I had to forgive him every single time. I reflected on the words Jesus spoke to the crowd a short time ago. If anyone would follow me, he must love me even more than his own life. If you begin and cannot finish, you will be ridiculed by all. If you cannot defeat the other king, it would be better to surrender than be defeated. Not fit for either fish or manure pile but thrown out. I wondered how many of these men and women would slip out of camp before morning and return to their homes.

Peter threw his cup to the ground and stood. "Seventy times seven," he muttered as he walked away.

"Peter, where are you going?" Andrew asked.

"Capernaum. It seems I have some business to take care of. I will meet you when you get there."

"Wait, I will go with you." Andrew stood.

"Good, brother," Peter laughed. "You probably need to see the same people I do."

I watched the two men walk into the darkness with their arms around each other's shoulders. This time, as Jesus turned to leave, I know I saw a smile on his face.

Everyone sat quietly around the fire, lost in their thoughts, until, one by one, they each began to drift away to find a place to sleep. I sat there long after everyone else left. I thought about my dad and mom. I thought about Angela and Becky. I not only had a lot of forgiving to do, but I needed to ask for a lot of forgiveness too. I wondered if I would ever get the chance to see them again and do what Peter and Andrew were on their way to do. And then there was Bethsaida. According to Chuza, I left my fiancée to follow Jesus. I had no idea how those events transpired. Had we agreed together, or had I left her standing at the altar? Would I see her if we went to Bethsaida? How would I even know who she was? Would I need to ask her to forgive me, or was it too late? What a mess. After seeing what Mary did and hearing Jesus's words tonight, I realized this discipleship thing was a whole lot tougher than I originally thought.

CHAPTER 18
Capernaum

As we prepared to leave Magdala the following day, about twenty adults approached the camp, and their leader spoke to James. The group consisted of four families with children, eight single men and four women who stood apart from the others, their faces hidden behind the shawls they wore over their heads. The youngest of the children appeared about five years old, and the eldest of the men could no longer walk upright but leaned heavily on a large wooden staff.

James spoke with them for some time, nodding and pointing north toward Capernaum. When he finished, he left them standing there on the beach and returned a few minutes later with Jesus. Jesus spoke with the same man and began to walk among the group, frequently stopping to pray. He knelt and laid his hands on each of the six children, then directed the four women to join Joanna and Mary, who were packing up the camp supplies. Lastly, he stood in front of the old man and spoke to him quietly. I wasn't close enough to hear, but I could see the panic in the old man's face when Jesus gently took the staff from his trembling hands and let it fall to the ground. The man strained to look up at Jesus's face, but his crooked spine kept his body bent, so he could only stare at Jesus's hands holding his. After a few moments, the man's back began to straighten, and by the time Jesus finished praying, he stood straight and tall. Jesus spoke with him and the other men for several more minutes, pointing and gesturing as if giving instructions, then Jesus turned and walked off the beach and away from Magdala for the last time.

A few minutes later, James returned to camp for a piece of bread warming on one of the large rocks circling the fire.

I approached him. "What's happening, James? Are those people from Magdala?"

He accepted a cup of the fish broth I poured for him.

I decided the best way to deal with the men's mockery was to face it head-on. After all, I was the only one in the group who had the benefit of observing history from the perspective of both the first and twenty-first centuries. It seemed pointless to deny any longer that some higher power had brought me here. But why? I knew there had to be a reason and was determined to find it out. In the meantime, I decided it would be irresponsible not to use the knowledge I had to influence the men around me and help confirm Jesus's respect for every person. I brewed a large pot of broth in a kettle borrowed from the women's camp and served each of them a cup of broth and some bread as they came to the fire. The night before, I kept Joanna up well past her bedtime, begging her to teach me how to do it.

By the surprised expression on James's face, I must have learned my lesson well. "Not bad, Thomas. Not bad at all." He held out the clay cup and inspected the amber-colored liquid. "And yes, most of them are from Magdala. A few are from some of the surrounding villages. They wish to follow him." He pointed in the direction Jesus walked. "He gladly welcomed them to our number. There are over fifty with us now." He put his hand on my shoulder. "Now, come with me. We must get everyone ready to move."

We reached the outskirts of Capernaum by late afternoon. Jesus and several others had already started setting up a base camp that would remain our on-and-off home for the next two years. Philip directed folks to different areas around the rocky, sparsely wooded hillside overlooking the Sea of Galilee. He sent couples and families with children to one site and unmarried men and women to their separate locations.

I followed Philip's directions, trying to process all the helpful information I'd picked up from James as we made the six-hour walk from Magdala to Capernaum. He confirmed he and John grew up in Capernaum, where their father, Zebedee, operated a successful fishing business. Several years ago, they had teamed up with their competitors, Andrew and Peter, when Peter bought a house near his wife's family. Like Philip and me, Andrew and Peter were initially from Bethsaida, another six to seven miles past Capernaum along the northeastern coastline on the other side of the Jordan River. It made sense Andrew and I would have known each other if we both grew up in Bethsaida. He had probably brought me to follow Jesus like he had his brother,

Peter. If that were so, perhaps I could learn something from him about the woman the original Thomas had left behind.

James was reluctant to reveal too much about the other men, but I discovered many had stories similar to Thomas's. Thaddeus left a wife and children in Caesarea to follow Jesus, while Nathaniel's wife, the cousin of the bride at the Cana wedding, camped with Joanna, Mary, and the other women. Their three children were still in Cana with Nathaniel's parents.

Judas was the only one of Jesus's close companions from Judea rather than Galilee, so counting the other James, called James the Younger, and the other Simon, called the Zealot, that made eleven of us including me. Of the twelve apostles, only Matthew was still missing. If my recollection of the Bible was correct, he should be a few miles away in Capernaum, working as a tax collector.

I found where the men would be bedding down and began gathering wood for the fire. When I returned with my first load, Salome stood with a large clay bowl in her arms. It looked like one of my mother's big flower pots that sat on either side of the front steps back home in Ohio.

"Thank you, Thomas." She put the bowl on the ground and gathered several large rocks to encircle the fire. "The sun will be down, and Sabbath starts soon. We need to have the stew and bread ready before then. Everyone will be gathering here for prayers. Do you want to start the fire or get more wood?"

Start the fire? I pictured the fire stick sitting on the mantle in my living room. It would be a cold, dark night if people were counting on me to get a fire started without matches or some other technology from the twenty-first century. I would have loved to stay and see how Salome did it, but I couldn't take the chance she might ask me to help.

"Ah, yeah...well, I think I better get more wood. If everyone is meeting here, we'll need a lot more. Can you handle the fire alright?"

"Of course, Thomas. When you get back, start another fire next to this one. Joanna will be here shortly with the stew."

When I returned, Salome had the fire started, stacked high with the wood I'd brought in earlier, and was working some dough from the pot she'd carried. She completed the circle of stones around the fire and placed three of the largest stones inside the outer ring. I copied what she had done, borrowed a burning branch from her fire, and started the second fire as Joanna arrived. James and John were with her, carrying a large copper-colored pot between them. It was about the size of a five-gallon bucket but shaped more like the pot-bellied spittoons I'd seen in old western movies. There were two holes cut into the very top of the pot opposite each other, and the brothers had placed a large branch through the holes so they could carry the heavy weight between them.

"Just leave it there next to the fire, John," Salome said. "We'll get it on the fire once it burns down a little more."

"Alright, Mother. We'll gather everyone together and be back at sundown." The two men kissed their mother on the cheek and walked back to the other side of camp where the families were setting up.

Twenty minutes later, both fires had burned down to red hot coals. Joanna and I lifted the copper pot onto the fire, where the round bottom balanced perfectly on the three large stones inside the circle. I pulled the branch out of the top while Joanna added fresh wood to the fire, sending flames curling up the pot's sides. Then she helped Salome flip the flower-pot-shaped clay vessel upside down, balancing the lip on the three stones, creating something like a round pizza oven. I wondered how they would get anything inside the oven without getting burnt. They continued kneading Salome's dough, eventually dividing it into two dozen tennis-ball-sized portions. Joanna and Salome each took one of the balls and began working it between their fingers in a circular motion until it flattened to about six inches in diameter. Then they slapped the flattened dough to the side of the clay pot, where it stuck, sizzling and smoking. A few seconds later, they used two small sticks to peel the dough off the pot and turn it to finish cooking. I watched this fascinating process until I heard Jesus's voice drawing closer, reciting familiar words.

"Father, holy is your name," he said to a group of men walking with him. "May your kingdom come. Give us each day the bread we need to live, and forgive us our sins, for we also forgive everyone who sins against us. And lead us not into temptation." He stopped and squatted to face Salome. "Will we have enough for everyone?"

"Yes, Lord. Mary is bringing more dough, and there is plenty of stew. Several of the fishermen from Magdala were very generous." She handed him one of the pieces of warm bread.

He took it but only held it gently in his hands. Then he looked up at the men he'd been talking to. "Suppose one of you has a friend, and you go to him at midnight and say to him, 'Friend, lend me three loaves, because another friend of mine has come from a long way off, and I have nothing to set before him.' But from inside the house, your friend answers, 'Do not bother me. The door has already closed, and my children and I are in bed. I cannot get up and give you anything.' I tell you, even though he will not get up and give you anything because he is your friend, yet because of your persistence, he will get up and give you as much as you need." Jesus stood and pulled off a small piece of bread for each of us, leaving none for himself. "So, if you can hear me, I say, ask, and it will be given to you, seek and you will find, knock and it will be opened to you. For everyone who asks receives, and he who seeks finds, and to him who knocks, the door will be opened."

"It's Jesus! It's Jesus!" A group of children ran into the light of the fire, shouting and laughing. They grabbed Jesus around the legs, knocking him to the ground.

"Stop that!" several disciples shouted, grabbing the children and pulling them away from Jesus, pushing them back toward their parents.

"Philip, Judas, please! Let them be." Jesus motioned for the children to come back to him. When they did, he drew them onto his lap and pulled them close to his side, stretching his arms around them all. Then he looked at his disciples. "You must always allow the children to come to me and do not try and stop them, for the Kingdom of God belongs to such as these." He placed his hands on each of the children and prayed silently. When he looked up again, he continued, "You see, whoever does not receive the Kingdom of God like a child will not enter it at all. Now let us enjoy being together tonight as friends and as children. Tomorrow will bring enough trouble. But for tonight, let us be at peace."

CHAPTER 19
Sarah

Staying at the main camp southwest of Capernaum served several purposes. Most importantly, it allowed Jesus time to spend with his mother and family in the city. Though he rarely spoke of it, the distance between him and his brothers and sisters was growing more painful with every visit. His sad eyes and solemn mood when he returned and his longer than usual stays out in the hills praying concerned us.

"He carries too much," Mary observed, coming to stand beside me when she found me staring in the direction Jesus had gone to pray. "He carries his own pain, and also the pain of everyone who has suffered losses to follow him."

Mary was right. Nearly everyone in the camp had paid a high price to be there. None more than her and Joanna. Even I missed home more than I ever thought I would. Salome must have noticed because she began including me with James and John when they went into the city to resupply the camp or to see Zebedee.

The other benefit of the Capernaum camp was it allowed us to reach almost anywhere in Galilee, upper Samaria, or Decapolis, east of the Jordan, in one or two days. So that's what we did. For the next several months, we followed Jesus to every town and village throughout the region and listened and learned while he taught the people about his father's kingdom. Occasionally, we would take longer journeys as far north as Tyre and Sidon or south to Caesarea and Joppa along the coast.

We had just returned the night before from an exhausting month in Judea when Jesus's touch woke me. "I am going to pray," he said quietly. "Meet me on the road to Capernaum an hour after sunrise. Bring James, John, and Philip. Also, ask Mary and Joanna to meet us at Peter's house by midday. If I know Salome, she left last night to go straight to Capernaum to be with Zebedee. She can meet us later." He squeezed my shoulder and walked away.

"Why only the three of us?" James asked when I told him what

Jesus said. "If he will be teaching in the synagogue again, everyone should be there to help protect him."

John and Philip echoed James's concerns, but none of us felt comfortable disobeying Jesus's instructions. After speaking with Joanna, I rejoined the three men, and we headed for the road to meet Jesus.

It was still early when the five of us arrived in the city and made our way to the synagogue. Jesus found a shady place to sit on a low stone wall alongside the steps leading up to the synagogue. It would be the perfect place for him to speak quietly to those arriving early. The calm serenity of the morning was abruptly interrupted by a mighty roar of laughter coming from a large, broad-shouldered man who drew James and John into a passionate hug, kissing them both on the cheeks several times before slapping them so hard on the back I feared they might be injured. I couldn't help but laugh at the joyous reunion between James, John, and their father, Zebedee. He held each of his boys out at arm's length nodding at them approvingly, then cupped their cheeks in his meaty palms, wiping the moisture off their faces with his thumbs. Finally, as his smile faded, he turned away from his sons and knelt on one knee in front of Jesus, taking Jesus's hand and kissing it. "Welcome back, Rabbi. You should try to get some rest while you are here. You look tired."

"I will, Zeb. I will. Did Salome make it home safely?"

"Oh yes," He chuckled. "She would never miss the chance to wake me from a sound sleep. A mind of her own, that one. But I admit, I was glad to have her back. Will we see you at the house before you go back on the road?"

"You will, Uncle. Perhaps a day out on the boat with you and the boys would do me good."

"Then I will hold you to it, Rabbi." Zebedee turned back to his sons. "So, you two runaways, how goes your fishing? Do you find men easier to catch than the fish of the sea?"

"Not easier, Father," James said with a smile, putting an arm around his father's shoulder. All three of them walked up the steps. "But I do not recall the fish we caught ever thanking us as men do."

Zebedee threw his head back and roared with laughter again.

"Could it be the fish knew they were headed to the fire, whilst these men you seek know you are trying to save them from it?" Zebedee laughed again, giving James a gentle push with his shoulder.

I watched the three men ascend the steps to the synagogue, feeling a disturbing anger and emptiness building inside me. I looked at Jesus, speaking with another father and young boy, wondering if he could sense the raging jealousy tormenting me. I turned back to watch Zebedee and his sons enjoying something my father and I had never experienced. Even something as mundane as fishing became a source of bonding between them and had launched James and John into the new life they pursued, clearly with their father's blessing.

I spiraled deeper and deeper into self-pity before being rescued by Jesus's words to another man, "I see you took my advice and found Zebedee."

Micah and his oldest son walked up the steps. He looked wonderful. Strong and healthy, wearing a clean robe with not a hint of blood on the sleeves. I threw my arms around him, "It's wonderful to see you, Micah," I said, then bent down to hug his boy. "It looks like fishing agrees with you far more than the quarries, huh?"

"Thomas the Judean," he said, returning my hug and nodding at Jesus. "You still follow the Master, I see. Good for you. I have thought of you often since that day, and I think you were right, after all, Thomas. Perhaps God has not forsaken us altogether." He looked at Jesus again. "I still intend to be there when—"

"Come, you two," Jesus interrupted. "It is time to go."

The rest of the morning went off without a hitch. Jesus healed several people outside the synagogue before going inside and many more after leaving. During the service, there were several readings before Jesus took the scroll. He taught for at least an hour, throwing in several stories he often told to make his message clear. Everyone was taken with him. "Who is this man who speaks with such power and authority?" I heard several people say.

Afterward, while we were standing outside the synagogue, several men came to Jesus, wishing to follow him. He gave them directions to our camp and told them he intended to remain in Capernaum for several days but would send some of his disciples to get them when time came to move on. Once Zebedee and his sons rejoined us, we headed toward the city. We walked about two blocks when I saw Peter up ahead, running toward us.

"Lord, we have been waiting for you," Peter said, grabbing the sleeve of Jesus's robe. "Come quickly. Sarah is gravely ill. Andrew and I found her sick when we arrived last night. Leah is beside herself with worry. She and Andrew are with Sarah now. She may not have much time. Please come quickly, Lord."

Jesus reached up and covered Peter's hand with his own. "Then let us go to her."

Peter did his best not to run too far ahead, constantly checking for Jesus over his shoulder. I could almost hear the words he wanted to say as he fought to keep them inside. This was a completely different Peter than the one I had come to know. On the deck of a fishing boat or in charge of a group of men, Peter could be relentless. He accomplished any task Jesus gave him, and when he came face to face with an obstacle, there was no doubt the obstacle would lose the battle. He didn't always get the job done right, but he didn't have room inside him for not getting the job done somehow. When Peter supervised and took control, there was only one place for everyone else to line up: behind him and out of the way.

But this Peter was no longer in control. He couldn't control whatever ailment had befallen Sarah, who I assumed was his mother-in-law. He couldn't control how fast Jesus walked to get to her, and he couldn't control what would happen once Jesus got there. The uncertainty and doubt left him broken and helpless. Desperation and fear of the unknown robbed Peter of the strength many of us had come to rely on.

I had the unique perspective of knowing how this story would end, just like I knew the outcome of most stories about Jesus. Anyone who spent any time in Sunday School knew the story of Peter's mother-in-law and how this event turns out. Jesus was going to get there on time, and with a single touch on the hand, Sarah would be healed of her fever. Then she would get up and offer to take care of everyone, like she always did.

As I walked with Jesus and watched Peter struggle with his doubts, trying to will Jesus to walk faster, my mind raced back to the morning before I arrived in Galilee. Pastor Nelson's words brought me face to face with my fate. Or at least the fate of the man whose place in history I had taken. Words that, if this timeline remained true, Jesus would one day say to me. "See the nail holes in my hands, Thomas. Now, reach here with your hand and put it into my side. Because you have seen me, you have believed. Blessed are they who do not see and yet believe."

Blessed are they who do not see and yet believe, I thought. *Blessed are those who believe without knowing.*

I took a quick look at the men around me. James, John, Philip, and Peter, dear relentless Peter. As I watched Peter's back, it dawned on me, they were the lucky ones. They didn't know how things would develop or how the story would end. They hadn't heard a hundred sermons on how everything would turn out. I thought about his words and realized how right Jesus was.

Faith was better than knowing. Believing is better when you don't see the end.

All these men possessed was their trust in the man they were following.

I stopped, causing John to run into me, nearly knocking me to the ground.

"Sorry, John," I apologized as I regained my balance, letting him pass by. As I stood there trying to piece it all together, a light began to break through.

That's it, isn't it? I said to myself. *That's what this is all about.*

Faith! Faith is better than knowing. What is known may never become a reality if there is no faith to bring it into existence. Faith is the power that transforms "maybe" into "is." From "might be" into "will be." From "I hope" to "I see."

I took off running, intending to catch Peter before getting to his house. "Peter," I called, coming up beside him.

"Not now, Thomas."

I had to get through to him somehow. But this was relentless Peter on a mission. Well, I wasn't going to get out of his way this time. Maybe I needed to approach this differently, and perhaps I needed to use a few of Peter's methods to do it.

"Yes, now, Peter."

Peter kept walking. "I said not—"

"Just shut up and listen, Peter. You don't have to stop walking, just close your mouth and listen for once."

Peter's eyes opened wide, but he didn't say anything more.

"Do you remember what happened in Nazareth, Peter? I wasn't there, but Andrew told me about it. You were there. You saw what happened. Jesus wasn't able to do many healings or miracles there. Right?"

Peter kept walking. Finally, he answered, "Yes, so?"

"Why? Why couldn't Jesus do many miracles, Peter? Did he lose his power? Did God desert him? Why couldn't he heal the people in Nazareth, Peter?"

Peter remained silent. I could see Andrew and a woman standing outside his house a few blocks away.

Peter looked at me, "Because the people there did not believe he could do it."

"That's right, Peter. They didn't believe. They kept asking him for a sign. But he wouldn't give them one, would he? He told them the same thing he tells the Pharisees whenever they ask him for a sign. Do you remember what he says to them?"

"Of course." Peter looked up toward the sky. "When it is evening, you say, 'The sky is red, so it will be fair weather tomorrow.' And in the morning, if the sky is red, you say, 'there will be a storm today.' You know how to discern the appearance of the sky, but are you unable to discern the signs of the times? You seek a sign, but no sign will be given to you except the sign of Jonah."

"That's right," I said. "But you don't need a sign, do you? Why don't you need a sign, Peter? Why don't you need a sign like the others?"

I swam in uncharted water now. I wasn't even sure I knew what I was talking about. But I knew I was teetering on the edge of discovering something vitally important for me and maybe for my friends as well. I began to realize I was at a disadvantage because I observed the events around me from a position of knowledge. They were living it from a place of faith in the moment. And that's where the power is.

"You don't need a sign," I continued, "because you know who he is. You follow him because of who he is, not what he does. Listen to me, Peter." I was beginning to see things more clearly now. "You have seen him heal a thousand people, but that is not why you follow him, is it? No, of course not. A few weeks ago, you watched him feed five thousand people with a few loaves of bread and a couple of fish. But that is not why you follow him either. You were there when he turned the water into wine. Is that why you follow him, Peter?"

"No," Peter whispered.

I grabbed Peter's arm to stop him. I expected him to pull away from me, but he didn't. He paused and stared at me. I put my hand on his chest. "You follow him because in here"—I patted his chest—"you know who he is. You made a choice before you saw him heal anyone. Before even one miracle. Did you leave your boat the day he called you to watch him perform signs and miracles?"

"No." Peter answered so quietly I could barely hear him.

"Then why, Peter? Why do you follow him? Why have you left everything important to you to follow this man from town to town?"

Peter's eyes reflected his turmoil. Then his focus cleared, and the Peter I knew returned. He put his hand on my shoulder and squeezed it, his best attempt at saying "thank you."

"Because this man is the Christ." he confessed.

"That's right, Peter. Miracles happen because we believe. We don't believe because miracles happen."

I saw the group with Jesus only a few steps away. I turned back to Peter. "Now, do you have any doubt what will happen in your house today is what his father intends to happen?"

Another squeeze of my shoulder. "None, my brother, none at all!"

At that moment, Jesus and the others reached us. "I believe Sarah is waiting for us, Peter. Is she not?" Jesus said.

"Yes, Lord, she is. Welcome to my home."

With the slightest feeling of envy, I watched the small group of disciples enter Peter's house. Whatever was about to happen for them; it would happen purely because they believed in the man who walked in with them.

CHAPTER 20
Levi

The following days, events played out exactly as I expected they would. Jesus healed Peter's mother-in-law, and she spent the next few hours making sure we were comfortable in her home. Her daughter, Leah, cooked everything the day before because of the Sabbath, so most of Sarah's time was spent making her guests feel comfortable. Mary and Joanna arrived right after the healing, and Leah insisted they stay with her and her mother. A short time later, Salome took the men a few blocks away to her house, where we were taken to the roof to rest.

"It is time to return to Peter's house," Jesus said, waking those who had dozed off. "The Sabbath is nearly over, and people will be coming as soon as the sun sets."

Light began illuminating the horizon the next morning when Jesus finally finished praying for and healing all those who came to him the previous night. He thanked Sarah for her graciousness, and we walked back to Zebedee's house, where Salome made us a quick breakfast of date bread and grapes. John and James led us down a narrow path between houses to the beach, where a large fishing boat belonging to their father was moored.

We set sail with the sunrise over our left shoulder, so I guessed we were headed for the northern shore of the Sea of Galilee. When Jesus fell asleep in the front of the boat, I found myself keeping a close eye on the sky, wondering if this boat ride would be the one when he calmed the storm, but the lake remained still and peaceful for the entire trip.

We spent the next several months visiting small towns and villages, preaching and healing. After a particularly tiring week where the crowds grew dangerously large, Jesus gave the order to sail back to Capernaum.

When James anchored the boat where we'd found it, I thought we might be going back to Peter's house, but Jesus led us farther down the beach toward the synagogue.

"He's going to see that thief Levi again," Peter whispered from behind me. "Why he gives that shameless parasite a moment of his time, I will never understand. I tell you this, James, if the people see him befriending a Roman minion like that tax bandit, they will leave him for certain. We will be the only ones left."

"You sound like a Pharisee, Peter," Jesus chided over his shoulder from twenty feet in front of us, talking with Phillip.

I could barely hear what Peter said and never imagined Jesus could hear him from so far away.

Jesus stopped and waited for us to catch up.

"Forgive me, Lord," Peter murmured meekly. Then he dug an even deeper hole for himself, "But why do you waste our time on this traitor. He robs his own people to—"

"Tell me something, Peter," Jesus interrupted. "Who among the men and women traveling with us does not have something in their past bringing them shame? Do you think I named your fishing partners the 'Sons of Thunder' because they are meek and reasonable men? Or did the Zealot earn his name working as a peaceful innkeeper? Do I need to remind you of your words the day I stood in your boat and watched you draw in a sizable catch?"

"No, Lord."

"It is not those who are healthy who need a physician, Peter, but those who are sick. I did not come to call the righteous, but sinners to repent." Jesus glanced around at his followers and smiled. "It appears I have succeeded." Then he turned to Andrew. "You were there the day Matthew went to see the Baptizer at the Jordan, were you not, Andrew?"

"I was there, Lord."

"What did John tell the tax collectors when they came to him for baptism? Did he tell them to leave the service of Rome?"

"No, Lord. He told them to collect no more than what they had been ordered to collect."

"Since the day he returned from the Jordan, has Matthew collected one cent more than what is due?"

Andrew shook his head. "No, Lord. But before that, he—"

Jesus raised his hand to silence Andrew, then turned his gaze on Peter, James, and John. "You men lived in Capernaum much longer than I. Has Matthew collected anything more from you than what was due since John baptized him? Has he threatened you or brought a single soldier to your door?"

Each man conceded Matthew had not tried to cheat them since he saw the Baptizer.

Jesus turned and continued down the beach. "Then, if I wish this one to follow me, what is that to you?"

"He will not follow you, Lord," Peter predicted. "He owns much property in Capernaum. His house is one of the grandest in the city. You yourself have said it many times. 'It is hard for the rich to enter the Kingdom of Heaven.' It will be impossible for this one."

"What is impossible with men is possible with God. Come and see," Jesus replied.

We left the beach, turned back toward the city, and approached the main road leading into Capernaum. On our right, built on a low dune with access to both the beach and the main road, a small building with large open windows emerged. A man dressed much like the Pharisees but with a plain outer tunic stood inside, counting coins being collected from travelers by his servant. He wrote a receipt once he finished the count, and a servant delivered it back to the traveler. The travelers then continued on their way, obviously distressed over their encounter with Matthew.

Jesus watched for several minutes, then approached the building, waiting at the open window for Matthew to look up. When he finally did, Matthew quickly pulled the turban from his head and lowered his eyes. "Lord, I was not expecting you today."

"It is time, Matthew. Come with me." Jesus did not wait for a reply but turned south and led us down the road toward camp.

I slowed my pace to observe what Matthew would do. He swept the remaining coins off the table into a small bag and handed it to one of the servants. He spoke briefly to each of them, then stepped out of the building with nothing more than the clothes he wore and ran to catch up with us. He fell in beside me.

"Welcome, Matthew," I greeted, putting my arm around his shoulder. I thought back to the morning I arrived in Galilee. Even though my initiation was less than warm and friendly, at least Andrew's presence helped me survive the shock of waking up among Jesus's disciples. I intended to pass the favor on to Matthew. "I'm glad you're with us."

"Thank you. You do me a great honor, Sir."

"Honor?"

"Yes, of course, friend. You have afforded me much esteem by using the name the good Rabbi has bestowed upon me." His face beamed with pride. Then as quickly as it had appeared, his smile faded as he stared at the group in front of us. "I fear, to the rest of these men, I shall remain, Levi, the wretched tax collector, unfit to even eat among true Israelites, much less these stiff-necked Galileans." He laughed without humor in his voice. "And to which of the Master's worthy disciples am I speaking, sir?"

"Thomas," I resisted the urge to stick out my hand.

"Ah! Loyal Thomas. I have heard the good Master speak of you. From Bethsaida, if I remember correctly."

"Yes, Bethsaida," I agreed, savoring the name "Loyal Thomas" like one of my mother's Sunday afternoon pot roasts. Could it be loyal was the nickname Thomas had been known by before he uttered those fateful words of doubt that labeled him for the rest of time? "And you, Matthew. Where are you from, and how did you come to know Jesus?"

"Caesarea, originally. In Capernaum for over fifteen years now. And in my business, it is incumbent upon one to be familiar with all the residents in his jurisdiction. I met the sons of Zebedee when John was just a boy and James joined his father in the fishing business. I became acquainted with Peter and Andrew several years ago when they moved to Capernaum. I have known Jesus less than a year. He sought me out at the tax office. His family is too poor to have dealings with the likes of me otherwise. But I confess, Thomas, I have provided the others ample reasons to hate me, as I have most of those who call Capernaum home."

CHAPTER 21
The Reception

Less than an hour later, we arrived back at camp. As we approached, I could see our numbers increased substantially. The family camp had doubled, and over a dozen men were waiting to speak with Jesus. He urged them to wait where they were, then approached Matthew and me.

"Thomas, I would like to go and pray. Would you show Matthew where the men are camped and help those men over there find a place to bed down? I will return for the evening meal and would like to have everyone gathered."

I told him I would take care of it, and he walked toward the hilly ground to the west.

Mary and Joanna, who returned ahead of us, had bread prepared and were waiting. And true to Matthew's prediction, the men turned their backs on him, refusing to acknowledge his presence. The untroubled look on Mathew's face told me it bothered me a lot more than it bothered him. I figured he had long ago grown accustomed to being ostracized by his fellow Jews, and if only a part of the story he told me was true, the scorn seemed well deserved.

I showed him where I slept and we both spent the afternoon resting. I woke to the sound of Jesus returning to camp. The group of men who had been waiting regathered and began asking Jesus questions or pledging to follow him. There were also several women with Joanna, Mary, and Suzanna. After Jesus pulled himself away from the men, Joanna approached and introduced the new arrivals.

When Jesus finished speaking to the women, I saw Matthew walk toward Jesus. They talked for a long time, Matthew often pointed back in the direction of Capernaum. It looked like Matthew was weeping, but I was too far away to hear what he said. Finally, Jesus nodded, and Matthew left our camp, heading back in the direction of Capernaum. I was about to chase after him to ensure he wasn't leaving us when Jesus walked up to me.

"Gather everyone here, Thomas. I will be teaching before our meal."

I did as Jesus requested, and after everyone gathered, he spent the remainder of the afternoon welcoming the new arrivals and teaching about the Kingdom of God. I heard much of what he taught many times before, but it was always entertaining to watch the faces of those who heard it for the first time. As Jesus finished the Parable of the Sower, the smell of fish stew drifted our way. He encouraged everyone to enjoy their meal and get to know one another, then he had one final announcement.

"Tomorrow, I will be returning to Capernaum," Jesus announced. "Matthew has invited me to his home for a reception. Those who wish to come are welcome."

Jesus spoke briefly with Peter before leaving camp. Then Peter spoke with me. His angry tone made it clear he was unhappy about the message, "Jesus expects you to be there tomorrow, Thomas. He expects all of us who have been with him from the beginning to attend Levi's little party. We will stay in Capernaum tomorrow night, and then we will be leaving the city and not be coming back here for some time. He wants you to bring nothing with you. If you have anything you value, find someone staying here and leave it with them."

I laughed as I patted myself down as though looking for my valuable possessions. Peter smiled. It was good to see.

"I will spend the night in my house with Andrew. There is a place for you on the roof if you would like. I am sure Sarah and Leah would be pleased to see you again. I told them about the words you spoke to me."

"Thank you, Peter. I would like that very much."

"Shall we find Andrew then? It will be dark soon."

As it turned out, Peter's assessment of the size of Matthew's estate was grossly understated. I imagined the villa's Spanish-style stucco walls and red tile roofs would fit nicely in Beverly Hills or Palm Beach. Nestled among rolling hills thick with vineyards and groves on the northernmost edge of the city, the view of Capernaum and the Sea of Galilee below was fantastic. The large open courtyard at the center of the structure held stone benches and tables under eucalyptus and cypress trees that could easily accommodate a hundred people. The seating area was nearly half full with well-dressed guests already. Servants led our group of five to a low pillowed table near Matthew and Jesus, who was speaking with a group of men. They stared at Jesus, captivated by his words.

James, John, Zebedee, and Salome sat at a nearby table with Nathaniel and a woman I'd seen in camp and assumed was his wife. I scanned the courtyard and recognized many who were part of our group by the shabby tunics and robes they wore. I realized much like the world I came from, a great deal could be learned from observing what people wore. The group standing behind Jesus with colorful robes and headgear were definitely the religious leaders of Capernaum. Scribes, Pharisees, perhaps a priest or two. The ones dressed like Matthew were likely also leaders in the business world. Perhaps other tax collectors, bankers, or accountants? Their simple utilitarian garb quickly identified the store owners, farmers, and fishermen. The occupation of a group of ladies at the very back table was easily inferred by their attire. While modestly dressed in simple robes, they were the only women in the courtyard showing even a wisp of hair. They could not have been more recognizable if they had dressed in miniskirts, halter tops, fishnet stockings and stilettos.

Our meal was remarkable, not only because of its excellent flavor but because it contained the first piece of real meat I'd eaten since arriving in Galilee nearly a year ago. It tasted like savory lamb. The bread consisted of finely ground wheat flour rather than the coarse, gritty barley flour I'd grown accustomed to eating. And the wine could have easily occupied a space in the locked glass cabinets of any high-end gourmet wine shops back home.

After the meal, Jesus moved from table to table, talking patiently with everyone, including the working ladies at the back. He lingered with several groups for long conversations, and by his gestures, he appeared to be making arrangements for some of the guests to return to our base camp.

After most of the guests excused themselves and the sun lowered below the horizon, Matthew stood and asked if we would come and sit together near the head table.

Once we were gathered, he bowed. "I wish to thank each of you for attending today," he began. "I am under no illusion regarding your presence here. I know most of you would have refused to defile yourselves had the Rabbi not required it of you." He nodded toward Jesus. "I understand how you must feel. Truly I do. I have wronged all of you and would undo it if possible. But I have been instructed by our wise teacher no power in Heaven or on Earth can cause the sins I have committed to be undone." Again, Matthew looked at Jesus.

Jesus nodded, encouraging him to continue.

"But, while they cannot be undone, my sins can be forgiven. Our Lord has forgiven me and assured me his father has done the same in Heaven. I...I...can only beg each of you to also forgive me."

Peter opened his mouth to say something, but Matthew raised his palm and said, "Please, sir, be so kind as to let me finish." He reached inside his cloak and pulled out a rolled piece of paper. "This is a bill of sale for this house. The man who owns the surrounding vineyards has been after me for many years to acquire it. It will become his at midday tomorrow." On a table behind Matthew sat three bags of coins. Matthew took the first one, stepped around several guests, and set it in front of Zebedee. "This is the money I have stolen from you over the years, sir. I know you require another boat or two. This should be quite adequate." Matthew placed the other two bags before Andrew and Peter. "I cannot undo the suffering I have caused you both. I cheated you more than most because...well...because you opposed me more than most. Please forgive me." He returned to the front. "The man to whom I sold this property is a good man. He has agreed to distribute the rest of the funds from the sale to the citizens in Capernaum whom I defrauded. I have kept nothing for myself. I only ask you to allow me to join you in your service to God."

Matthew stood in silence.

I saw two men near the back leave the courtyard.

Another stood and said, "My father is dead because of you. I will never forgive you, traitor!" The man spat on the ground and stomped out. We sat in stunned silence.

Finally, Peter slowly got to his feet and faced Matthew. After what seemed like an eternity, he picked up his bag of coins and handed it to his mother-in-law. Then he turned to Jesus. "Not everyone who says, 'Lord, Lord,' will enter the Kingdom of Heaven. But only those who do the will of God." He pointed at Jesus but turned to address the rest of us. "This man has taught us many will say to him on that day, 'Lord, did we not prophesy in your name, and did we not cast out demons and perform miracles in your name?' And he will declare to them, 'I never knew you. Leave me.'"

Peter approached Matthew and took the bill of sale from his hand, holding it high in the air. "If we hear his words, we must act on them. If we do, we will be like a wise man who builds his house on a strong foundation. The rains may fall and floods may come, but that house will not fall because it has been built on the rock. But those who hear his words and do not do as he teaches will be like a foolish man who builds his house on the sand. When the rains fall and the floods come, and the winds blow and slam against that house, it will fall. And the loss will be very great."

Peter lowered the paper looking at it for a long time before continuing, "Matthew's house was built on sand." Another long pause. "So was mine and everything else I have ever put my hand to." He looked at Jesus. "But you have forgiven me and given me the chance to rebuild. I confess I do not know if I will be able to do all you require of me, Lord. I only know I can do no less for this man, whom I have hated, than you have done for me." He turned to Matthew. "It will be an honor to walk with you, brother." Then he looked back at us. "Which of you will stand with me?"

Another handful of men and a couple of women left.

Then Andrew rose and joined Peter putting one arm around him and the other around Matthew. Next were James and John. Then Philip and Nathaniel. Then Thaddeus, Simon the Zealot, James the younger, and finally Judas. I found myself standing with them as well, but I don't remember how or when I got there. I looked around at these men with more pride and happiness than I had ever known.

There we were for the first time as a group. Standing in solidarity with one another, doing something none of us could have done a few months ago. Maybe even a few hours ago. The twelve disciples were finally together.

CHAPTER 22
The Sending

Before going off to pray, Jesus sent most of the men and women back to camp. To the twelve, he gave instructions to spend the night in Matthew's house. Then he sent the women home with either Salome or Sarah. Just before sunrise, James woke us.

"Jesus wants us to meet him on Mount Arbel." He turned to Matthew. "Do you know this place?"

"Yes, of course, it is very near," Matthew said. "Less than an hour."

We grabbed some bread and fruit the servants collected the night before and followed Matthew as he left his home for the last time. He led us north into the hills adjacent to his estate. When we arrived at the top of Mount Arbel, we could see Capernaum and the Sea of Galilee to the south and the beginning of the Chorazin Plateau in the north. We were surprised to find the women already there.

"What are you doing here?" Simon the Zealot demanded of Mary Magdalene. He stood with his arms crossed over his chest. If he thought he could intimidate her by stepping to within a few feet and staring down at her, he was about to learn a very painful lesson.

"We obey him as you do, Simon," Mary said, stepping forward and closing the gap between them. "Or perhaps you would like to instruct our Lord regarding who he may and may not call to follow him."

I knew many of the men felt the same as Simon did, but the sight of Mary with her hands on her hips staring up at Simon's chin, daring him to question her further, caused most of them to break out laughing.

"She is correct, Simon," Jesus said as he came up behind us. "Like all of you, she has chosen to follow me and has been entrusted to my care. Now, come sit with me." Jesus stepped between us, found a large rock to sit on, and we took seats on the ground in front of him.

"Who do the people say I am?"

We looked around at each other, not speaking at first.

"Some say John the Baptizer!" Philip finally called out.

"I have heard some say you are Elijah or Jeremiah," Andrew added.

Jesus raised his hand to silence us. "I have heard those things as well. But who do you say I am?"

Peter looked at me and nodded. He remembered our conversation. "You are the Christ. The son of the living God."

"You are a blessed man, Peter, because you did not come to this understanding on your own. Only my father in Heaven could have revealed it to you." Jesus addressed us, "There have been many others who have come before me: Simon of Peraea, Athronges, Theudas. Even now, there are others. Why have you not followed them?"

Once again, Peter answered, "Lord, to whom shall we go? Only you have the words of eternal life."

The rest of us added our agreement.

"And yet you still find my words difficult to accept and my ways beyond your understanding," Jesus said, looking at each of us. "Surely you heard the Pharisees challenge me last night! 'Why does he eat with the tax collectors?' they asked. 'Why does he sit with prostitutes and sinners? Why do his disciples not fast like our disciples do, as did John's?'" Jesus got up and came and sat on the ground with us. "How did I answer them, Philip? You were there next to me."

"You answered them as you have answered many times before, Rabbi. It is not those who are healthy who need a physician but those who are sick. You have not come to call the righteous but sinners." Philip looked around at us and smiled. "For which every one of us is grateful."

"Do you trust me, Phillip?"

"Yes, Lord, you know I do."

"Do you trust me?" He looked at each of the men until they nodded.

"Yet, you still question my wisdom when calling these daughters to follow me." He gestured toward the women. "Have you not yet come to understand I am preparing the way for a new kingdom? I did not come to abolish the old ways but to fulfill them. And that which is fulfilled and complete must step aside and make way for that which is to come. I am the new covenant—the new affirmation between Heaven and Earth. No one sews a patch of unshrunk cloth on an old garment; otherwise, the new patch will pull away from the old, and a worse tear results. And no one puts new wine into old wineskins; otherwise, the wine will burst the skins, and the wine is ruined, and so are the skins. But one puts new wine into fresh wineskins. Listen to me. I am telling you the truth. I am the new wine. If you try to contain all I teach you in old skins, it will be lost and have no effect. You cannot contain my new ways within old ways of thinking. Many say my words are hard to understand and difficult to accept. But to you twelve and these women who follow me, I have made my meaning clear and known. There is no more time to decide. Now it is time for you who have been with me from the beginning, my apostles, to take the message of the Kingdom of God to all of Galilee, Peraea, and even as far as Judea. I am sending you out in pairs, but perhaps not as you wish."

Jesus stood and walked among us, laying his hands on us. "Peter, Andrew, James, John, Philip, Nathaniel, Matthew, Thomas, James, Thaddeus, Simon, Judas. I give you power and authority over demons and all sickness and disease. Do not take anything for your journey except your staff: no bag, no bread, no money. Do not even take two tunics. Wherever you find those who welcome you, enter that house and stay there until you leave that city. As for those who do not receive you, when you leave that city, shake the dust off your feet as a statement against them." The last man Jesus approached was Peter. He knelt before him and placed his hand on Peter's arm, speaking the exact words he had said over each of us. "And when you come to a house that receives you, Peter, and you find the man of that house sick with a fever, as we found Sarah, what do you intend to do?"

"I will do as you did, Lord. I will place my hands on him and heal him in your name."

"And what will you do if the woman of the house has fallen ill? What will you do then, Peter?"

"I will...well, I..." Peter hung his head and admitted, "I do not know, Lord."

"Leah," Jesus called.

Peter's wife stepped out from among the women and joined the men. "Yes, Lord?"

"What would you do?"

Leah smiled at her husband. "First, I would spare my husband the anguish of questioning the woman by sending him and her husband out of the room." All of the women and several men laughed, obviously causing Peter some of the anguish Leah hoped to spare him from.

"Then," she continued, despite Peter's embarrassment, "once I knew what she suffered from, I would lay my hands upon her and bring healing to her in your name."

"Thank you, Leah." Jesus moved on to James and John. He knelt in front of them. "John, do you remember what happened a few days ago when we left Capernaum and the woman who had suffered from a hemorrhage for twelve years touched me?"

"Yes, Lord."

"Can you tell me what the Law of Moses says regarding her?"

John looked at James, who shrugged his shoulders. After a few moments, John looked back at Jesus. "Forgive me, Lord. I am a simple fisherman. I have known the commandments since childhood, but regarding this woman, I do not know."

"Do any of you know?" he asked the men.

Matthew spoke up. "It is found in the book of the Law, Rabbi," he said. "If a woman has a discharge of her blood for many days, not at the period of her menstrual impurity, she shall continue as though in her menstrual impurity, she is unclean. Likewise, whoever touches her shall be unclean and shall wash his clothes and bathe in water and be unclean until evening."

Jesus turned to Philip, "Why was I not made unclean when she touched me, Philip?"

Philip thought about it. "I do not know, Lord. Though I have heard many who were with you that day ask the same question. Why did you not follow the ways of the Law and wash?"

Jesus looked toward the women. "Salome, will you join us?"

Salome joined Jesus, kneeling beside her two sons.

"Would you explain to James and John and everyone here why I was not made unclean when the suffering woman touched me?"

Salome bowed slightly toward Jesus, then raised her voice, "Because of the flow."

Matthew spoke again, "Forgive me, Lady Salome, but how can that be? The Law states plainly her flow caused her to be unclean."

"It is not her flow of which I speak, Matthew. It is his." Salome pointed at Jesus. "Do you not remember what he said when the woman touched his robe? 'Who touched me? Someone has touched me, for I am aware power has left me.' "The power of God flowed out from him," Salome explained, "into the woman and at the same time prevented anything from flowing back toward him. It is why, in almost every case, he must touch those he heals. And why you also must lay your hands on those who need healing. The gift he has given you will flow from you into them." She looked at Jesus, who nodded for her to continue. "It is also why he is trying to teach you that you cannot go alone. Few fathers and husbands would allow you to touch their wives or daughters. It is not the Law, but the Pharisees and priests have made it seem so, and we cannot leave the women of Israel to suffer. Therefore, we must travel together. Men laying hands on men, and women on women."

Jesus rose. He and Salome joined the women, and Jesus laid his hands on each of them, speaking the same words he had over the men. Then he spoke to everyone, "Listen to me, all of you. I have cared for you as a shepherd cares for his sheep. But now I am sending you out among wolves. I will not be with you, so you must be as wise as serpents but as innocent as doves. Always be careful, but do not be afraid, because it is not you who is speaking, but the spirit of my father speaking in you. Remember, those who receive you, receive me, and the one who receives me receives him who sent me."

Jesus turned to Peter. "Peter, you and Nathaniel will travel with your wives. Take Andrew and Mary of Magdala with you. Take what I have taught you to the villages of Judea surrounding Lydda. Thaddeus, you should return home to Caesarea. I believe you will discover your wife has had a change of heart. Take her with you and travel down the coast toward Joppa. You will find good fishing there. James and John, you may travel together with your mother and mine. Take my message to Jerusalem and as far south as Beersheba. I will go with you as far as Bethany, where I intend to stay with Lazarus for a time."

Jesus assigned the rest of us a traveling companion and a general direction to take his message. He gave us clear instructions on how to conduct ourselves on the road, always being careful to arrive in a village early enough to get separate accommodations before sunset. We were told to stay at that abode until our work was finished. Clopas and his wife, Mary, would be traveling with Philip, Judas, and Junia throughout Galilee west of the sea, while Matthew and Suzanna would stay in Capernaum. Joanna and I were sent to Chorazin and Bethsaida.

After giving us our final instructions, Jesus said goodbye and sent us back to Capernaum. The women stayed at Peter's home with Leah and Sarah, and the men stayed with James and John. No one spoke very much that night as each of us dealt with our own fears, wondering when we would see Jesus again. He assured us we would know when to return to the base camp, where he would meet us. After Zebedee feasted us on the day's catch, I found a quiet place on the roof to sleep but lay awake most of the night, worried about what Joanna and I were going to find when we got to Bethsaida.

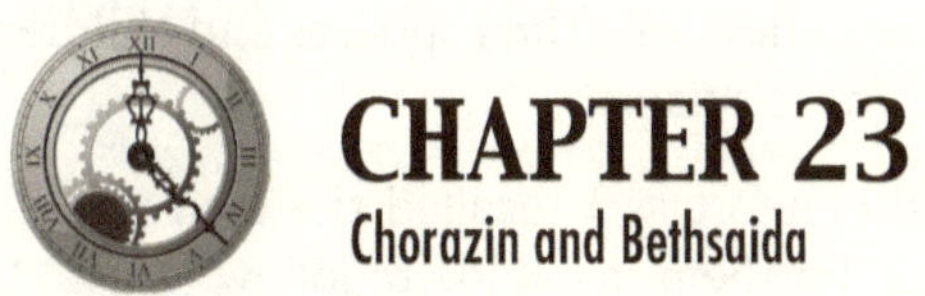

CHAPTER 23
Chorazin and Bethsaida

Joanna and I spent the first few months of our journey in Chorazin. We used her father's estate as a base and traveled to the small villages and settlements on the plateau during the day. Both of her parents were in Jerusalem, representing Antipas's interests at Pilate's court. We had great success preaching the Kingdom of God wherever we went, even among the servants and hired laborers on the estate. Many people were healed and delivered. The sight of Joanna walking on her own and the reports of other great works Jesus did caused a lot of excitement and celebrating, but there was great sadness when time came for us to leave for the next village. Many of the servants begged Joanna to move back permanently or at least stay until her parents returned, but she stood firm in her decision to finish the task Jesus gave us.

"The Kingdom of God must be preached in all this land before the Master calls us to return to Capernaum," she told the servants. "You must tell everyone in Chorazin what we have told you about Jesus and what you have seen with your eyes over these last days. Others will come to you soon to teach you more about what God is doing in Israel and how he wants you to live. Perhaps when I return, Jesus will be with me. Keep the faith as I am."

"You seem troubled, Thomas," Joanna said to me after about an hour on the road to Bethsaida. "Do you fear your betrothed will no longer wish to wed you, or do you fear she will?"

Joanna's attempts to comfort me were genuinely kind and thoughtful, but she had no idea how complicated her question was to answer. I didn't even know the woman or the circumstances under which I'd left her behind. While I was certainly not the only person among Jesus's followers to have complicated relationship issues to address, at least the others knew who their spouses and children were. I didn't even know my fiancée's name.

I found some small comfort as I recalled the men's stories about how difficult it had been for them to decide to follow Jesus. Many had lost everything. Wives, parents, children, farms, lands, and livelihoods had been surrendered to follow him. And I knew from talking with Joanna and Mary Magdalene the same held true among the women. Every sacrifice and loss was a burden my companions carried silently without complaint and served as a constant reminder of how different reality was from perception. How sterile and trivial the words I heard in church seemed to me now.

I shook my head as I pictured Pastor Nelson reciting Jesus's words, "I honestly am telling you, there is no one who has left house or brothers or sisters or mother or father or children or farms, for my sake and the gospel's sake, that will not receive a hundred times as much now in the present age, houses and brothers and sisters and mothers and children and farms, along with persecutions, and also in the age to come, eternal life."

Easy for you to say, Pastor, I thought as I pictured the congregation at Riverview Church on a typical Sunday morning, following along in their Bibles. *So easy for you to say.*

To the modern Christian, these were merely words on a page read by a man in a suit standing behind a pretty pulpit. Words, in most cases, that would cost them nothing. After church, they would go home to their comfortable suburban homes and enjoy a lavish family dinner with all the trimmings. Not a single one would lose their children, parents, or spouse because they decided to follow Jesus. Not one of them would be required to make a single change in their lives to continue as faithful church members.

I wondered how different they would feel if they could spend one night with the people I now considered my new family. How would they respond after looking into the pain-filled eyes of a wife and mother who left her husband and children? Or after listening to a man lying nearby trying desperately to keep his sobs as quiet as he could so as not to increase the suffering of his fellow disciples and friends. Not to mention what these dear people would have to go through when the man they loved was taken from them, tortured, and killed. No, I could not think of a single similarity between the Christianity in the twenty-first century and what these men and women were going through now.

And with this in mind, I still had to deal with my current reality. I didn't even know what the woman the other Thomas abandoned looked like. Had we grown up together or was the marriage arranged for us? Did my parents live in Bethsaida, or had I moved there to work in my fiancée's family vineyard? Did I have brothers and sisters or friends who had listened to Jesus on the day he passed through who made a different choice? What did Jesus say or do that caused me to leave everything behind to follow him?

Joanna's voice brought me out of my reflections, "Thomas? Are you alright?"

"Yes...yes, I'm fine," I sputtered, realizing how self-centered the last few minutes had been. "I'm sorry. I was thinking about your question. I guess I don't know which would be better. But my troubles seem small compared to all you have gone through to be here."

Joanna gently touched my arm and then drew her hand back quickly, looking around at the deserted countryside. "Your troubles are not small to you, Thomas. And they are not to me either. And I can assure you, they are not small to God either. That is what being a part of his family is about. None of us have to carry our burdens alone. Now, tell me, what is troubling you so?"

As I searched for the words to share with Joanna, I realized how taxing always telling the truth really was. I would have given anything to be able to confide in her. To tell her the whole crazy story about waking up in her time not knowing a single person or having the slightest idea why I was there. But that was impossible. It would only draw another person into my confusing world and wouldn't solve anything. Yet, being alone all the time, even among friends, was beginning to wear on me.

"I guess I'm just not the same person I was when I left Bethsaida, Joanna," I admitted honestly. "This last year traveling with Jesus and hearing him preach has changed me. I don't know what I want or expect to find when I get home. I wonder if my family will even recognize me."

Joanna touched my arm again. This time she left her hand there and stared directly at me, obviously not caring if the whole world saw her crossing cultural boundaries. "We are all different, Thomas." She gave my arm a gentle squeeze. "No one who follows Jesus can remain the same. You can never return to the same place you left before you met him."

"Thank you, Joanna. I couldn't ask for a better friend than you."

Joanna smiled and nodded and then walked silently beside me the rest of the way to Bethsaida.

About an hour before arriving in Bethsaida, the road split. The left leg continued up into the hilly countryside north of the village. The right path took us northeast along the shore of the Sea of Galilee. We could see many vineyards, olive groves, and barley fields on the hillsides above as we approached the town. I wondered how much of Thomas's life had been spent happily working in one of those vineyards. For the first time, I actually found myself envious of the man who lived this life before me.

While considerably smaller, Bethsaida looked much like Capernaum, especially from the perspective of the seaside. A dozen fishing boats with nets were strewn across the shore along with the fishermen they belonged to. Another five or six boats floated about half a mile out on the lake. Several fishermen nodded in my direction as we passed and I wondered if they were men I knew or simply being friendly.

We ascended one of several stone steps leading up the steep hillside into the central part of the old, weathered village. If the buildings of Bethsaida had been built of wood instead of stone, it would have looked very much like the old western towns in movies. One long main street divided the town with several side streets branching off to the right and to the left. The main road bustled with people. Several men pulled or pushed hand carts filled with fish or bags of grain or barrels, possibly containing wine or olive oil. If I had grown up in Bethsaida, nothing about it looked even the slightest bit familiar.

I was about to ask Joanna where she thought we should start when I heard a woman shout my name.

"Thomas! Thomas!"

I spotted the woman working her way through a large crowd in front of an open market about thirty yards away. Once she made it to the dirt road, she lifted her skirt and ran toward us, weaving between carts and people. Young and pretty, she appeared to be maybe twenty-five or twenty-six. She wore a skull cap, much like Mary Magdalene's, but long strands of dark wavy hair stuck out in several spots, and she wore it too far back on her head, freeing much of her hair in the front. When she reached me, she grabbed my arms, stretched up on tiptoes, and kissed both of my cheeks several times. Then she took one step back, looked me over from head to foot, and shoved me so hard in the chest it knocked me flat on my butt, leaving me gasping for air.

"You mangy goatherd!" she screamed. "Do you have any idea how much trouble you have caused so you could run off pretending to be Moses or Joshua or some other fool prophet? Of course, you don't. Have you ever cared about any of the messes you left for others to clean up?" When I opened my mouth to speak, she threw her hands up. "Do not dare make any of your feeble excuses, brother. I have heard them all before from you or Mother more times than I wish to count. She still refuses to hire a single new hand to take your place because she keeps believing your sanity will return and you will come home. Have you seen her yet?"

"Uh, no...I...uh, no," I stuttered, getting to my feet.

"Well, come on then. It would put her in her grave if she discovered you were home and did not see her straight away." She turned and walked back toward the market, still talking and waving her arms.

I looked at Joanna, who had a huge grin on her face. "You'd best follow her, Thomas. Next time, she may not be so gentle with you. Besides, I think we have found our accommodations for tonight."

When we reached the market, the woman exited with three baskets of greens, grains, and fruit, one in each hand and one in the crook of her elbow. She set them down in front of me and started down the road toward the center of town, still talking over her shoulder. "Mother has aged since you left, Thomas. Try not to let it show on your face when you see her."

I grabbed two baskets, Joanna took one, and we followed. I could only imagine what trouble I would have caused if I hadn't seen her take one of the side streets about forty yards ahead. By the time we reached the turn, my sister had traveled far up the road leading to the vineyards.

Half an hour later, the road turned into a footpath weaving through vines and groves. The next time we saw her, she was waiting for us near two stone pillars separating the lush green vineyard from a dry, barren patch of land about the size of a football field with a large stone villa in the center and several barns, granaries, and stables around it.

Joanna made a slight bow when we reached her and said, "Please forgive me. My name is Joanna. I did not hear your name."

"I am Dahlia. Goatherd's sister." She walked on. "Are you his new wife? He must have forgotten he already has one of those here in Bethsaida. Perhaps he failed to tell you that."

Joanna nearly choked, getting the words out as quickly as she could, "No, no, Dahlia. Not his wife. We serve Rabbi Jesus together. We are merely traveling companions with a common mission."

Dahlia stopped and turned. She looked at Joanna as though seeing her for the first time. "He sends you out together? To speak for him? This teacher? He sends a woman?"

"Yes, Dahlia. Jesus treats us the same way as he does the men." Joanna paused and smiled. "Even though some of them still resent it."

Dahlia's eyes widened, and she pursed her lips. "Well, perhaps this rabbi of yours is not so bad as I thought, Thomas. I will hear more of him tonight after supper."

As we approached the house, Dahlia explained to Joanna the path we took through the vineyards and groves was the shortcut. The main road, located on the other side of the house, wound around the hillside from the east. We entered, and Dahlia led us through the large, richly furnished house where an older woman sat alone under a pile of tousled blankets. Dahlia introduced her to Joanna as Anna.

Thomas's mother could not have been more different from his sister. She appeared mousy and quiet and wept when she saw me. I knelt in front of her and kissed her cheeks as she cupped both sides of my face with her hands, whispering over and over, "I knew you would come home. I knew you would."

After a quiet meal, we moved to the veranda outside the rear entrance, where servants served wine in glass goblets and Dahlia forced me to listen to every hardship my decision to run off and follow the crazy preacher had put my family through. It seemed Thomas the apostle and Tommy Evans were far more alike than I realized. Both were huge disappointments to our families.

Joanna tried to change the subject, "My family is also in the wine business. Our vineyards are on the plateau northwest of here. But I do believe this wine is even better. You should be very proud."

"We are," Anna said. "Though it has been nearly impossible to keep up with all the work since Thomas left." She looked at me. "I am so glad you have come home."

I began to wonder if Thomas had more than one motivation for responding to Jesus's call to follow him. As the evening wore on, I became more and more eager to discover the answer to my most important question. Surprised the topic had not already been brought up, especially considering Dahlia's earlier comments, I asked, "You mentioned my fiancée earlier, Dahlia. Is she well?"

A chill descended on the room. My mother and Dahlia stared at the floor.

"What is it? What has happened?"

Anna left the room, taking her wine with her.

After waiting to make sure Anna would not return, Dahlia began her story, "She was as confused as the rest of us when you left, Thomas. Everyone was. We thought you were happy here. Like Mother, we believed it would not take you long to realize you made a mistake and come home. Then about three months after you left, it started."

"What started, Dahlia? What happened to her?"

"Some say she finally lost hope when you did not come back. Others say the grief she carried when you abandoned her caused her mind to give up and leave her. The priest at the synagogue says she has a demon. Whatever it is, Thomas, she is truly mad. Her parents have tried to care for her, but it is becoming even more than they can bear. She never leaves her room, rarely eats, and refuses to speak with anyone. Even her parents."

Shocked as I was by what I was hearing, it didn't compare to what Dahlia said next.

"Rebecca does not recognize anyone from Bethsaida. Not her parents, not me or her other friends, not even her three brothers. She claims she does not belong here. She says she comes from another place. Even from another time. And she says things about other places I have never heard of and other strange things no one can explain. I fear you will find Rebecca a very different person from the woman you left, brother."

My breath caught in my throat. The room spun around me, and the meal I'd eaten threatened to come up. I lowered my head onto my knees, trying to get control of myself. How could this be happening? There was no way what Dahlia described could have been a coincidence. This had something to do with me. Something to do with me being here in this time and place with Jesus. Had the same thing happened to this Rebecca? Had a person traveled back and...Rebecca! Rebecca? Becky? Oh, dear God, no! It couldn't possibly be, could it? Could the woman Dahlia described, the woman I was betrothed to here in Bethsaida before I chose to follow Jesus, be the same woman I left behind in Ohio? The Becky from home? My Becky? I ran to the door.

"I want to leave as soon as it's light."

"If that is your wish, Thomas." Dahlia's eyes widened. "I will be ready."

"Joanna, will you come with us? If this is a demon, I'll need..."

"Yes, of course, Thomas," Joanna answered. "I will be waiting with Dahlia in the morning. And Thomas?"

"Yes?"

"Do not be afraid. This is why he sent us here."

CHAPTER 24
Rebecca

Dahlia and Joanna were waiting for me when I stepped out the back door. Joanna handed me a piece of bread and a skin of wine. I looked at Dahlia, hoping she would take the lead since I had no idea where we were going.

"Come on, Joanna," Dahlia called. "Let goatherd eat his breakfast. I will show you part of the vineyard on the way."

Dahlia led Joanna around the front of the house, out the main gate, then left at the road leading further up into the hills. I lagged far enough behind to not hear their conversation, wanting to concentrate on my own thoughts. If the woman we were about to meet did turn out to be my Becky, Dahlia's description suggested she dealt with time-traveling entirely differently than I had. Perhaps that's because I left nothing I truly valued behind in Ohio besides her.

On the other hand, Becky got along great with her parents, with the possible exception of the nights I brought her home too late or the occasional argument over her future plans. She had been an exceptional student and leader of several high school groups supporting rights for minorities and women. Because she was an overachiever in almost everything she touched, her parents hoped she would choose a career garnering respect among her peers and colleagues and owning multiple bank accounts. But Becky decided to wait a year or two before choosing a college and major to pursue her love of art and reflect on what life meant to her and how she wanted to live it.

Well, Beck, if this is you, somebody jumped in and interrupted your plans and made some decisions for you. I thought. *Now, what part do I get to play in your life?*

Dahlia and Joanna turned down a path similar to the main road in front of Thomas and Dahlia's house. This house was even larger, with several more outbuildings. I counted at least a dozen men working in or around the grounds. I quickened my steps and came up alongside Dahlia.

She looked at me, "You better let me go in first and explain to Rebecca's parents you are here. The last time I talked with them, you were not likely to be welcomed back again."

A servant met Dahlia at the door and quickly ushered her into the house. Even from a distance, I could see contempt in the woman's eyes when she glanced at me. Joanna and I waited beneath one of the two giant eucalyptus trees on either side of the path leading from the house to a cluster of small buildings in front of two large barns.

Joanna opened her mouth to speak just as Dahlia came out, followed closely behind by a man and a woman, most likely Rebecca's parents. Under the circumstances, I would have understood if an ugly scene developed. Several months ago, I watched Benjamin confront Jesus in front of the fish tower in Magdala, but unlike Benjamin's face, hard and full of rage, nothing ugly could be seen on the faces of these two people. The only thing I could sense, as I looked into their empty eyes, was pain and desperation. They were both middle-aged, and while the man was tall, he seemed small and almost hidden within his heavy, drab robes.

They stopped in front of me, and the man grabbed my upper arms. "Thank God you have returned, Thomas. Thank God indeed. I told Martha many times that a man of religion such as yourself would listen to Almighty God and do the right thing." The man shrugged and pursed his lips. "All in God's good time, of course. I understand, Thomas. I do. All in God's good time. But where is the healer?" He looked left and right and then over my shoulder. "Where is he, Thomas?" His tone changed from excitement to suspicion as his grip on my arms tightened. "Surely he is with you? That is why you have returned, is it not? To deliver us from the dark curse befallen our daughter. Is he coming later, Thomas? I have ordered the servants to prepare a room for him even now."

He looked at his wife, who made a slight gesture toward Joanna and me.

"And you too, of course, Thomas. Yes, yes, of course, rooms for all of you. When will he be here, Thomas? The healer? Surely, he is coming as he did before, yes?" The fear intensified in his voice as he continued to look around, seeing no one except Dahlia, Joanna, and me. He looked into my eyes and must have seen the answer to his question there. His hands began to tremble as he clung to me, trying to keep himself from falling. When he could stand it no longer, he buried his head against my chest and wept loudly.

I put my arms around his shoulders and drew him close as his body convulsed in long agonizing sobs. I never felt such love and compassion for any person in my entire life. As I traveled with Jesus over the last year, I experienced more changes than in all the years before combined. I met and became friends with many beautiful people, went through harrowing experiences with Roman soldiers, came face to face with death, watched as Jesus performed miracles, and saw people recover from horrible diseases at his touch and now mine. Still, nothing prepared me for this moment. Rebecca's father's pain reached into a part of me I did not even realize existed. I caused this pain. It didn't matter that a different Thomas decided to follow Jesus. Everything the former Thomas ever did was my responsibility now. I would never be able to enjoy the fruits of this new life without also embracing the ramifications of the life of the man whose place I had taken.

I opened myself to this poor man's pain. I drank it into my soul, hoping to relieve a tiny sliver of the torment he felt. I'd watched Jesus do it hundreds of times in a single day and marveled he could take upon himself so much suffering. This one man's pain was nearly more than I could bear.

As he began to quiet and his breathing became shallower and more controlled, I lifted a silent prayer to God. *Thank you, my Father, for bringing me here to this man. Thank you for letting me meet him. Thank you for your son, who has taught us to love better. Yesterday I healed because I could. Today and from this day on, I will heal because I understand more of your love and compassion.*

"Reuben," Martha tried to pull her husband away from me. "Come, Reuben. We should return to the house. There is nothing for us here." She shook her head at me. Then she turned to Dahlia and pointed to a door on the side of the house. "Your rooms have been prepared for you there. You should rest. You will find some fruit in your rooms to sustain you. I will have you summoned when supper is ready."

"Where is Rebecca?" I asked. "May we see her? I believe we can help." I gestured toward Joanna.

Martha stared at me as she struggled to hold her husband upright;

his sobbing had returned. Dahlia joined her, taking Reuben's other arm. "She will not know you, Thomas. She does not know any of us. She does not even know herself." Martha turned toward the house, supporting her husband's weight. About halfway to the door, she stopped. "But you cannot make things any worse. If you wish to see her, follow us."

She led Joanna and me into the house and pointed down a narrow hallway. "She is in the last room."

Joanna and I hurried down the hall. When we reached the last door, we stopped and looked at each other. The only other time I'd seen such deep concern and compassion on Joanna's face was by the light of a torch when we stood in the cold, dark dungeon passing a tiny loaf of bread through the bars to John the Baptist.

"I'm afraid," I whispered.

"I know you are, Thomas. But remember what Jesus taught us. You must not be like the servant who hid his master's money in the ground. Be like the others who did well. You must understand the ones who did well with their master's money were also afraid. The difference was they did not let their fear stop them from doing the right thing. Your courage and..." she hesitated, "your love for this woman has brought you to her door. Jesus would not leave her broken, and neither must we."

I wanted to wrap my arms around Joanna and thank her for being there for me when I needed her most. Instead, I sucked in my breath and nodded, "Thank you." I reached for the bar on the door and pulled it open.

The room felt small and sparse compared to what little I saw of the rest of the house. A bed even smaller than my single bed at home sat on the floor in the back corner, its straw-filled mattress rumpled and torn. The only furniture in the room consisted of a square wooden chest at the foot of the bed and a small wooden stool against the stone wall on the right. A woman sat on the bed with her back to us. Her legs were crossed yoga style under her white linen tunic. Her dark hair fell long and unkempt across her shoulders. She didn't turn or acknowledge us in any way.

Joanna took a seat on the stool and motioned me forward. When

I reached the chest at the end of the bed, I sat and waited. I wasn't sure why or what I waited for. Maybe I wanted to sense some kind of familiarity or connection with this stranger sitting with her back to me. There wasn't any. Once I accepted the fact Jesus wasn't going to suddenly walk through the door and rescue me from the situation I whispered her name, "Rebecca."

Rebecca continued to stare at the back wall for several minutes as though I was not even in the room. Finally, she turned her head slightly, "Leave it on the stool and go."

I didn't know what she meant, but it didn't matter because her words faded to nothing as I gazed at the side of her face. I'm not sure what I expected, but this woman looked nothing like the one I knew in Ohio. She was a few years older with wavy dark hair instead of Becky's blond curls. Her skin was a rich olive color and the eye I could see was black as coal. As I ran my hand over my balding head and full beard, I reminded myself I didn't look anything like the twenty-year-old college kid she would remember either. All I know is when I saw Rebecca's face, every feeling I ever had for Becky filled my heart, and I knew it was her.

"Becky?"

The woman's shoulders lifted as if someone had thrown a glass of cold water on her. I wasn't sure whether I helped or did more damage to an already frightened and confused person. Joanna's words came back to me, *'Do not be afraid. The difference was they did not let their fear stop them from doing what was right.'*

I took a deep breath. "Becky, it's Tommy." I looked over my shoulder at Joanna and smiled. Helping one person could confuse another. *How would I explain this to Joanna? Well, too late now.* I plowed ahead. "It's Tommy from Springfield."

Becky spun around and looked at me for the first time. I'm embarrassed to say as she stared at me with her dark eyes, my biggest hope was she wouldn't be disappointed in what she saw in me. Fortunately, I saw no sign of disgust as she searched my face for any sign of the person she knew. What could I say to convince her I was who I said and not sound entirely crazy to Joanna?

"The last time we saw each other, we were leaving the Red Iron,"

I said, hoping while it wouldn't make sense to Joanna, it wouldn't give me away either.

I watched Becky's forehead scrunch together as she thought about what I said. She continued to search my face, looking deep into my eyes, her mind racing to put the pieces together. I saw the moment it came together in her head. I don't know how she did it, but in one swift movement, Becky leaped from the head of the bed to the foot and wrapped her arms around my neck, nearly knocking me off the wooden chest.

"Tommy, Tommy! Thank God! Is it really you?" She took my face in her hands and looked into my eyes again. When she knew for sure, she kissed me on the lips and wrapped her arms around me again. "How did you get here? How did we get here?" She kissed me again. "Did you come to take me home? Can you get us home? Tommy, I want to go home. Oh, please, Tommy, take me home with you."

As soon as Becky touched me, I saw Joanna stand quickly. Becky's behavior was totally unacceptable. Joanna knew it, and I knew it. Hopefully, she would see it as part of Rebecca's illness. I pushed Becky away and held her at arm's length as Joanna came up beside the chest.

Becky looked at her suspiciously. "Who is this, Tommy?"

"Rebecca, this is Joanna. She is a very good friend of mine."

Wow, I thought. *This could spiral out of control fast. I need to make this work, and I need to make it work now.*

"Joanna, ah... I think Rebecca is going to be fine now. I think you should go and get her parents and Dahlia."

Joanna turned to leave.

"And Joanna?"

She turned with a smile on her face. "Yes, Tommy?"

Oh boy, this is getting worse.

"Could you take your time? I need to help Rebecca remember a few things before seeing her parents. So just go slow, Okay?"

"Of course, Tommy," she smiled again. "I think I need to step outside for some air anyway. I will be back soon." She left the room and closed the door.

I looked at Becky and saw desperation. "What do you mean, see my parents, Tommy? What things do I need to remember? Take me home. Get me out of—"

"Stop," I said as firmly as I thought Becky could handle. "We have maybe five minutes before Joanna returns, and I need you to be quiet and listen to me."

Becky started to say something more, but I put my fingers on her lips to stop her, an action she used dozens of times back home when we were dating and she needed me to be quiet to let her get her point across. She understood the significance and nodded.

"I don't know how we got here, and I don't know how to get us home." I watched tears fill her eyes and flow down her cheeks, but she remained quiet. "I'm sure you've figured out by now, this is not Springfield. Somehow, we have traveled back in time to first-century Galilee. We don't look like ourselves because we've taken the place of real people who live here, in this time period."

Becky opened her mouth to speak.

"I don't know where they are. They might have taken our places in Springfield. I don't know. I've taken the place of one of Jesus's companions, the apostle Thomas and have been traveling with him and a group of his disciples for over a year and a half."

Her eyes became as big as saucers.

"The woman you are now was Thomas's fiancée before he left her to follow Jesus. I had no idea you were here and took her place until yesterday. I came as quickly as I could."

I could hear excited voices from another part of the house. I was running out of time.

"No one knows I'm not the real apostle Thomas, and no one knows you are not the real Rebecca of Bethsaida. And we need to keep it that way for now. If we have any hope of ever getting home, we have to play the parts we've been given until we find a way. Do you understand?"

I watched as the panic on Becky's face began to fade. "Yes, I think so. But how—"

"We don't have time for questions now, Beck. By the sound of those voices, we have about a minute before the curtain goes up. Can you do it?"

She thought about it for a few seconds and then nodded.

"Good. Everyone thinks you've been sick or demon-possessed or gone mad since you got here and took Rebecca's place. Some people think you've been overwhelmed with grief since I left. Whatever happened before, you must play the part of the healed daughter now. That's the only thing able to buy us time to figure out what's going on."

"But why are we here, Tommy? How did we get here? Who brought us here?"

"No time, Beck. We'll find time to talk later. I know we can figure this out together. We just have to wait for the right time."

Becky looked up. The voices were nearly at the door. "I can do it, Tommy. You can trust me, okay?"

"I do, Beck." That's when one more piece of the puzzle clicked into place. "I have one more thing I need to ask you before they get here." I gestured over my shoulder, expecting Joanna and Rebecca's parents to step into the room any second.

Becky nodded again. "Anything, Tommy."

"Will you marry me?"

Becky's eyes widened. I could see dozens of questions, fears, and doubts pass through them. Then she smiled. "Of course, I will, Tommy Evans or Thomas the apostle, or whoever you are. In this time or any other time, I will marry you."

I gave her a quick kiss and reached the stool barely before the door opened and Joanna led Dahlia and Rebecca's parents into the room.

CHAPTER 25
The Plan

If there were a version of the *Academy Awards* in first-century Palestine, Becky would have walked away with the Oscar in every category. In the brief few minutes we spent together, she processed the essential information and arrived at the only logical conclusion: I was right, everything happening was real, and her best shot at ever seeing home again was to join me in accepting our present circumstances. She set aside the doubts and fears crippling her since arriving in this time period and became Rebecca of Bethsaida. Hope is an awesome force, and now that Becky had some, she took on the challenge.

Reuben entered first after Joanna, shoulders back and chest expanded, the look of a protective father sternly on his face. When he saw his daughter sitting alone on the chest at the end of the bed and me, seated a safe and proper distance away on the wooden stool, much of the concern in his eyes disappeared.

"Mother!" Rebecca cried, jumping up and running to the older woman behind Reuben. The dour, disapproving look on Martha's face melted away as she and her daughter embraced, sinking to the floor clutching each other tightly. They touched one another's faces and wiped tears from each other's cheeks.

The look on Dahlia's face was priceless. I understood the relationship between her and her brother was complicated. But as she looked back and forth between the newly restored Rebecca and me, she saw me in a whole new light. Was that respect I saw in her eyes?

When I looked at Joanna, she had the same smile as when she left the room to retrieve Rebecca's parents. These were not the first miracles she'd been a part of, including her own and her son's. A silent offering of thanksgiving passed between us as we acknowledged God's hand in everything. I hoped she'd go back to calling me Thomas in the days ahead.

"Father," Rebecca said, taking Reuben's hand as he helped his daughter and wife to their feet.

Reuben held his daughter out at arm's length and looked at her from head to toe. "How is this possible?" Then, he looked at me. "Did you do this?"

A simple "yes" would not have been a lie. I had undoubtedly played a part in what happened to his daughter, both in her illness and recovery.

Becky must have seen me searching for the answer and jumped in, "Of course he did, Father. Did you know Thomas has been traveling with Jesus since he has been gone? Jesus sent him here to help me. I am so sorry for the trouble I have caused you and mother."

Reuben drew Rebecca close. "Do not concern yourself with that, child. All that matters now is you have come back to us."

Becky looked past her father at me with a "what do I do now" look on her face.

I returned it with my best "I don't have a clue" look.

"Thanks a lot," she mouthed silently. To her father, she said, "I still don't remember very much from before I got sick. I remember you and Mother, of course, but not much else. I'm going to need your help to put my life back together, Papa."

Reuben looked at her for a long time, slowly shaking his head.

Had she said something wrong? I remembered Joanna telling me my speech sounded strange when we first met. I wondered if Reuben sensed the same thing in his daughter, who was not really his daughter.

Then he broke out laughing and crying at the same time. "Papa," he laughed again, wiping his eyes. "Papa. You have not called me 'papa' since you were a little girl." He turned to his wife, who was still weeping. "Almighty God has been good to us today, aye, Martha. He has blessed us and caused his face to shine upon us, has he not? Yes, yes, indeed he has. As the great king himself wrote in the Tanakh." Reuben covered his head with his hand and raised his voice, sounding a little like an excited Pastor Nelson, "'You have turned my mourning into dancing. You have untied my sackcloth and encircled me with joy. Lord, my God, I will give thanks to you forever.'"

He grabbed one of Becky's hands and one of his wife's and began dancing in a circle causing Martha to burst out laughing. Even Becky laughed as he spun them around the room. "Yes, yes. Tonight we celebrate. Tonight we put on clean clothes and give thanks as David commanded." He put his arms around his wife and daughter and led them toward the door. "I will go to the cellar. Only our best wine for tonight."

Their voices faded down the hall, leaving Dahlia, Joanna, and me standing there looking at each other. Then we began to laugh.

A short time later, several servants arrived and took us to our rooms. I was glad to be alone as I needed some time to piece together what I'd do next. I knew almost nothing about marriage customs in this time. Chuza told me Rebecca and I were betrothed. Being betrothed in Jesus's time was a lot weightier than an engagement in the twenty-first century. The whole Mary and Joseph story made that pretty clear. I thought it safe to assume whatever arrangements were made had been settled at the original betrothal. Nothing I learned about Thomas so far led me to believe his father was alive. So, the agreements were either made by Thomas himself or a close male relative. However they had been decided, I'd be expected to know what those arrangements were. That would be my biggest challenge. But I thought I knew someone who might help.

I knocked on Dahlia's door.

"Come."

Dahlia's room appeared identical to mine, which was identical to the room where we found Rebecca. Dahlia sat on the wooden chest, so I took the stool and leaned back against the wall. "I intend to keep my promise to marry Rebecca." I sat quietly, hoping Dahlia would take over the conversation, as she was inclined to do, and fill in the blanks. It didn't take long.

"And after the wedding, do you and Rebecca intend to take the west end of the house and manage the vineyard? That was always Father's plan, was it not, brother?"

I hesitated, wondering if Dahlia had always been the more dominant between us. I needed to be cautious. I wanted her to see me differently from the brother she remembered but not so much she wouldn't continue to lead the conversation.

"No," I answered, allowing a degree of uncertainty to enter my voice. It was an honest answer considering I wasn't sure of anything. "No, after the wedding, Rebecca will be traveling back to Capernaum with Joanna and me to rejoin Jesus and the others."

Dahlia shook her head and stood, putting her fists on her hips. For a moment, I thought she might shove me again. "How do you expect Mother to maintain the vineyard if you go running off again?" she growled through gritted teeth, keeping her voice low. "We have been falling behind every day since you left. Reuben sends laborers down to help us, but it is not nearly enough to prepare for the harvest. Mother hates to take his charity even though he and Father were close. If you leave again, there will be no one to help her." She sat and put her head in her hands.

"I know it has been difficult for you, Dahlia, but you have done a great job. I'm sure you will—"

She looked up, anger gone and replaced with stubborn determination. "I have already spoken with Joanna." She crossed her arms over her chest. "I will be traveling with her to Capernaum. I want to meet this Rabbi of yours who treats everyone the same. Father could never make a match for me, and I turned away every suitor Mother brought by the house since he died. Joanna says this prophet you follow accepts even the unmarried."

"He does," I admitted. "In fact, he teaches it is more difficult for those who have husbands or wives or children to follow him than those who do not. You will be welcomed among his disciples, Dahlia, and free to remain as you are or to marry if you choose. But that still leaves Mother with a vineyard to tend and no children to help her. Perhaps we can hire a manager from one of the other farms who will hire laborers in Bethsaida to come and—"

"She will hate it, Thomas. The vineyard was always Father's dream, never hers. She stays in the house only because it is where she and Father made a life together. She always hated the fields because they took him away from us so much. She will hate them even more now. The constant worry is killing her. If we both leave, she will not be able to stay at all. We must find another way."

What other way could there be? I couldn't stay in Bethsaida. My destiny was with Jesus. I certainly couldn't discourage Dahlia from her decision to join us. That's exactly what we'd been sent out to do. I wondered what Jesus would say if he were here now. As I let his words pass through my mind, I smiled. How wise he was. How wonderfully and intentionally contradictory he was. Always teaching in a way that forced us to think about God's Kingdom and find the correct answer for each specific situation. Over and over, I had heard him say, "Anyone who loves their father or mother more than me is not worthy of me." Then he would turn right around and say to the Pharisees, "Why do you neglect the commandment of God and hold to the tradition of men? Does not Moses say, 'Honor your father and your mother'? But if a man says to his father or his mother, 'whatever I have that would help you, I am giving to God,' you no longer permit him to do anything for his father or his mother, thus invalidating the word of God by your traditions."

How was I supposed to do both? How could I follow Jesus and honor my mother—Thomas's mother—at the same time? That's when it hit me.

"What was her dowry?" I asked Dahlia as the idea began to percolate in my mind.

"The what?"

"The dowry." I wondered if I spoke the correct word for this time period. "Did I give Reuben something so I could marry Rebecca?"

"The bride price?" she raised an eyebrow.

"Yes, of course, the bride price."

"You know very well what it was, Thomas. Father's favorite piece of land. The vineyard on the high hillside closest to Reuben's property. It was the first piece of land our great grandfather purchased when he arrived here from Judea. You nearly refused to give it, but Reuben would take nothing less."

That was it!

I knew the way to reach Reuben. As I pictured each of the other actors in this crazy play, I thought I had a pretty good guess about how to reach each one of them. All I needed was time to pull it off. Time to learn as much as I could about Reuben's family. Yes, now I needed to start playing my part. Becky took on the role of Rebecca of Bethsaida; now I needed to become the grateful son-in-law.

"Thanks, Dahlia," I said, leaving her sitting there with her mouth open. I needed to get back to my room and think things through.

Late that afternoon, Reuben sent a wagon for Anna, who arrived before supper. She was as delighted with Rebecca's recovery as Reuben and Martha were. I learned as much as I could about the relationship between the two families earlier during my conversation with Reuben. Now I could only hope the connection between the two families ran deep enough for my plan to work.

I also learned Rebecca had three brothers, two of whom owned small villas in other parts of the vineyard and would be arriving tomorrow. But the youngest brother was the key to everything. He worked on one of the large fishing boats in Bethsaida. Reuben sent a message to him, but being out on the boat, it could be days before he received news about his sister and returned home. Martha grieved over his situation. She wanted him home, not out at sea. He would be the final piece of the puzzle if things worked the way I hoped.

After the meal, we moved to the veranda, where more wine was served along with a very spicy hard bread and sweet date jam. I listened patiently to stories about Rebecca's childhood, picking up a few helpful ideas along the way. As soon as there was a lull in the conversations, I asked Reuben if he would mind taking a walk with me. We excused ourselves and stepped out into the night, where he listened quietly as I revealed my plan.

An hour later, I followed Reuben back onto the veranda. Everyone could see by the look on his face he had something important to say, and they fell silent.

"There is going to be a wedding after all!" he shouted, throwing his hands in the air then wrapping them around me and squeezing the air out of my lungs. I couldn't tell whether it was his way of welcoming me into the family or punishing me for putting him on the spot to explain the rest of our agreement.

"Thomas and Rebecca will be married as soon as preparations can be made, and then they will be leaving to rejoin the Rabbi. We must make plans quickly. We will send messengers out first thing tomorrow to invite—" Reuben stopped talking when Martha jumped up.

"What do you mean 'leaving,' Reuben?" Martha cried, shifting her piercing glare between her husband and Rebecca.

Anna jumped up next, "You just came home, Thomas. You cannot leave again! How will we ever be ready for the harvest if you leave your sister and me alone again?"

It was Dahlia's turn to stand and add to the chaos. "I will be going with them, Mother. I must meet this prophet they follow."

Well, now all the cards were on the table. So far, so good. All that remained was to see who had the winning hand.

"This will not do, Rebecca!" Martha warned. She moved quickly from shock to anger. "Your brothers will never allow it." Fists on hips, she turned to her husband. "Have I been blessed to see one mind restored today only to see another lost to madness, husband? What are you thinking, Reuben?"

Anna sat back down in her chair and began to wail, "How can you do this, Thomas? Was it not bad enough you left your sister and me to do all your work, and now you come home only to steal the little bit of help I have? The grapes will rot on the vines. We will be ruined. I will be begging on the streets of Bethsaida along with the lepers." She got to her feet again. "You cannot do this! You cannot!"

I hated seeing everybody's life thrown into such a tailspin. But sometimes, it's necessary to endure a few moments of turbulence to truly appreciate a safe landing. At least that was my hope. I went to Anna and held her hands while she wept, "Let Reuben explain, Mother. It's going to be alright."

"Yes, please explain, Reuben," Martha glared at her husband.

I looked at Joanna. She fought hard to keep a smile from forming on her lips. Somehow she must have put the pieces together from her many conversations with the other women and had a good idea where all this was going. She was a good judge of character, and she probably already figured out the secret motivations among the family members. Every eye turned to Reuben.

"Yes, yes, everyone sit down, please. Let me explain." When everyone finally settled back into their seats, he continued, "Like all of you, it grieves me to say goodbye to our precious Rebecca when we have only today welcomed her back after such a long illness." He paused as though reconsidering the deal we made, but then he continued, "But... but we can see from what has become of Thomas, who loved neither the vine nor the field, mind you"—he put his arm across my shoulder again—"he has chosen the better path. He has become a true man of God, has he not? A man of healing, even as his teacher." He smiled at Rebecca, then looked at Martha. "How can we deny our daughter the same opportunity, woman? How can we stand in the way of their happiness? How do we know this Nazarene who Thomas follows is not the one we have been waiting for? The one Israel has been waiting for? How can we deny our daughter the opportunity to walk in the footsteps of Miriam, who stood with her brother Moses? Or Deborah, the greatest of the judges, or Ruth, or Esther, who saved our people?"

"I do not wish to hinder anyone," Anna cried. "But I still have a vineyard to care for. I must—"

"I will care for the vineyard," Reuben said softly.

The moment of truth had arrived, and now Reuben had everyone's full attention. They knew Reuben was not a man to make a poor business decision.

"Thomas has increased the bride price. The entire vineyard belongs to me now. I will hire new workers, and the harvest will be completed on the day the grapes are at their finest." He looked at Martha. "We now have the largest vineyard south of the Chorazin Plateau. And thanks to you," he turned to Rebecca, "and your sacrifice, your brother in Bethsaida will be able to return to the land."

Reuben's announcement of the youngest son's return sealed Martha's agreement. She put her hand on her chest as though having difficulty catching her breath.

"Think of it, Martha," Reuben said, kneeling before his wife. "Abram will be able to come home again, where he belongs. There will be land enough for each of our sons now."

Martha began to cry, reaching out to embrace Rebecca. I could see the wheels already spinning in her head. There were wedding plans to make and a new villa to build for Abram. It was one of the crucial things I learned while talking to Reuben and Dahlia that afternoon. Martha grieved the loss of her son to the sea every bit as much as she suffered Rebecca's illness. Abram was by far her favorite. Losing a daughter, who would eventually leave home to marry anyway, in exchange for Abram coming home was more than a fair trade in her mind.

Reuben rose and approached Anna. She sat frozen with a frightened daze on her face, her arms wrapped around her as if trying to protect herself. He went down on one knee. "The vineyard is mine now, Anna. You need never worry over it again. I will care for it in the same manner Seth did. It will remain as your husband always intended it, with the finest grapes in all of Galilee. The only property Thomas has not pledged to me is the house and the courtyard west of the barns. That will remain yours for as long as you or one of Seth's heirs live." He swallowed hard. "And I will pay you a fair portion from each year's harvest so you can live there without concern. You will always have a home for Dahlia and Thomas and Rebecca to return to."

Anna's shoulders relaxed, and for the first time since I arrived in Bethsaida, she looked happy. The winds tossed us about, but the landing touched down safe and smooth. The turbulence of a few moments ago were forgotten and the discussion turned toward future plans. As the plane rolled smoothly up to the gate, the only thing left to complete was the wedding.

The room broke into cheerful chatter, and I offered a prayer of thanks. Somehow, I did it. I kept my commitment to Jesus and honored my mother at the same time.

CHAPTER 26
The Wedding

I met Rebecca's brothers the next day and did my best to pretend I knew what they were talking about as they recounted stories of our past. Fortunately, they couldn't stay long because Reuben needed to send each of them out to announce to the residents of Bethsaida, family, and friends in nearby villages the wedding chamber was prepared and the date set. They mounted mules and rode out the following morning. I was sent home with Anna, Dahlia, and Joanna with instructions to return in one week.

Dahlia and Joanna became invaluable resources over the next few days. Dahlia took my total ignorance regarding what to do for granted, often answering my questions with a sarcastic "Did Father teach you nothing, Thomas?" She quickly fell into the role of big sister tending to her dim-witted brother. By the end of the week, I felt exhausted but educated.

I learned it was customary for the groom to announce to his future wife and her family during the year-long betrothal: "I am going to prepare a place for you, and I will return for you when it is ready." Then he would return to his father's house to build a living space for his new bride. The official date of the wedding could not be set until the groom's father approved the new construction, leaving the bride unsure when the groom would return for her. Much of that had been a formality for Rebecca and Thomas, because Thomas's father died a few years before the betrothal, and adequate living quarters already existed in the family home they would share with Anna and Dahlia. No official date had been set when Thomas originally left to follow Jesus, and now that the wedding was back on, Reuben worried he would be shamed when not enough guests came on such short notice. Plus, the harvest was just around the corner, and many families would be busy preparing for the most crucial time of the year.

"The proper time for weddings is after the harvest, Thomas," Reuben explained as we walked together that night. "When the hard work is over, people can relax and enjoy the cool evenings."

Only the size of the newly negotiated bride price and my insistence the three of us needed to return to Capernaum immediately after the wedding persuaded him to risk embarrassment.

I had no idea what was happening with Becky. We hadn't been able to steal even a second together since those first few moments in her room. I knew she was strong, but I constantly worried about her.

On the afternoon of the seventh day, Rebecca's three brothers and two other men, who I learned were Thomas's best friends, arrived to prepare me for the wedding. They mounted me on a mule, and the six of us rode to a remote area by the lake where they stripped me, scrubbed me from head to toe with coarse brushes, and dressed me in my wedding clothes. Finally, they adorned me with a crown made of flowers like those growing near Anna's and Martha's homes.

When we got back to my mother's villa, Anna, Dahlia, and Joanna were gone, but about half the male population of Bethsaida was waiting for us. Their boisterous shouting and singing told me more than a few already had a head start on the celebration. The mules were handed over to servants, and I was stationed in the middle of the crowd of men as if they were saying, "If you have second thoughts about this wedding, you should give them up now because there is no escape for you." We marched together for the thirty-minute hike between Anna's villa and Reuben's estate, singing and banging on every conceivable type of percussion instrument. As we entered the back gate, one man raised a long curved instrument made of an animal's horn and blew several long, loud notes.

"Behold, the bridegroom comes!" everyone shouted. "Behold, the bridegroom comes!" The horn blowing and the shouting continued until we stood outside one of the side doors of Reuben and Martha's home.

The door opened, and ten women in white dresses exited, each carrying an oil lamp. The last woman was dressed in a long white flowing gown with colorful ribbons at her wrists and elbows and a crown of flowers on her head similar to mine. A silky white veil completely hid her face. I have to admit the first thought that came to my mind was the story of Jacob. I feared Rebecca had a somewhat less attractive older sister Reuben wanted to marry off first, and I was being tricked into marrying her. I dreaded having to spend the next seven years serving him in order to marry Rebecca.

Strange, I thought, *how some Bible stories I'd learned as a child stuck with me for my entire life.* I smiled to myself, hoping Becky was under the veil but also realizing I could do nothing to change the events unfolding around me.

The ten women led the veiled woman through the crowd of men, past me, out the rear gate, and down the path toward Anna's villa. With me still in the middle, the band of men followed, resuming their shouts, singing, and horn blowing. About halfway between the two homes, we found Reuben, Martha, Anna, Dahlia, Joanna, and about fifty others under a small group of trees. The veiled woman sat there with her ten attendants. They sang as we approached and the crowd pushed me to the front under the trees. Reuben joined us when the song ended and offered prayers and blessings that seemed to go on forever. When he finally finished, he said something to the bride and stepped away. The veiled woman turned to me and recited loudly, "Let him kiss me with the kisses of his mouth, for your love is more delightful than wine. Pleasing is the fragrance of your perfumes. Your name is like perfume poured out. No wonder the young women love you! Take me away with you—let us hurry! Let the king bring me into his chambers."

As soon as she finished, everyone shouted, "We rejoice and delight in you. We will praise your love more than wine."

I was so relieved to hear Rebecca's voice come from the veiled bride I nearly forgot the words Dahlia had insisted I memorize. One of the men finally gave me a sharp poke in the ribs from behind. "Like, uh... like a lily among thorns is my darling among the young women," I stammered. "Arise, come, my darling, my beautiful one, come with me. My dove in the clefts of the rock, in the hiding places on the mountainside, show me your face, let me hear your voice, for your voice is sweet, and your face is lovely."

Becky stood when I finished, and Reuben rejoined us, reciting another blessing. By the smiles on everyone's faces, I figured that meant we were married. Two of Becky's attendants stepped to either side of her to help lift her veil, and I finally gazed upon the woman I knew I loved more than life itself. It didn't matter whether she was in Rebecca's body or that I was the apostle Thomas instead of Tommy Evans. Whatever the future held, we were going to face it together.

Here in the first century or in the twenty-first century, if we ever found our way back home. In Galilee or Springfield, Ohio, or on some remote planet in another solar system, it didn't matter. We were going to make it together. Becky smiled at me as though she were having the same thoughts. I took a step toward her and chaos descended.

In a matter of seconds, every male there came between Rebecca and me.

"Whoa, whoa, whoa, no, no, no. First, we celebrate!" the men shouted with suggestive smiles.

The bridesmaids joined hands with one another and any other woman close enough to grab and danced in a circle around us. Everyone shouted as a horn blew. Even Reuben looked happy as he watched the crowd of several hundred begin to march toward Anna's villa.

In preparation for our arrival, long rows of low tables were set up and covered with food. Becky and I sat at the same table but on opposite sides. Several more musicians began playing, and after the meal came more dancing—men with men and women with women. I was nearly exhausted when the music finally stopped. Rebecca's attendants surrounded her, and my five companions walked me to stand by her side. Anna approached first. She kissed Rebecca on the cheeks and gave me a slight bow. Rebecca's mother stepped forward next and did the same. Finally, after dozens of bows and kisses, Reuben stood before us. He kissed his daughter on the cheeks and did the same to me. Then he took Rebecca's hand and placed it in mine. He stepped back, smiled his warmest smile, and walked away.

We were ushered by the ten attendants and the five men to the outer door of the bedroom I prepared for us during the seven days we waited for the wedding. Rebecca and the ten women entered the room and closed the door. Rebecca's three brothers came, kissed me on the cheeks, and left. One of Thomas's old friends did the same, leaving the other friend, Yoel, alone with me. The attendants exited the room without stopping or saying anything to me, leaving Rebecca inside.

Yoel stepped to the door and opened it without looking in. "I will stand guard for you, Thomas. I will not leave your door nor sleep until Rebecca's parents come to retrieve the bed clothing in the morning." He stepped aside, and I walked in. Yoel closed the door behind me.

CHAPTER 27
The Honeymoon

We stood there staring at one another for a long time, taking in the incredible moment. Finally, Becky walked across the room and gently rested her head on my shoulder.

"We did it," she whispered. "I didn't think I would have to travel back in time two thousand years to get you to marry me, but it was worth it." She looked up into my eyes, then pulled me into one of those kisses that should be reserved strictly for married people in this time or any other time.

"We need to talk first, Beck," I gasped when she finally let me come up for air.

Becky stuck out her bottom lip and put on her puppy dog face, which looked every bit as cute on Rebecca of Bethsaida as it ever did on Becky of Springfield.

"C'mon, Becky. Stop it." I pleaded, drawing on all the willpower I could muster. "You know we have a lot to talk about."

"I know." She laughed, exchanging her puppy dog look for her "you had your chance" look. She kissed me again, let go of me, and sat on one of the stools. "Okay, so what have you been able to figure out? Do you think we have a chance of getting back home?"

I wanted to give her hope, but she also needed to hear the truth. "I have no idea how we got here or how to get us back. But there's no doubt in my mind something supernatural is behind all of this. So the one thing I'm pretty sure of is if God brought us here, he has something important for us to do. There has to be a reason. God doesn't just..."

Becky chuckled and shook her head. "Wait a minute, Tommy. Do you honestly think God brought us here? Geez, the Tommy Evans I knew didn't even believe God existed. And now you think, of all the people in the whole wide world, the God you didn't believe in picked you to come here on some special mission? Don't tell me. I'll bet you discovered a magical stone pillar from the Scottish highlands in your backyard or a mysterious tape recording from a guy named Phelps, right?" She laughed hard. It was wonderful to see her laugh, but we weren't getting anywhere.

"C'mon, Becky, this is serious," I urged, trying not to laugh along with her at our crazy situation. "A lot has changed for me since I got here. I've seen things I never thought possible. I know it sounds nuts, but I've been traveling around Israel with Jesus, Becky, and yeah," I shook my head at what I was about to say, "I can't come up with any other explanation than God brought me here, brought us here, and I think my mom knew it was going to happen."

"Your mom? What could she possibly have to do with this, Tommy?

"I don't know for sure," I paced back and forth. "But I've been thinking a lot about some of the things Mom said the day before it happened. Because of her, I went to church Sunday morning. She said God had something special for me. Then when we got there, the preacher's whole sermon was on Doubting Thomas, and he's the disciple who—"

"Whose place you took, right?

"Yes, exactly!" I could see in her eyes some of the pieces were starting to fit together. "And listen to this. The last thing Mom said to me was she knew I would be there for him when the time came."

"For him? Him who?"

"That's just it, Beck. Him who? I thought maybe she meant my dad at the time, but now I'm almost sure she meant Jesus. I think maybe sometime in the future, Jesus is going to need me."

Becky's eyes widened.

"I know, I know, it sounds totally weird. But I think that's why I'm here. I think I have to do something or say something important. My mom knew about it and warned me so I would be ready when the time came."

Becky nodded. "Okay, it kind of makes sense. I mean, I can't deny we're here, and I want to believe there's a reason for it." She thought about it for a few moments. "Okay, so if you're here to help Jesus, why do you think I'm here?"

"I don't know for certain, Beck. But I do know this. You wouldn't be here if you didn't have an important part to play. God must know I can't do what I need to do without you. That we need to be here together. Like a team, I guess. We might not even know what we have to do until the moment it happens. We might not even know it then. Geez, I don't know. We have to be ready, Beck. If there's any way to get us home, that's it. When the time comes, if we do what we need to do to help Jesus, then God won't need us here in this time anymore, and maybe he will send us home."

Becky stood and wrapped her arms around me and rested her head on my shoulder again.

"What's the matter, Beck? Do you think I'm crazy?"

She held me tight for several minutes. "No, I believe you...I do, Tommy...It's just..."

"What, Beck?"

"I guess...I'm scared. What if I mess it up? I could ruin it for both of us. We might end up here forever. I wish God picked someone else."

"No way, Becky, please don't wish that. You don't have to be afraid. You're here because he knows you can do whatever he needs you to do." I smiled, amazed at myself. I was no longer the frightened, confused boy I had been when I arrived in the first century. I studied under the greatest teacher of all time and he'd chosen me as one of the twelve to be with him through everything—me, the timeless apostle.

"Let me tell you a story, Becky," I began, taking her hands in mine. "I was afraid once too, but Jesus taught me the Kingdom of God is like a man who prepared to go on a long journey. Before he left, he called three of his servants and entrusted his wealth to them. He gave the first one..."

And so I told her the story of how the third servant lived in fear and how it kept him from doing what he needed to do. I told her about how seeds grow differently in different types of soil and how people who build towers need to take stock of their ability to finish before they begin to build. I told her everything I could remember about the places I'd been and the things I'd seen Jesus do and teach.

"He is everything he claims to be, Becky. I was so wrong not to realize it before. I can't wait for you to meet him."

"He sounds wonderful, Tommy. When will we leave?"

"Tomorrow morning. So I need to tell—" She put her fingers on my lips like she'd done so many times before when she had something important to say. Except this time, it wasn't more talking she had in mind. She kissed me softly.

CHAPTER 28
Downpours and Revelations

Reuben and Martha arrived at sunrise to relieve an exhausted Yoel of his guard duty and collect the evidence of Rebecca's virtue. Anna prepared an excellent breakfast for us. After many tears and well wishes, Dahlia, Joanna, Rebecca, and I left Bethsaida.

The base camp outside Capernaum had nearly tripled in size since our departure four months ago. Salome met us as we approached and led Joanna, Dahlia, and Rebecca to the women's area to get settled.

"Jesus is with the others," she pointed east. "He asked you to join them."

I thanked her, headed for the men's camp. I was surprised to see Jesus sitting alone.

When I got close, he stood to greet me. "Welcome back, Thomas. He who finds a wife finds a good thing and obtains favor from God. Will you and Rebecca be remaining with us?"

"Yes, Lord, of course. But how did—?" That's when the first one jumped me. I think it was John, but regardless of who came first, I soon found myself under eleven shouting, laughing, and very hefty men. Thankfully, they pulled me to my feet before I passed out.

After a great many kind and encouraging words, hugs, and cheek kisses, Jesus finally got everyone calmed down and seated. We spent the rest of the afternoon sharing stories of what had happened to each of us on our journeys. All the stories were wonderful. Thousands of people heard the message of God's Kingdom and hundreds were healed in the months we'd been gone. Most of the time, the men were serious as they told their stories, but the single apostles felt compelled to end their account with "but I did not find a wife," which made everyone laugh again. All in all, it was a great afternoon.

Several days later, after a teaching session with the apostles, Jesus informed us he intended to leave for the eastern side of the lake shortly after sundown. "Thomas, would you please go to the women's camp and let Joanna, Mary, Salome, and Rebecca know I would like them to join us."

That brought a chorus of objections from the men. "Lord, are you sure you want to send the newlywed?"

"If you send Thomas, he and Rebecca are likely to miss the boat completely. Perhaps you should send Peter, Lord. He has been married so long—"

"Thomas will do, brothers," Jesus said, smiling. "I will see you at the boat later."

I still felt uncomfortable traveling by boat. As we drew near the lake, a sudden sense of panic and queasiness in the pit of my stomach came over me. I bent over, put my hands on my knees, and swallowed hard. Peter, Andrew, and the other fishermen spent countless nights on the lake as part of their business, and for them, it would be simply another night at sea. For me, it meant losing my supper and spending most of the trip draped over the side of the boat.

"I do not enjoy these voyages either." I looked up to see Judas beside me. He was one of the friendliest of the twelve, but we hadn't spent much time together.

"Not much water where you grew up?" I asked.

"Not unless you consider the well in the center of town." He laughed. "No, I never saw water like this until I came to Galilee."

"Where are you from?"

"Carioth, in the south of Judea."

"Is that where you met Jesus?"

"No, my father, Simon, does business in and around Jerusalem. I first heard Jesus preach in Bethany. When he left there, I followed him to Galilee and have been with him ever since. You arrived shortly after if I recall."

"You land lovers can stand there and wait for us to get back if you like," Peter offered as he walked past us. "But if you plan on sailing, it is time to get wet."

Judas looked at me and shrugged. Then we both stepped into the water.

The trip began well enough, as I sat with Andrew, Mary, Joanna, and Rebecca, marveling at the sunset, its orange fire dancing on the waves. We continued to reminisce and tell stories about our adventures on the road and were utterly oblivious to the darkening clouds rapidly forming and moving toward us from beyond the eastern cliffs.

It began with the rising wind innocently buffeting our sail but quickly became more severe until powerful waves slammed into our starboard side, threatening to fill the boat. Sheets of rain drenched us, and I could feel concern rising even among the seasoned seamen as they struggled to control the spar and tie down the sail to keep it from ripping apart. Their shouts were drowned out by the howling, gale-force winds. The storm became a monster, intent on devouring us, and everyone knew it. Andrew and I ushered the women into the hold. If the ship broke apart, they would be no safer than the rest of us, but it was the best option we had.

I looked around for Jesus and found him exactly where I expected: sleeping peacefully on a cushion in the back of the boat. Knowing how the story ended with Jesus happily rescuing everyone, I should have felt more confident. But, as I came to realize, there is a vast difference between reading a story about an attacking lion and actually finding your arm gripped tightly between his teeth.

I was thrown from one side of the boat to the other, desperately trying to keep my feet under me on the wet planks. I tried helping Philip hold the tiller in place, but the handle kept ripping out of our hands. Everyone stumbled about in the darkness, groping for anything they could find to hang on to and avoid being thrown over the side. That's when I heard angry voices above the roar of the storm. Dimly, I could see Peter and some of the others standing in the back near Jesus. The look of panic on Peter's face could not be mistaken.

After listening patiently, Jesus stood and made his way to the prow of the boat. He stood unmoving, his hair whipped by the wind, his face like stone as the lightning flashed and illuminated his peaceful expression. He raised his hand and spoke into the darkness.

Then, as if we were suddenly transported to another part of the world, the wind subsided, the waves slowed their movements, and the rain tapered off. Finally, everything went silent. Jesus continued to look out over the calm, dark sea. The others were silent as well, edging away from him, looking as terrified now of him as they had been of the storm.

Jesus turned his burning eyes on us. "You have such little faith. How is it you have learned so little from me?"

No one said a word. Most of us looked down and away from his convicting eyes.

"If you have faith, even as small as a mustard seed, you can say to a mountain, 'Be removed!' or to the storm, 'Be calm!' and it will be as you say." His voice seemed quieter now, but his tone remained solemn as he walked among us. Finally, he returned to the back of the boat and sat alone.

"I have seen him do some amazing things," Judas whispered as he came and sat on my left along the outer rail.

Rebecca and the other women arrived from below deck, and she took the spot to my right.

I looked at Judas curiously.

He went on, "I have seen him return sight to the blind and hearing to the deaf and cause the lame to walk again. I was there when he fed thousands of people with a little boy's basket of fish and bread. I drank fine wine, which a few moments before had been water." He sat silently for a few minutes, thinking. "But what kind of man is this who can order the wind to stop, and it obeys?"

I was unsure how to answer Judas, but the far-off look in his eyes told me he wasn't really looking for an answer. He sat beside me for several more minutes, staring at the calm, glassy sea, nodding his head.

"There is no power on Earth that can oppose him, Thomas. Not the Sanhedrin, not the Pharisees, not Antipas. Not even the power of Rome can resist someone who can call on the winds to do as he wishes. Surely he is the salvation of Israel, my brother. We must find a way. We must find a way!"

"A way?" I repeated.

Judas got up and smiled at me, "Nothing, my friend. Nothing for now." He looked around the boat. "But it would be best not to repeat our conversation for now." Then Judas walked away.

"That's weird. Did you understand any of that?" I asked Becky, who had been listening closely.

"Sure, didn't you?"

"No, not really. Jesus sent Judas out just like the rest of us. He understands the power Jesus gave us. He's healed people in Jesus's name just like we all have."

"That's not the kind of power Judas is talking about. He's referring to a different kind of power, Tommy." She looked around the boat for anyone close enough to hear her. "I mean, Thomas."

"A different kind of power? What do you mean? I still don't get it."

Becky had only been with Jesus for a few days, and already she was seeing things I did not. I wondered how I'd ever gotten along without her"

"Almost everything Jesus does, whenever he uses his power, it's for other people, right?

"Yeah."

"Healing people, feeding people. Even the water-to-wine story is about what he did for his mom and the wedding guests, right?"

"That's true."

"But tonight was different, Thomas. Even though he saved us, tonight was about raw power. Think about it. Like Judas said, Jesus talked to the wind, and the wind did exactly what he told it to do. Even the weather obeys him. Can you imagine what power like that would mean in our time? Every military commander in the world would see Jesus as either the source of world peace or the source of world domination. I think that's what Judas sees."

"World domination?"

Becky rolled her eyes in frustration. "Not the whole world, Tommy," she corrected. "But definitely his part of it. That's the only world he knows about or cares about." She thought for a couple of moments. "Do you remember the story you told me about the man you met on your way to see Jesus right after you first got here? I think you said his name was Micah."

"Sure, I remember."

"He was dying, right?"

"Right."

"And Jesus healed him, right?"

"Yes."

"What was the last thing he said to Jesus?"

As soon as she asked the question, a light came on for me. "'When you raise your army, I will be there. I will come and fight beside you.'" I quoted Micah. "And you think Judas..."

"I think many people in this time hate the Romans," she said. "And a lot of people around Jesus are hoping his kingdom is going to be right here on Earth with him as the king. And after what I saw here tonight, there's no doubt in my mind if Jesus wanted to drive the Romans out of Israel, he could do it by the weekend."

Now, I saw it. A lot of other things I'd observed but didn't understand began to pop into my mind. "And I don't think Judas is the only one who thinks that way," I conceded.

"What do you mean? Who else?"

"The one we call the Zealot would join Jesus's army in a heartbeat. I've heard him say so when Jesus wasn't around. And just before Jesus sent us out, a big fight broke out among some of the men. John and James asked Jesus if they could sit on his right and left when he came in glory. I didn't understand what they meant at the time, but I think they were asking Jesus if they could sit next to him when he ruled in his kingdom. Not in heaven, but right here on the earth. All the others were upset about it. I think they want to rule with him. They want Jesus to be a real king. He keeps telling them that's not why he came, but they don't seem to get it. I think I've made the mistake again of looking at things through the eyes of someone from our time rather than someone from here and now. How stupid!"

"Don't be so hard on yourself, Tommy. Maybe helping them understand is part of why we're here."

I thought about it. "Yeah, I agree. And I also think we need to keep a close eye on Judas."

"He's the one who turns Jesus in at the end, isn't he?" Becky asked.

"Yeah, according to the Bible, he does. But why would he do that if he sees Jesus as the answer to Israel's situation? Does that make any sense to you?"

"Not really. But I agree with one thing Judas said."

"What?"

"We need to keep this to ourselves for now."

We spent the remainder of the night in small groups, sleeping or manning the oars. The storm had driven us to the west, increasing the length of our journey. The sudden calming of the wind made the sail useless so rowing was the only option. It turned out to be a needed distraction, as no one was in the mood for conversation. Jesus's rebuke still burned inside each of us. I felt incompetent and ashamed. But like with so many of Jesus's lessons, I was drawn by the hope and love he had for me. He called Thomas to follow him. Whoever the original Thomas was, I was the one following Jesus now. And I knew despite tonight's failure, Jesus wouldn't give up on me. On any of us. I felt peace filling me as I breathed in the cool night air and prepared to get some sleep until my shift at the oars. Yet, what I didn't know was the battle with the sea was only the beginning of an even greater conflict brewing."

CHAPTER 29
Legion

"Thomas, wake up." The voice sounded familiar but distant, distorted, and filtered through the sleepy fog in my mind. "You fell asleep at the oars," Andrew said, his smiling face now recognizable to my tired eyes.

"Huh? Oh yeah," I mumbled, straightening up and wincing at the sharp pain in my back.

The light of dawn tinged the edges of the high cliffs above us in shades of pink and promised to bring the sun's morning light to the hills and lake, along with the oppressive heat of the day. The gentle, rhythmic splashing against the sides of the boat brought it all back to me, including the memory of last night's storm.

"Good morning, Thomas." Nathaniel laughed, waving a piece of bread over his head. "Breakfast?"

"I have dates," Phillip called, stepping onto the deck from below. Salome and Rebecca were filling cups with wine. They must've been up for an hour already.

While I slept at my post loafing, I thought. *Loafing Thomas will become my new nickname if I'm not more careful.*

A meaty hand gripped my arm, and Nathaniel shoved a hunk of bread into my hand. "Not much longer, Thomas," he said, pointing across the water toward the hazy shoreline south of the cliffs. He answered my question before I could ask, "It is called Decapolis. Ten cities designated free by the Romans. Mostly gentile, but there are some Jews who live in the smaller towns and villages, though I doubt we'll see either. This area is pretty remote."

Peter told us before the storm, Jesus arranged today as a time for teaching and refreshing, away from the large crowds in Galilee. I was looking forward to spending time with Jesus like we had before he sent us out. It would also be a chance for Becky and me to learn together.

A dull scraping shook the boat's hull. James, John, and Peter jumped out and hauled the boat onto the sand, securing it with an anchor.

Those still aboard got out and waded through the tall reeds growing near the water's edge and onto the beach. Beyond the shore, a gently rolling plain rose steadily for about half a mile, then elevated into round, dune-like hills, covered with dry grass and rocks. Each was dotted with olive and sycamore trees. It was a tranquil place to rest. There were no houses or buildings in sight, only a large herd of pigs grazing on the grassy foothills to our left, about halfway up the mountainside. The foothills were punctuated with large, rocky outcroppings, shallow crevasses, and wide-mouth caves. After the harrowing night at sea, I was beginning to relax when I heard a screeching sound coming from among the caves. Several of the others looked up, scanning the area for the source.

"Is that a…bird?" Rebecca asked, coming to stand beside me.

"None I've ever heard," James answered skeptically.

So much for the peaceful setting and quiet morning with Jesus, I thought as a loud, bellowing roar exploded from somewhere close.

Rebecca screamed, dropped the armload of wood she was carrying, and ran back toward the boat. I heard branches snapping among the woody thickets and tall grass, but I still couldn't see what was causing the sound. Then, out of the brush at the base of the hills, two men burst out, running toward Jesus.

The men appeared otherworldly and supernatural in the worst way imaginable. They ran with uncanny speed, but their movements were ungainly and spastic. Their limbs weren't broken, but it seemed as if extra joints had been added in places they didn't belong. They slowed as they approached the group gathered around Jesus with the women behind them in the surf. I signaled for Becky to stay put. James and I raced over to join Jesus.

When we reached him, the two men were stopped a few feet away. They wore the remains of what was once their clothing but now was nothing more than rags providing little to cover their nakedness. One man was large, bigger than Peter, while the other was smaller. Both were malnourished, their bones and bulging joints visible beneath skin covered with old scars and fresh wounds, which looked pink and festering. Their hair and beards were thickly matted; and their fingernails were jagged and packed with dirt. The remains of old manacles and chains hung from their bloody wrists and ankles. But as gruesome as their bodies looked, their faces revealed even worse. Their mouths were open, lips moving as if trying to speak, but no words came out. Their sunken eyes stared blankly, and I doubted they saw anything clearly. A series of jerks and spasms shook them, causing their eyes to roll back in their heads, drool dribbling out of their mouths and down their chins onto their bare chests.

As they stared at Jesus, I thought I saw a moment of sanity flash like a ripple across their faces, as if they could almost remember something... maybe who they were. Then the moment of internal clarity was quickly snatched away. I'd seen Jesus heal many different ailments, but in all the hundreds of broken and needy people, I'd never seen anything like this.

Rebecca took a position behind me; her arms wrapped tightly around my waist. The rest of the disciples bunched together behind Jesus. Peter alone was in motion, reaching down and grabbing a large piece of driftwood. He stepped toward the two men, jaw set, eyes focused.

"No," Jesus said, loudly but calmly, breaking the silence. His hand was out, blocking Peter's way, but his eyes were unmoving, unblinking, fixed on the men in front of him.

"But Rabbi," he began.

Jesus cut him off by shaking his head, never taking his eyes off the two men.

"You are safe," Jesus spoke, taking a step toward them.

"Does he mean us?" Rebecca whispered in my ear.

"No, I think he means them, and I think you're about to see—"

Before I could finish my sentence, intense seizures shook the big man's body sending waves of emotion flowing across his face: panic, desperation, hopelessness, confusion, fear, and raging hatred. The small man mimicked his companion as if they were somehow linked together. Without warning, the big man tensed, crouched, and then lunged forward, arms outstretched to attack. The other man followed.

Before they'd taken two steps, Jesus calmly raised his hand, and they stopped in mid-stride. They appeared momentarily suspended as if they'd slammed into an invisible wall before reaching Jesus. The large man slowly crumpled to the ground at Jesus's feet.

"Do not be afraid," Jesus encouraged as he knelt beside the man.

"What do you want with us, Chosen One?" the man growled. "You have no right! Our time is not yet come. This one belongs to us, and we will have him! He is not of Israel. No covenant protects him."

"He is a child of my father," Jesus answered. His words were gentle but filled with authority. "And it was not you who brought me here, but these you claim are yours. All those the father calls come to me, and they are mine." Jesus's words rang louder now, like hammer blows on an anvil. "No one can take them out of my hand!"

The man growled again.

"Now, come out of these men!" Jesus ordered

A scream ripped from the large man's throat. "Do not torment us! We have an agreement. You cannot... Our time is not yet come! You have no—"

"What is your name?" Jesus demanded.

"Legion," the creatures hissed, "for we are many. Perhaps too many even for you, eh?"

The man's eyes cleared for a moment and flickered. I saw something unsaid pass between him and Jesus. Then his eyes grew wide again in terror.

"No! No! You cannot! We must stay here. Near the desert." He glanced around wildly, finally spotting the herd of pigs on the mountainside. "Pigs! Into the pigs! Not the abyss! It is not our time. It is not our time. We have an agreement!"

Jesus stared at the man; then he followed his eyes and looked intently at the herd of pigs. It seemed as though time slowed as Jesus and the herd communicated. Finally, Jesus nodded toward the pigs and whispered, "Thank you."

Then he turned back to the man, "So be it, Legion. Go quietly, then. Go!"

Both men shrieked and convulsed simultaneously. I shut my eyes and covered my ears when I thought I could not bear the sound a second longer. Finally, silence! When I opened my eyes, the two men were lying motionless on the ground. They were so still, I couldn't tell if they were alive or dead. Then a sudden sound came from the mountainside; the previously peaceful herd of pigs was stampeding toward the cliffs above the lake. Squealing loudly, they ran heedless of the edge and never slowed as one after one they dove off the cliff, plunging into the water below and disappearing beneath the waves.

For a moment, all we could do was stare. No one said anything.

Slowly, one after another, the lifeless bodies of the pigs began to bob to the surface.

"Thomas, look," Rebecca pointed toward the two men.

"A miracle!" Joanna exclaimed, taking Rebecca's hand and pulling her closer to Jesus and the men who were beginning to sit up.

The big man gazed up at Jesus and tears began to fall, slowly at first, then in torrents.

The smaller man hugged himself, face buried in his rags and wept.

Mary walked back to the boat and returned a few moments later carrying an arm full of robes. She handed one to Joanna, and the three women helped the men cloth themselves. Salome arrived a few minutes later with food and water.

We spent the rest of the morning listening to Jesus talk to the two men about life and forgiveness in the Kingdom of God. As the noon hour drew near, a group of about twenty men walked down the beach toward us. Since they were dressed differently than most of the Jewish peasants and farmers I saw in Galilee, I assumed they were gentiles from one of the nearby cities. Jesus met them and talked with the group beyond my hearing.

They kept waving their arms and pointing at the lake, then pointed fearfully at the two men sitting on the ground, now clothed and calm. After a few minutes of discussion, the crowd left the way they came. Jesus returned and told us we should prepare to sail.

Even as we began the final preparations to leave, the two men huddled close to us like frightened children seeking comfort and protection.

I pulled John aside and asked, "Does Jesus intend to take them back to Galilee?"

John shook his head, "The master hasn't said, so..."

"No, Lord." The big man shouted and began sobbing hysterically. "Let us come with you. Please, please."

Jesus gently held the man's shoulders, then put his hands on the sides of his face, looking at him compassionately. The man's tears washed over Jesus's fingers.

"Galba, listen to me. You have received much today. You are free of Legion. They can never return to harm you again because you have heard my words of the Kingdom and the father and believe."

Galba blinked through tear-filled eyes as Jesus motioned toward the rest of us.

"These friends of mine travel throughout Galilee and Judea with me, teaching others what you heard today. And I have many more who follow me in Israel who do the same. But I have no one to send into this region." Jesus motioned for the other man to come closer and put his hand on his shoulder. "Caspius, Galba, the people here are wary of Jews, as you saw from the men who were here and asked me to leave. You are my disciples now, and only you can tell the story of what happened here today. I am a stranger here, as are these men and women with me. But you are not. You are known by all. And soon, the story of your deliverance will be the most famous in Decapolis."

Caspius began to nod as the vision Jesus was planting in his heart began to take shape. "Yes, Lord. We will serve here as those men do in Israel," he pointed at us.

"Yes."

"I can be a brother to Galba and he to me just as they are to one another?"

"Yes," Jesus repeated, "But you are also brothers to us now, even when we are apart."

"Many will join us!" Galba announced, the fear and sadness gone from his voice. "Yes, Lord, we will serve here. Many will join us. I promise you, many will come!"

Jesus smiled and nodded. "You have a family, Galba, as do you, Caspius. I know you love them."

Galba nodded, tears again brimming his eyes.

"When you return home, you will be as one coming back from the dead, will you not?" Jesus asked. "The sheep that was lost is now found. The prisoner set free. And when your family and friends ask why and how this happened, tell them the truth about what you experienced and what we talked about today."

Galba's face continued to brighten.

Caspius took his friend's arm. "Yes, Rabbi. It will be as you say."

Galba nodded. "It will be as you say."

Jesus drew them into an embrace, placing his hands on the backs of their necks and he prayed, "Father, I know these two sons are yours. I give them the power to deliver those in bondage even as they have been delivered. Put your words in their mouths and give them courage to face the darkness when it comes." He gently put his hands on their chests. "My peace will be with you, brothers, even in this world of trouble. Take heart for I have overcome the world."

Galba and Caspius thanked Jesus profusely and Jesus turned to walk back to the boat.

We were ready to sail within the hour. Rebecca and I were preparing to wade out to the boat when Judas came up beside me.

"Did you see that, Thomas?"

"See what?" I asked. But I knew what he'd say.

"He cannot be hurt. You saw it. The possessed man could not reach him." Judas smiled and slapped me on the back. "He is the One, Thomas! Oh yes, he is the one. He is here to deliver us. Nothing can defeat such power as this."

"Pardon me," Rebecca interrupted, in the most deferential tone she could muster. "I am new among you, Judas, but you have been with him for nearly two years. Have you ever heard him say that was his plan?"

"No, no, of course not, you foolish woman. He does not dare reveal himself yet. He is not ready. But soon, yes, very soon, when the time is right, he will declare himself, and we must be prepared to stand with him when he does." Judas turned to me. "You are a good man, Thomas. I know you will be there for him when the time comes."

I felt Becky squeeze my arm as Judas slapped me on the back again and ran into the surf to board the boat.

Becky pulled me to a stop and stared up at me. "Those are the same words you told me your mother said to you before you came here. She said you would be there for him when the time comes."

"I know, Beck. I know. What do you think it means?"

"I'm not sure, Tommy. But how could Judas know those very same words? Maybe he's the one we're here to help.

"Help him do what? Oh man, this isn't getting any easier, is it?"

"No, it isn't. Now, come on. Peter's standing on the boat waiting for us."

CHAPTER 30
The Cross Before Me

If Jesus planned on changing his message, as Judas hoped, the next few months did nothing to reveal it. If anything, Jesus became more transparent than ever. He knew exactly what he came to accomplish and was determined to finish the work.

"I must suffer many things and be rejected by the elders, chief priests, and scribes and be killed and raised on the third day," he told us one night when only the twelve were together.

As far as I could remember, this was the first time Jesus had spoken the words, "I must be killed." The words had about the same effect on the other disciples as if he'd said, "I'm going up into the hills to pray." They completely missed the significance.

A couple of the men looked as though they hadn't heard him. A few others looked at one other and shrugged with a look, "I don't get it, do you?" Others shook their heads. Only the glare on Judas's face suggested he alone among those close to Jesus understood what Jesus said.

Over the next few months, Jesus spoke of his death often. "It is necessary for me to go to Jerusalem and to suffer many things and be killed then raised up on the third day," he repeated to the whole camp one night after Sabbath.

His declaration was the last straw for Peter, who must have been stewing over what Jesus was saying. Perhaps Peter realized Passover rapidly approached, or maybe he was sick of hearing Jesus proclaim his death. Whatever the reason, he couldn't hold back any longer. "God forbid it, Lord!" he objected, the anger and frustration evident in his voice. "This is never going to happen to you! Never!"

Jesus looked directly at Peter. "Get behind me, Satan! You are a stumbling block to me. You do not have your mind set on God's purposes but your own."

After that, no one attempted to question Jesus when he mentioned his coming death. I could hardly blame them. No one wanted to be reprimanded the way Peter had been. To be accused of supporting the enemy was difficult to hear. Peter still had not recovered from the harsh rebuke, spending most of his time alone or with his brother. The whole camp seemed unsure of what to say or do at Jesus's proclamation. The only exception was Judas, who doubled his efforts to draw me into whatever scheme he planned on hatching.

"All this talk of suffering and dying is just a ploy, Thomas," Judas declared as he sat down beside me after finishing our evening meal. "What could possibly be accomplished by his death, I ask you? Nothing! Nothing good at all. No, my friend, Jesus is planning something big, and whatever it is, it will happen this year in Jerusalem. That much is clear. This is why he was so angry with Peter. Peter must know something and nearly gave it away. That's why Jesus corrected him so harshly in front of us. Let me ask you, Thomas. Have you ever heard Jesus speak to any of us like that before, especially Peter?"

"No, I guess not," I stammered, realizing the truth.

"You see, it will be this year in Jerusalem," Judas continued. "Jesus may not think he is ready yet, but I know he is. He is simply making sure he can finish what he begins, just as he has taught us. We must be there for him, Thomas. We must help him finish." Judas hesitated as though considering whether or not to continue. He must have decided he could trust me and went on. "But if he wavers, I have been working on a plan to encourage him." Judas stood and began to walk away. Over his shoulder, he added, "Deliverance is coming, Thomas. Be ready."

"Be ready for what?" Becky asked, sitting down in the spot Judas left.

We watched Judas disappear into the night. "Honestly I'm not sure," I answered once he moved out of sight. "But I know he's planning something."

"Let's think it through. You know the Bible better than I do. What does it specifically say Judas does? I know he's the one who betrayed Jesus, but not much more than that."

"I don't remember the details either, Beck. I know he took money and led the Jewish leaders and a group of soldiers to where Jesus prayed with his disciples. Judas kissed Jesus, and that's how the soldiers knew who to arrest. Really, that's all I know. I don't remember ever hearing anybody say why he did it. I never thought much about it. Judas seems pretty much like everybody else around here. Sure, he isn't perfect, and I've heard rumors he helps himself to some of the group funds now and then, but he doesn't seem like a terrible guy either. It's obvious he's hoping Jesus is going to drive the Romans out of Israel by force, but half of these guys are hoping for the same thing. I heard the Zealot say he could have a hundred men here in a day if it came to a fight. And we already know that's what Micah is hoping for. John and James want to pick a fight with someone almost every time we go out, and Peter still doesn't buy his 'I'm going to Jerusalem to die' business even though he'll never confront Jesus about it again. You can bet on it."

Becky sat on the ground, crossed her arms over her knees, and rested her head on her arms. "How will we know what to do if we don't even know what's supposed to happen? Are we here to make sure things go the way they did before, or are we here to change things?"

I sat next to Becky. She was exactly right. "That's the question I've been asking myself every day since I got here. But there is one thing I know for sure, Beck."

"What?"

"If we get the answer to this question wrong, it will be the biggest mistake we've ever made. Maybe the biggest mistake anybody ever made."

Becky put her arm across my back and laid her head on my shoulder, but she didn't say anything.

A few minutes later, I got up and helped her to her feet. "It all boils down to one thing, Beck," I reminded her before we parted ways for the night and went to our separate campsites.

"What's that?"

"Who do we really believe Jesus is?"

The next month whirled with activity. We were on the road constantly, revisiting every town and village from Capernaum in the north of Galilee to Hebron in the south of Judea. Hundreds followed us wherever we went and hundreds more came to meet us in every town or village we visited. We rarely stayed in one place more than a day, but when we did, the crowds grew into the thousands, leaving Jesus completely exhausted by the time we managed to spirit him away to a secluded spot where he could rest, pray, and regain his strength.

One thing became evident as the weather began changing from the oppressive heat of summer to the cool days and cold nights of fall. Jesus's message grew colder right along with it. Every stop brought more and more conflicts with the Pharisees and other Jewish leaders. Even his message to the people became increasingly hard to accept.

"I am telling you the truth," he would teach, "I am the good shepherd, and the good shepherd lays down his life for his sheep. All those who came before me are thieves and robbers. The one who is a hired hand and not a shepherd sees the wolf coming and flees because he does not care, and the wolf scatters and kills the flock. I am the good shepherd, and I know my own, and my sheep know me. I lay down my life so that I may take it back again. No one takes my life from me. I lay it down on my own. I have the authority to lay it down, and I have the authority to take it back up again."

"Why do you listen to this fool?" a man in the crowd shouted. "He is insane."

"He has a demon," another yelled.

"You're the fool!" a third man cried out. "These are not the words of one who is demon-possessed. A demon cannot open the eyes of the blind, can he?"

Everyone began arguing with one another. Some people within the crowd started shoving others who disagreed. We were barely able to get Jesus out of the mob before the fights broke out.

Fighting among the masses became a pattern almost everywhere we stopped. Jesus tried to impress upon the crowds he wasn't here to only heal them and feed them. He had come to teach them. "I am the good shepherd," or "I am the light of the world," or "The Kingdom of God is like this...." But the people quickly became bored or annoyed with his message while waiting for the healings to begin. But the angriest rejection came when he began teaching on the bread of life.

"I am the bread of life," Jesus proclaimed. "Anyone who comes to me will not be hungry, and the one who believes in me will never be thirsty. For I have come down from Heaven, not to do my own will, but the will of Him who sent me."

"This is fool's talk. How can this man say he came down from Heaven?" I heard one man bellow.

"Do not listen to this nonsense. This man comes from Nazareth. We know his mother and father. How can he say he comes from Heaven when we know better? He is a liar. Do not listen to him." another yelled.

"I am telling you the truth," Jesus shouted to the crowd. "I am the bread of life. The living bread came down from Heaven. If anyone eats from this bread, he will live forever. And the bread which I give for the life of the world is my flesh."

"How can you give us your flesh to eat?" jeered a man from Magdala. "We are not cannibals!" Many in the crowd began to laugh at the thought, agreeing.

"I am telling you the truth," Jesus declared again. "Unless you eat the flesh of the Son of Man and drink his blood, you have no life in you. My flesh is the true food, and my blood is true drink. The one who eats my flesh and drinks my blood remains in me, and I in him."

The crowd fell into stunned silence.

Even Jesus's loudest critics couldn't find words for the horror at the thought of drinking his blood. Jesus's statements were another one of the things I became numb to in my twenty-first-century world. To me, the words had merely been part of the ritual repeated every first Sunday before communion. But they were shocking beyond belief to these people, hearing it for the first time, especially for the Jews with dietary restrictions in the Mosaic Law against eating or drinking blood.

"This is too much!" a disciple named Silas turned to me. We'd been traveling together often over the last year. "How can I listen to this? He asks us to do what the law forbids? To heal on the Sabbath is one thing, but this! To drink blood? It is impossible. He asks too much, Thomas." Silas turned his back and walked away. After that day there were many men and women who never returned to our camp.

Several nights later, Jesus noted the number of disciples in camp had fallen by more than half. When he called the twelve of us together, he asked us if we were going to leave him also.

"Where are we going to go, Lord?" Peter replied. "Only you have the words that bring eternal life. We must stay."

As it turned out, those were merely the opening rounds of the long fight Jesus was starting. The next bout came a few weeks later in Jerusalem at the Feast of Dedication. During a contentious conversation with a large crowd, Jesus asserted his divine relationship to his father, and soon we were fleeing an angry mob intent on stoning him. Wherever Jesus went after that the scribes and Pharisees were there. They crafted subtle religious land mines to try and trap him in his words, revealing a well-orchestrated resistance to his teachings was growing among the Jewish leadership. The Sanhedrin opposition was gunning for him with the express intent of stopping him any way they could.

Jesus's popularity and the anticipation of his arrival began to slowly ebb away over the winter months. It left us trying to pick up the pieces of his ministry and shore up our own faltering visions of what we thought it should be. What made things even more difficult was Jesus's evolving relationship with those of us who followed him. He seemed to be of two minds: one of purpose and confidence, and the other of a solemn, isolated introspection. It was as if he tried to deal not only with the present moment but also his inevitable future at the same time.

I watched him, as if from a grandstand seat, play out the real drama of confronting his own death. This was no divine Son of God floating effortlessly and serenely above the trauma. I witnessed a fully human man experience the loss of close friends and followers. I saw him struggle with doubts and fears clawing at his heart as he dealt with the fact real people with real power were plotting to kill him. It shook me to the core. Becky and I talked about the tension often, but it brought little comfort. Jesus, along with the rest of us, was beginning the long, steady slide into the darkness ahead.

CHAPTER 31
Lazarus

With violence escalating in nearly every village, we stopped at in the hostile territory around Jerusalem, Jesus decided to travel north to the region of Perea.

We walked for three days and made camp on the outskirts of a village east of the Jordan River called Pella. The blooming flowers on the hillsides and the steadily warming temperatures gave us the hope of spring. We were looking forward to a much-needed time of rest after the discouraging past several months and were hoping to dispel the feelings of anxiety growing among us since the Feast of Tabernacles. Jesus hadn't spent much time in Perea, so we weren't as well known and didn't attract much attention in the area. Our camp nestled among olive and fig trees on small hills about two and a half miles east of the river. We were a day's walk from the Sea of Galilee to the north. The predictable routines of cooking, cleaning, and listening to Jesus teach was helping us all to recover.

We'd been there nearly a month when a messenger from Bethany arrived. I saw him talking to Matthew and Nathaniel, who took him directly to Jesus.

"That doesn't look good," I whispered to Becky, as she sat beside me embroidering a colorful design into the hem of her tunic.

"No, it doesn't. Let's see what's up."

By the time we reached the group, Jesus was sending the messenger on his way. "Thomas, I am going to pray. Would you and Rebecca make sure everyone is together for this evening's meal?"

"Yes, of course, Lord."

"A messenger came this morning with news; my friend Lazarus is gravely ill," Jesus said after Mary and Becky distributed fish stew and flatbread to everyone. "His sisters Mary and Martha asked me to come to him in Bethany." He paused for a moment, then continued. "As you know, Bethany is only a short distance from Jerusalem."

As soon as Jesus said the word "Jerusalem," I felt the ripples of alarm flow through the camp. Our vacation was over.

"I plan to leave in a few days. You are all welcome to come, but I will understand if you would rather stay here. Those who have been with me from the beginning will travel together. Lazarus's family is prosperous and can provide accommodations for us."

Preparing to leave and assisting the others kept my mind busy for the next few days. The journey from Jerusalem to Pella had taken three days, so I expected the same timeline in returning. We would travel south along the main road through the Jordan Valley, turn west at Jericho, where we could resupply, then head up through the dry foothills to Bethany. Arriving that way would make us less conspicuous to our enemies in Jerusalem, and being less noticeable right now was good.

The night before our departure, Jesus called us together to inform us Lazarus was dead. As Becky and I approached the group gathering around Jesus, I could already hear Peter making his case.

"Then why are we still going, Rabbi?" Peter said. "Just a short time ago, the Jews there tried to stone you. Do you still intend to go back? You know how the priests and Pharisees oppose you. Many people in Jerusalem who once followed you have turned away." Peter laid out his case methodically and cautiously, trying to make his point yet avoid any further rebuke from Jesus. "If word reaches them you are coming, they will have time to lay traps for you."

Or stones, I thought to myself, remembering the mobs we encountered.

"Peter," Jesus said gently, "there are twelve hours each day to walk, and the father has given you light none of those who oppose us possess. Moses led the Israelites by a pillar of fire at night that protected them. Is not my father able to keep us safe by the light he gives? And I tell you, Peter, one greater than Moses is here." Jesus addressed us, "If I ask my father, will he not give me twelve legions of angels? Is that not enough?

Am I not enough? Now, let us go without fear."

No one said anything, but I watched as Judas and Simon the Zealot whispered back and forth. No doubt they were calculating the size of the angelic force Jesus revealed was at his disposal.

"He could rule the whole world if he wants to," Becky whispered.

"But that's not why he came," I reminded more strongly than I intended. "At least not to rule it that way."

Becky crossed her arms over her chest and looked up at me. If she could have put her fingers on my lips without making a scene, I knew she would have. She needed to make a point and I needed to be quiet and listen.

I nodded for her to continue.

"You're thinking like someone who knows the Bible too well again." she pointed toward Judas and Simon. "Try listening to Jesus from their perspective."

I was about to object, but this time she did raise her hand, threatening to silence me with her fingers. "Sorry, go ahead."

"It must be why I'm here, Tommy." She pulled me away from the group so no one would hear us. "I know you didn't pay much attention in church. You think you don't know the Bible very well, but that's not true. You were there every Sunday for almost twenty years." She put her hand on my chest. "But in here, you know it. You can't help it. Even if you weren't listening, it has somehow become a part of you. You know the story. You know how it ends, or at least how it's supposed to end. So everything you see and hear happening now, you're interpreting from that perspective. But, I don't."

She paused to gather her thoughts. "That's gotta be why I'm here with you. I never went to church. My parents didn't go and never made me or my brother go either. So everything I see and hear is new. I see Jesus through fresh eyes. I hear him with new ears. I'm more like these people than you." She gestured at the group around Jesus, "I'm experiencing everything that happens more like them than you ever can because you know too much."

"So, how does that help us know what to do?" I asked, knowing she was right.

"I don't have everything figured out yet, Tommy, but we will. The important thing is, you have to stop seeing Judas as the betrayer. I know that's hard because all your life, you've thought of him that way. He may be the one who betrays Jesus, but it's not because he wants Jesus to die. I think it's the opposite. He wants him to rule. He knows Jesus is powerful enough to keep an army fed with a few fish and a couple of loaves of bread. He's watched Jesus control the weather and command the underworld. Even demons as powerful as the ones we encountered in Decapolis were no match for him. And now Jesus admits he commands an army of over sixty thousand angels. Judas isn't planning to stop Jesus, Tommy. He's planning to use Jesus to start a war. And everything he sees and hears keeps confirming to him Jesus can win it."

"So do we let Judas do what he's planning, or do we try to stop him?"

Becky took my hand and led me back toward the group. "If I could answer that question, we'd know exactly why we're here."

We left Pella early the following morning with about thirty-five people traveling south along the main road. An important trade route from Egypt to Syria, it required constant monitoring by the military. Farmers with pack animals and carts carrying produce and goods were familiar sights, along with priests and scribes trying carefully to avoid contact with the unclean people and animals traveling around them. Small herds of oxen, mules, sheep, and goats were being driven to market, leaving dung on and along the road. The manure added to the stench of sweat and dust choking the air. At our afternoon meal, I found myself sitting with the other apostles who were still unsure of Jesus's decision.

"The risk is too great in Jerusalem. We should return here as soon as he grieves his friend."

"He will not listen, James," Peter shook his head. "Our best hope is to keep him in Bethany. If we spread the word he is there, perhaps the people will come to him. That may be enough."

Nathaniel laughed. "You fool yourself if you think you can keep him out of Jerusalem. Especially now, so close to the feast. He cannot resist the large crowds."

"If he goes there, he may die," Peter predicted. "He has been speaking of it for months. We must try—"

"Then I say we all go with him. So that we can die alongside him." As soon as the words left my mouth, bells and whistles began going off in my head. I hadn't intended to say anything, let alone that. It was like the words were there all along, inside me, and couldn't wait to escape. As I reflected on what I'd said, it didn't surprise me how much I meant them. They hadn't come from my head, but from my heart.

The others sat there silently for a few minutes, thinking about what I'd said. Finally, one by one each man began nodding their heads, then got up and walked away after touching me on the shoulder, leaving me alone with my thoughts.

On the third day, the afternoon shadows were growing long when we finally reached the Mount of Olives, east of Jerusalem. Fig groves, vegetable gardens, and sheep pens signaled we were nearing Lazarus's estate. We passed several stone buildings designed for storage, carpentry, or smithing, along with those used to house servants and guests.

Jesus led us straight through the courtyard to the main house, where a servant boy carrying a sack of feed on his back saw us. He dropped his load and ran inside. A few moments later, a woman dressed in black stepped through the door. She stared at Jesus with burning eyes, then ran toward him, bursting into tears as she embraced him.

"That is Martha," Joanna said, stepping up beside Becky and me. "She is the older of Lazarus's two sisters."

Jesus spoke with Martha quietly for several minutes until she stopped crying. Then as they walked toward us, I heard him say, "Your brother will rise again."

Martha stopped and looked at Jesus shaking her head, a mixture of anger and disappointment on her face. "I know he will, Lord. I know he will rise in the resurrection on the last day. But if you were here, he would not have died."

Jesus put his hands on either side of Martha's face. "I am the resurrection and the life, Martha. He who believes in me will live, even if he dies, and whoever lives and believes in me will never die. Do you believe that?"

Without hesitation, Martha replied, "Yes, Lord. You know I believe you are the Messiah, the Son of God, foretold to come into the world." After a few more quiet words whispered between them, Martha returned to the house.

"We will wait here until Mary, Martha's sister, joins us," Jesus directed. "They will take us to where they have put him."

A short time later, Martha returned with a younger woman, also dressed in black. As soon as she saw Jesus, she rushed headlong into his arms, crying uncontrollably. I watched as Jesus tenderly embraced her, tears beginning to flow from his eyes. The pain coming from the three of them as they stood clinging to one another was heartbreaking. Becky must have felt it too because she took my hand in hers. I was about to say something comforting when she furrowed her brow and looked past me. "Who are they?" she asked.

I turned and saw a large crowd of women coming toward us. Like Mary and Martha, they were dressed in black robes and cried out or moaned loudly in despair.

"They are mourners," Joanna said, "friends who are here to grieve with the family."

When the mourners saw Jesus talking with Mary and Martha, they stopped. When Jesus and the sisters turned toward a well-worn path weaving between several buildings and into the rocky hills beyond, Joanna, Becky, and I fell in behind them. We walked until the path opened into a small box canyon where dozens of small trees and shrubs were planted, creating a comfortable garden with stone benches and prayer altars. Several caves had been cut into the rock wall ahead of us, each sealed with large stones.

We stopped in front of the largest stone, where Jesus continued speaking to Mary and Martha, giving most of his attention to Mary, who finally cried out, "Yes, Lord, I believe you." Then she fell to the ground, wrapped her arms around his feet, and wailed. "But if you had only been here, Lord. If you had only come sooner!"

Jesus looked down at Mary, then at Martha. Then at the group of mourners and guests who filled the small canyon. Finally, he turned and looked at us, the men and women who spent much of the last three years with him. His eyes grew red and moist as he continued to look at the people who gathered to say goodbye to Lazarus. After a few moments, he gently stepped out of Mary's grasp, leaving her lying on the ground weeping. He touched Martha's cheek and took a step toward Lazarus's tomb. He wavered several times, nearly losing his balance, before dropping to his knees and burying his face in his hands. I could see his body shake and hear his agonizing sobs as he grieved. Everyone remained silent as the sun slowly began to set behind us, bathing the canyon in soft orange light. In the quiet, I could hear the whispers from the mourners around me, some speaking in admiration of Jesus's great love for Lazarus while others were still questioning why he had taken so long to arrive.

"Why is he crying?" Becky asked, standing on her tiptoes to whisper in my ear. "He's going to raise him from the dead, isn't he? Even I know this part of the story."

I thought about it for a long time as I watched Jesus continue to weep bitterly. When I looked around the canyon, I couldn't find a single face without tears. Then when I looked at Becky, my own tears began to stream down my cheeks and into my beard as I finally understood.

"He's not crying for Lazarus, Becky. You're right; Jesus knows what he is here to do. He knew it when he left Pella. He's crying for us, and maybe a little for himself. The people standing in this canyon are his closest and dearest friends. His only friends, really. For three years, we have eaten with him, slept beside him, watched him perform miracles, heal the sick, and even command the storm. He has given us everything he has, often to the point of complete exhaustion. He would stay up late, teaching us well into the evening, and then spend the rest of the night praying. He's taught us and shown us every day about God's Kingdom and how it works, and yet everyone he cares about, everyone he loves still doubts him. He is about to perform one of the greatest miracles in history, and he's out there entirely by himself. Completely alone. Not a single one of the men or women he's traveled with all this time believes Lazarus will walk out of that tomb despite everything he's done. And he knows when word of this reaches Jerusalem and the scribes and priests hear about it, they will determine more than ever he must be stopped. If he goes through with this, he is sealing his fate to die. Most of these people he's never going to see again. Not in this life anyway."

When Becky squeezed my arm, I turned back to see Jesus struggling to get to his feet, using the sleeves of his robe to wipe away his tears. He stood on trembling legs, took a few deep breaths and stared at the grave where Lazarus lay rotting.

"Take the stone away," he said quietly.

Stunned, no one moved. After a few minutes, people began glancing around with embarrassed looks on their faces, as though they wished they hadn't come to see the great prophet fail.

"Take the stone away!" Jesus shouted at the top of his lungs. His voice echoed off the canyon walls. "Take it away now!"

Martha took a few steps toward Jesus and grasped his arm, trying to pull him away. "Lord, he's been dead for four days now. There will be a terrible stink. Let's go back to the house."

I could feel the electricity in the air as Jesus freed himself from Martha's grip and turned back to the tomb, his tears flowing again.

"Did I not tell you if you would only believe, you would see the glory of God?" Jesus cried without looking at Mary or Martha but raising his voice so everyone could hear it. "Take the stone away."

The servants who accompanied us looked bewildered, even after Martha finally whispered to them. "Go on. Do as he says."

After some prodding, they cautiously approached the stone and began pushing it away from the opening. Once the grave entrance was opened, they ran out of the canyon, leaving Mary and Martha clinging to each other, staring into the dark opening.

Jesus lifted his face toward the sky and threw his arms out to his sides. "Father," he shouted, "I thank you that you have heard me, as you always hear me." He paused for a moment, then went on more quietly. "But I say this for those who are here, for their benefit, so they may believe you sent me."

The air around me began to crackle with energy. The wind whipped through the canyon, blowing around but not making a sound. Everyone stood transfixed, staring into the black, empty mouth of the crypt.

"Lazarus!" Jesus shouted, causing several people close to him to cover their heads with their arms. "Lazzzzzarrrrrusssssss, come out!"

The following silence was overwhelming. Mary and Martha clung to each other, weeping softly. Many people were holding hands. A few had fallen to their knees, foreheads touching the ground.

But the gaping hole revealed nothing.

Jesus stared, unmoving, his eyes boring into the dark tomb with an intensity I had not seen since I watched him calm the storm.

Suddenly, Mary screamed! Then one hand covering her mouth, she pointed at the tomb with her other. I could hear gasps and cries from people around me, as the figure of a man, like a mummy in a Hitchcock horror movie, began to shuffle out of the gloom.

"Remove the bindings and let him go!" Jesus commanded.

Everyone rushed toward the tomb, each straining to touch Lazarus as though we were trying to convince ourselves he was real. Mary and Martha began tearing the wrappings off their brother. As the face cloth came off, he drew in several rattled breaths, his eyes closed, his face sunken and pale. Then, in a flash, life and energy filled him. He opened his eyes and inhaled deeply. Martha touched his cheek, and he smiled weakly in recognition. By the time the burial wrappings were off and Mary covered her brother in a long dark robe, Lazarus seemed fully recovered.

Jesus remained alone, still standing on the spot where he called for Lazarus. He looked utterly drained. His tears stains were still evident on his cheeks. When Lazarus looked around and saw him, Jesus smiled weakly, his eyes brightening. Lazarus began to laugh and cry and then laugh again as he walked toward him. Jesus met him and caught him in a tight embrace, laughing along with his friend.

Everyone around me dealt with what happened in their own way. Most were crying and praising God. Some were shaking their heads in disbelief or talking among themselves in small groups. Becky pulled me into a bear hug, her face wet against my cheek.

When she released me to embrace Dahlia and Joanna, familiar

hands spun me around, and a laughing Judas kissed me passionately on both cheeks; then, he drew me close and whispered into my ear, "Do you see, Thomas, nothing can stop him!"

It was absolutely clear to me now that Judas saw everything Jesus did and every move Jesus made through the eyes of a revolutionary who had discovered a powerful new weapon to unleash. Judas knew he had an overwhelming tactical advantage in the fight to come.

"Even if Rome comes against us with all its strength, we cannot be defeated." His eyes glowed with passion as he spoke. "If they strike us down, he will raise us up to fight and die again. Think of it, Thomas, an army that cannot be killed. Immortal warriors. Nothing like this has been seen in Israel. Not even Joshua or David possessed power such as this!"

I glanced at Becky, who broke away from Dahlia and Joanna and watched us with keen interest. She made a circular motion with her fingers, urging me to take advantage of Judas's excitement to probe for more information.

"But you know he does not intend to fight, Judas. He made it known that it is not his way. How do you plan to change his mind?"

Judas patted me lightly on the cheek several times, "I have a plan, my friend. Oh yes! Do not fear; I have a plan." Judas looked around to be sure no one was listening.

Becky smiled and turned back to rejoin Dahlia and Joanna.

"He will stay here for a few days with his friends, but then he will go into Jerusalem. I will leave for the city tonight to meet with Micah and the others. Simon the Zealot has arranged for his followers to meet us there in the next few days. When news of today's event reaches Jerusalem, the people will know they must choose. They can continue to follow the hypocrites who delivered our people into the hands of the Roman overlords or," he paused to smile and nod at Jesus, "or they can follow the true king who has come to bring freedom to our people." He pulled me to the side and whispered. "I will ensure he is well received in Jerusalem when he arrives. You make sure he does not tarry too long. Once in the city, we will provoke an attack by the Romans, and Jesus will use his power to protect us and lead us to freedom."

Speechless, I opened my mouth but couldn't find any words.

Judas gripped my shoulders once more and then disappeared into the crowd.

As the canyon darkened, I sat on one of the stone benches praying God would show me what to do. Was I here to help Judas or to stop him?

I know you'll be there for him.

For who, mom? Jesus or Judas? If Judas's plan succeeded, nothing would turn out the way history recorded. An armed conflict with the Romans would change everything. I knew every man who followed Jesus would do whatever Jesus asked, but I also knew deep inside, most of them shared the same thoughts and feelings I heard from Judas. They would fight if they thought it was the way to restore Israel's freedom. James and John already talked about raining fire from Heaven to punish those who didn't follow us. And I heard Peter tell Andrew he planned to buy a sword once we reached Jerusalem. The Zealot had plans of his own, and now I learned Micah, a man I brought to Jesus, had been drawn into the scheme. If Judas could rally a large enough crowd and Rome saw it as a potential threat, would they move against us? And if soldiers attacked, would Jesus use his power to protect us? No, this was not the way it was supposed to happen. But was I supposed to join the fight or try to keep history on course? And how was I even supposed to do that?

I listened to the crowd still celebrating. Jesus, Mary, and Martha stood together, smiling and laughing. Lazarus walked among the crowd embracing his family and friends. I felt like an island of regret in an ocean of joy.

Help me, Lord, I prayed again.

A few moments later, a hand touched my shoulder. "You okay?" Becky asked.

"No," I took her hand and walked with her out of the canyon. We left the empty grave and revelers behind. "No, I don't think I am."

CHAPTER 32
The Temple

We spent the next several days with Lazarus and his sisters in Bethany. It reminded me of how things were that first chilly evening on a hillside in Galilee. Everyone seemed happy and at ease, and the mission seemed to be back on track. Hope and excitement for the future permeated everyone. As word of Lazarus's resurrection spread, hundreds of new disciples came from Jerusalem, Emmaus, Bethlehem, and the surrounding countryside to see Jesus and Lazarus. Jesus spent his days teaching, and in the evenings, the twelve apostles, and many of those who had been with him from the beginning took meals together with Lazarus and his family while reminiscing about all the marvelous things we had seen and done. On the fourth night, the party ended.

"We go into Jerusalem in the morning," Jesus announced. "I intend to teach in the temple before the Feast of Unleavened Bread."

After Jesus left to pray, the mood shifted quickly from merriment to gloom. While none of the other disciples fully grasped Jesus's predictions about what would happen at the feast this year, everyone knew going into Jerusalem meant trouble. Every day, as crowds gathered at Lazarus's home to listen to Jesus preach, there were more and more priests and Pharisees among them. Jesus handled their arguments well, but the encounters were becoming more hostile with each passing day. There was little the religious leaders could do amid the supportive crowds gathered in Lazarus's courtyard. But now, the battle would shift to their home turf, the Jewish temple. Over the next hour, the disciples wandered off to find a quiet place to spend what we expected to be our last peaceful night for some time to come.

I found Becky sitting with Joanna and Mary Magdalene near the well south of Lazarus's manor house. Mary wept softly.

"Mary is afraid Jesus is going to die in Jerusalem," Becky informed me as I sat beside her. The warning look in her eyes urged me to tread carefully.

Mary deserved the truth. "I have heard him say so myself, Mary,"

I said. "Many times."

"'The Son of Man must suffer many things and be rejected by the elders and chief priests and be killed,'" Joanna recited, then added, "'and be raised on the third day.'"

"Those were his words, Joanna," I agreed. "We have all heard him say it."

"But do you believe him, Thomas?" Mary asked through her tears. "Do you believe that no matter what happens in Jerusalem, he will live?"

There it was. The question I'd been dancing around for months, for years really, afraid to come to grips with. The question Becky and I struggled with in hopes of discovering what to do. And now, Mary's grief forced me to face it head-on.

Through some strange twist of fate, I spent the last three years with the most incredible man I'd ever known. I watched him do things impossible for me to believe without seeing them with my own eyes. I heard him teach with wisdom that indeed seemed otherworldly. But who was he really? Was he a man, or God in a man's body? Was he simply a man who would die in a little more than a week or a God who would defeat death as he often promised he would?

In my life as Tommy Evans, I'd been so sure I knew the answers. As Thomas the apostle, everything changed. But had they changed enough to know for sure Jesus was more than a great man with extraordinary gifts?

If Jesus was just a man—a powerful man, no doubt—and I fell in with Judas, perhaps we could change history altogether. Israel and the Jewish people would be liberated, and the friends I made along the way, like Micah and Zebedee, would be free to live and worship as they pleased. Rome would be defeated 300 years before it fell, and Jesus, the man, would live out a long life, perhaps as a king, with the power and influence to spread his message around the world.

If, on the other hand, Jesus was God's son as he claimed, then the coming week needed to play out as Matthew and John originally wrote it, including seeing Judas abandon his hope of revolution and betray Jesus to the Jewish authorities as history originally recorded.

But another even more terrifying possibility loomed before me. If Jesus was a mortal man, deluded in his convictions of something more, and the coming days saw him go to Jerusalem, get arrested, and be crucified, and I did nothing to stop it, my friend would die. The man we had grown to love and depend upon would be taken from us. His life would be lost for nothing, and our lives ruined. If he was merely a mortal man, there would be no resurrection. How I answered these questions defined the very purpose for my presence in Jerusalem.

I looked toward the house and saw Lazarus standing on the veranda, looking up at the stars. "I'm pretty sure that man standing over there," I pointed in Lazarus's direction, "knows the answer to your questions and mine, Mary."

When we left Lazarus' home early the following day, hundreds were already waiting in and around the courtyard for Jesus. They fell in around us, shouting their loyalty to Jesus or begging him for healing or deliverance. Jesus reached out and touched as many as possible as we made the short walk from Bethany to Jerusalem. As we passed the Mount of Olives, Jesus called us twelve off to the side to speak privately. Technically, it was only the eleven of us because Judas left five days earlier and had not yet returned.

"Thomas, Matthew, go into the village up ahead. You will find a young colt tied there, one that has never been ridden. Untie it and bring it to me. If anyone tries to stop you, tell them the Lord has need of it."

We did as Jesus instructed and found the colt past the first building in a small corral. When the owner asked us why we were taking his animal, we told him the Lord had need of it. He laughed and waved his arms, "Then go on with you. If he needs it, he shall have it. Go. Go!"

By the time we returned to Jesus, the crowd had doubled in size, making it difficult for us to reach him and the others. Once we did, John and James threw their cloaks on the colt, while Matthew and I lifted Jesus onto its back. How the animal remained calm through it all, I don't know. The people squeezed us together, pushing and pulling us in various directions. Those who could reach Jesus touched him and walked away healed. Those who couldn't reach him pushed even harder against us, throwing the animal and us off balance. Peter, Andrew, Simon, and Nathaniel walked in front to open a path between us and the city gate about a half-mile away.

It was madness!

"Save us, Son of David! Save us now!" the crowd shouted as we inched our way toward the city that held all the answers to my troubling questions.

"Deliver us, Lord!"

"Blessed is the one who comes in God's name! Deliver your people, Lord."

"Salvation has come!"

"Save us, Lord!"

A group of men began climbing the palm trees along the road and cutting branches. As they fell to the ground, people picked them up, waving and throwing them onto the road in front of us. The closer we got to the city, the larger and louder the crowd became.

"Save us, Son of David!"

"Deliver your people, Lord."

"Blessed is the one who comes in God's name!"

"Rebuke your disciples, Rabbi," shouted a Pharisee dressed in colorful robes as he came up alongside the colt. "Tell them to be silent."

"Let me tell you the truth, Josiah," Jesus shouted, pointing at the people. "If they stop, the stones themselves will cry out. Would you like that better?"

Josiah pushed his way through the crowd and disappeared.

As we entered the city, the notable increased presence of the Roman military seemed to have little to no effect on the disorderly crowd. It felt like the whole city was about to descend into chaos. When Jesus slipped off the colt and headed straight for the temple, disappearing into the crowded courtyard, I got the horrible feeling he was about to add to our problems.

When we finally caught up with him, Jesus stood with Judas, who pulled out his money pouch. "Do you intend to purchase your offering now, Rabbi?" Judas asked.

"Put your purse away, Judas. We have no need of it today." Then Jesus turned to observe the people milling about the courtyard exchanging their foreign coins and purchasing offerings for the upcoming feast. He stepped up to the first table stacked with coins of various shapes and colors and looked the man in the eye.

"Why do you store up for yourselves treasures on earth, where moth and rust destroy, and where thieves break in and steal?" He grabbed the corner of the table and flung it into the air, scattering coins in every direction. Those standing close by dove to the ground, trying to gather as many spilled coins as they could reach.

Jesus watched them pushing and shoving each other as they fought over their treasures. He opened a cage of doves, releasing them into the air. Then another. And another. When he reached the next table, the seller came out from behind it intending to stop Jesus. He stood motionless as Jesus walked past him. He watched helplessly as Jesus flipped his table and his money into the air.

"No one can serve two masters!" Jesus shouted. "If he tries, he will hate one and love the other, or he will be devoted to one and despise the other. You cannot serve God and money." Another table went flying. More doves took to flight. Jesus climbed on another table, kicking the coins to the ground where more people scrambled to collect them.

"It is written," Jesus shouted. "'My house will be called a house of prayer, but you have made it a den of thieves.'" He stood there for a long time looking out over the crowd, his eyes brimming with tears as he watched many of the same people who only minutes ago cheered him as he approached the city fight over their precious pieces of bronze and silver scattered in the dirt and dung of the temple courtyard. An angry mob of money changers fought against the crowd to gather their scattered coins.

I watched as he silently prayed, his lips often forming the word "Jerusalem."

When he finished praying, he stepped down from the table, turned his back on the chaos of the temple, and headed for the gate we had entered earlier. When I caught up with Jesus about thirty yards ahead, I could see a company of Roman soldiers and a centurion blocking the exit from the city. They took up a defensive position, with shields at the ready and their hands on the pommels of their swords. My throat tightened as I recalled the prison guard's blade pressed against it back at the palace in Tiberias. My fingers came away from my neck damp with sweat, but no blood this time.

"Are you ready?" Judas asked, coming up on my left.

Simon boxed me in on my right, James the younger, behind me.

"Ready for what, Judas?" I stammered, realizing once again, events around me were outpacing my ability to anticipate and keep up. I looked at Judas, who nodded slightly, then lifted his eyes to scan the surrounding rooftops.

The first face I saw as I followed Judas's gaze was Micah's. He crouched behind the knee-wall at the top of a building on my left. He smiled, touched his forehead with his fingers, and gestured behind him with his head. The message was clear: "My men are behind me. We await your signal." I glanced to Micah's left and saw another man. He gave me the same sign.

I spun my head to the right. More men were hiding on the rooftops there. I checked the alleyways on either side— more men waited. There was no way to know how many rebels there were, but I had little doubt there were enough to turn the streets of Jerusalem into a bloodbath.

Judas grabbed my arm and shook it hard, "Keep your eyes ahead of you, fool. You will give away their positions. As soon as the Romans arrest Jesus, they will attack. We have over five hundred men in the city. Today we become free men, Thomas."

CHAPTER 33
The Centurion

The bile in my gut burned the back of my throat as we approached the Roman soldiers blocking our exit. I looked around for Becky, but she and the other women left us when Jesus announced he was going to the temple. I had grown accustomed to her wisdom and insights, which I desperately needed now. Five hundred men were about to attack one hundred well-armed, well-trained Roman soldiers who stood in our way, their leader poised with his spear at his side and his sword and dagger ready on his belt.

This would undoubtedly be the event to change history. If Jesus used his power to prevent his arrest and protect us, Judas would have his war. If Jesus did not intervene, the rebels still stood little chance. Despite their numbers, they would be put down quickly, but nothing would ever be the same regardless of the outcome.

Was this the moment I had been summoned to the past to either support or prevent?

I thought about catching up with Jesus and warning him but knew Judas, Simon, and James would stop me. When I looked back toward Jesus, I could see it was too late anyway. He walked only a few yards from the Roman centurion. I lifted a quick prayer of thanks that Becky and the other women were not with us. Very likely, many of us would not survive today's encounter.

Jesus stopped in front of the centurion and, after a moment, put his hand on the man's arm. I watched a number of the soldiers tighten their grips on their swords. Several directly behind the centurion had their blades halfway out of their scabbards when Jesus asked, "It is good to see you, Antonias. How fares your servant?"

The centurion smiled at Jesus, then dropped to one knee and bowed his head. "He is well, Rabbi. When I returned home, he was as you promised. He has resumed all his duties. I have no words to express my gratitude."

The Roman faces behind Antonias were frozen in shock and disapproval as they watched their commander humble himself before the Jewish troublemaker. Eyes widened even further when Jesus helped the centurion to his feet and embraced him.

"You have done well, Antonias," Jesus stepped back to look at him. "You served Antipas in Capernaum and now you command your eighty here in Jerusalem. Were you sent here to arrest me?"

I could feel the tension rise in both the disciples and the soldiers.

Antonias smiled again, "No, Lord, only to see you leave the temple in one piece."

"As you can see," Jesus laughed, gesturing behind him, "for now, it still stands." He looked at the men standing with Antonias, then behind him at the temple, then back at the centurion. "But I tell you this, my friend. Tear this temple down," Jesus put his hand on his chest, "and I will raise it up in three days."

Antonias stared at Jesus for a long time, considering his words. Then he nodded. "Be careful, Rabbi." He glanced up at the rooftops. "Had any other centurion been sent here today, things would have turned out much differently."

Jesus embraced Antonias once again then led us through the soldiers who stepped aside to let us pass. Jesus walked out of the gate toward Bethany, and by the time we reached Lazarus' home, the women had rejoined us. Somewhere in between, Judas, Simon the zealot, and James the younger disappeared. I described the scene at the temple and the confrontation with the Romans to Becky. After supper, we sought out a friend to help us understand some of the day's events.

"He is taunting them," Matthew said as he stirred the fire with a long stick. All the others had retired after the evening meal, and now the three of us sat around the fire alone, sharing its warmth and a cup of cool wine. Matthew was the most educated among us and knew the Jewish and Roman authorities well from his days as a tax collector.

"What do you mean, taunting them?" I asked

"The Pharisees study the Scriptures more than anyone, and Jesus is thoroughly aware of that. Everything he did this morning was shrewdly designed to deliver a message to Caiaphas and the Pharisees who were watching."

"What message, Matthew?" Becky and I spoke at the same time.

"A most dangerous one, I fear. Jesus openly declared himself to be the Messiah today. The Anointed One. The King of Israel. A most dangerous and antagonizing message indeed."

I didn't understand, but I knew I was learning something important. I encouraged him to continue. "The king! How?"

"You should study your scripture more, Thomas. When the great King David was in his last days, Adonijah, one of his sons, tried to make himself king in David's place, but David already promised the throne to his other son, Solomon. So, David had Zadok the priest and Nathan the prophet mount Solomon on David's donkey and ride into the city proclaiming him the true heir to David's throne."

"Just like Jesus did today," Becky said.

"Yes. Exactly. Just as the prophet Zechariah described it, 'See, your King comes to you, Jerusalem! Righteous and victorious, riding on a colt, the foal of a donkey.' Oh yes, the message Jesus sent today was unmistakable to anyone who knows the prophecies. Maybe not to the rabble along the roadside, but you can be sure the Pharisees got his message. He is here to rule. If there is going to be a resurrection as Jesus has alleged, it will surely be the resurrection of Israel and King David's throne. And you saw it for yourself today. The people support him. They love him. And nothing represents the corruption of our leaders more than the marketeers in the temple. When word of what he did today reaches the people, there will not be a Judean within a hundred leagues who will not rally to him. 'Make my Father's house a house of prayer' will become the new battle cry on every Jewish lip."

Becky and I looked at each other with a shared understanding of what we were hearing. The man sitting next to us had Matthew's face but spoke with Judas's words. Were the two of them conspiring, or was I once again doing what Becky warned me about? Was I looking at events through the eyes of someone who knew the story too well? Everyone around me interpreted events through the eyes of first-century Jews whose necks had been under the heels of their Roman conquerors for as long as they'd been alive. How could they not misinterpret Jesus's words and intentions? Their hopes of liberation and freedom kept them blind to Jesus's real message of suffering and death. Their eyes could only see their victorious king triumphantly riding into Jerusalem on King David's colt.

"Thomas told me what happened today in the temple courtyard, Matthew," Becky said. "Why didn't the temple guards stop Jesus? Could anyone else have gotten away with what he did?"

"Of course not, Rebecca. But Jesus is not anyone else, is he? He has too much influence with the people. The Pharisees fear him, and they fear the crowds who follow him. And as we saw today, the Romans have no stomach for confronting him. Pilate knows better than anyone the quickest way to end up as an exile on a Greek island is to lose the peace here in Jerusalem. The whole area of Judea is too important to the Roman economy for Pilate to risk an uprising. As long as Jesus does not start the fight, Rome will move cautiously. Without Rome's backing, the Jewish leaders have little authority to move against Jesus and will not risk igniting the crowds that support him. Whatever Jesus is planning, he has planned it well, and he should be able to move about freely as long as he stays in public places."

CHAPTER 34
The Turning Point

For the next four days, that is exactly what Jesus did. We made the short walk into Jerusalem from Bethany each morning and the loyal crowd gathered in Lazarus's courtyard to follow him. Jesus would go straight to the temple where he taught during the day and we would return to the safety of Lazarus's estate in the evening. Hundreds of new pilgrims arrived in Jerusalem daily to prepare for the Feast of Unleavened Bread and most wanted to hear Jesus speak. But even with the massive crowds cramming into the temple grounds, dozens of scribes and Pharisees always managed to find their way to the front to debate with Jesus. By midweek the crowd was divided.

"They must be bribing the people somehow," Philip commented as he and Nathaniel walked back to Bethany with Becky and me. "He wins every argument, but still, many are turning against him. Scribes and Pharisees from all over Israel are pouring into Jerusalem. While Jesus teaches in the temple, they plot against him in the synagogues."

"I will be glad when the feast is over. We cannot get out of this city soon enough," Nathaniel added.

Becky and I found a quiet spot to spend time together alone in the box canyon. We were running out of time and more confused than ever about what to do. After the crisis with the Roman soldiers had been avoided, we became even more sensitive to everything anyone said or did that could inform us about the purpose of our presence in the first century. When I saw Joanna and Mary Magdalene running toward us, the goosebumps on my arms told me the moment had arrived.

"Thomas, I am so glad we found you," Joanna began as she and Mary knelt in the grass beside Becky and embraced her.

"What's wrong? What happened?" I asked.

"Judas," Mary answered.

"What's happened to Judas? Where is he? What has he done?"

"He has not done anything," Joanna cried, anger in her voice. "He is leaving."

"What do you mean leaving? Where is he going? Back to Jerusalem?"

Joanna shook her head. "We are women, Thomas. He does not even speak to us. We learned it from Simon. Judas is returning home to Carioth. He is on the road south of Jerusalem toward Bethlehem right now. I do not—"

"Rebecca, let's go." I stood and pulled Becky to her feet. We ran out of the canyon, leaving Joanna and Mary sitting alone in the dark. There was no time to explain or to waste. I operated purely on instinct now, without a clue what to do next. All I knew was Judas held the key to everything. What he did or did not do determined the outcome for humanity.

"Where are we going?" Becky gasped for breath as we reached the road.

"We need to catch up with Judas," I bent over and put my hands on my knees.

"Why, Tommy? Maybe his leaving is what's supposed to happen."

"I don't think so, Beck. It doesn't feel right. Him leaving. I think he has to be here. One way or another, Judas Iscariot plays an important part in what will happen. He needs to be in Jerusalem. Come on." We ran in bursts, starting and stopping, for the next hour through the mountains south of Jerusalem. The almost full moon illuminated the road ahead and provided plenty of light to keep us from stumbling and falling. I knew I pressed Becky to the limit, but there was no way I was going to spend three years with Jesus and fail to find out why at the end.

"There he is," Becky wheezed. She let go of my hand and ran ahead like she'd gotten her second wind. When I caught up, she and Judas were staring at each other.

"What do you want, traitor?" Judas asked, turning to me.

The word "traitor" hit me like a hammer blow. I grew up believing Judas was the traitor. Now he'd turned the tables on me. But that would have to wait. "I want to know why you are leaving. Where are you going? What happened to that great plan of yours?"

Judas looked at Becky with contempt. I thought he might spit at her feet. Then he turned and continued down the road without a word.

I could feel anger building up as I watched Judas's back fading into the darkness. I'd never been in a fistfight in my life, but I knew that streak ended tonight. I rushed after Judas, spun him around, and looked at him long enough to see the shock register in his eyes. Then I pushed him hard in the chest with both hands knocking him flat on his back. I jumped on top of him in an instant, my right arm cocked and ready to strike, when Becky grabbed me.

"Thomas, stop," she whispered. "You won't help Jesus this way."

It was probably only a few seconds, but it felt like an eternity before I relaxed my arm, and Becky let go of me. I slid off Judas and sat beside him on the dirt road. I extended my hand. He took it, and I helped him sit up. Becky sat on the path beside me.

Judas looked at me for a long time, occasionally letting his eyes drift over to Becky. Finally, he hung his head in defeat, "There is nothing left for me here, Thomas. It is over. But you should know that. You were there. I assumed you must have had something to do with it."

"You mean in the city? What could I have done? You were right there beside me. What happened to your five hundred men? I thought they were ready to fight."

"They were ready to fight," Judas growled. "Right up until the moment that centurion knelt in front of Jesus. If he had made a single move against him—a single move, Thomas—they would have come from everywhere and fought. But instead of arresting Jesus, the Roman fool bowed to him." Judas laughed. "Of all the Roman commanders in Jerusalem, the one they send owes Jesus the life of his servant." He shook his head and scoffed. "It took the fight out of everyone. That was our one chance, Thomas. Afterward, we could not hold the men together. When Micah saw the centurion on his knees, he threw down his sword and walked away. Most of his men went with him. The last anyone saw of him, he walked the road back to Galilee preaching about love and forgiveness to anyone who would listen. Simon's men stayed another day, but now most have given up and gone home too." Judas got to his feet. "I intend to do the same." Judas brushed the dust from his robes as he prepared to walk away.

I had no doubt this was the moment in time I had been born for. Three years ago, like an arrow in the hands of a master archer loosed from the bow, this was my target. There was no more time for deciding. No more time for questions. Now, I needed to act!

If I let Judas walk away, history would change. There would be no kiss, no arrest, no trial, no cross, and no crucifixion. And if Jesus was who he says, no resurrection either. If I let Judas disappear down the road, I could return to Jerusalem and live out my days as one of Jesus's friends and companions while he continued to preach and teach throughout Israel and perhaps beyond. Not a bad life. Maybe Becky would even come to accept our circumstances and be happy here.

But if I learned anything from Jesus over the last three years, life was never about oneself. It's about the people around you. The people you love. The ones you care about and still have yet to meet. The family and community you are part of. Life was about the whole wide world we live in. In the next few seconds, the decision I made would affect practically every human being born on planet Earth for the next two thousand years.

If I let Judas walk away, future generations would never have the opportunity to face what I was facing right now. Never get the chance to ask the questions I'd wrestled with since arriving here. Never be given the opportunity to look inside themselves and decide: *What do I do about Jesus? Who is he, really? Is he a man, or is he more?*

As I watched Judas's back, I realized those questions were settled inside me now. All that mattered was to act. I had to do everything I could to ensure that tomorrow night my friend, the finest man I'd ever known, was arrested and killed. If I could somehow persuade Judas to return to Jerusalem and complete his historical role, a man would die... but a Savior would live.

I know you'll be there for him when the time comes, my mother's words echoed again inside my heart.

Those words had tormented me since the morning I woke up in Galilee. But now, for the first time, I remembered what she said next before she walked away to join my dad at the picnic table. 'Just remember all of us, son.' At the time, I thought she meant her, dad, and

Angela, but she hadn't. Like usual, I was thinking too small. But Jesus had taught me to see a bigger picture. To see the world and every soul in it. To make every soul valuable. It didn't matter whether Jesus talked to his closest companions or to a Samaritan woman with five husbands. A Roman centurion dressed in armor or a forgotten leper clothed in rags. A wealthy Jewish prince with much to lose or a despised Canaanite woman looking for crumbs from the master's table. A forgotten child or a lonely widow. To him, every person had infinite value. Everyone had a place in his father's kingdom. No, my mother didn't mean I should remember my family. She meant exactly what she said.

When the time comes, remember all of us. Remember the world. A world that needs a savior.

"Thanks, Mom," I whispered. The only thing left to do was to figure out how to get Judas to return to Jerusalem.

That's when I heard Becky call out, "Judas wait, I think there is still a way."

I looked at her, wondering what she had up her sleeve.

Judas stopped but didn't turn. I could feel him struggling with himself. Finally, he turned but addressed me instead of Becky, "There is no way, Thomas. After we failed in the city, our only hope was to get the Jewish leaders to act. I have friends in the Sanhedrin who say Caiaphas has decided not to seek Jesus's arrest until after the feast. By then, it will be too late. If Jesus leaves the city after Passover, there may not be another opportunity for Caiaphas to move against him for a year. They will not pursue him in the countryside, and there is no guarantee Jesus will return to Jerusalem next year. No, the opportunity has passed. We have failed. You can continue to follow him if you wish, but I am going home."

"Why won't Caiaphas arrest him during the feast?" Becky asked.

This time Judas spoke to Becky, "Are you such a fool, woman. You should open your eyes. Jesus has too many supporters in Jerusalem. In the temple, we could have used that to our advantage. But Caiaphas's objective is not the same as ours. He wants to silence Jesus, not crown him. Caiaphas wants a quiet arrest, not a riot. He fears if there is trouble, the Romans could take retribution on all the Jews in Jerusalem. The outcome is too unpredictable. Caiaphas has no choice but to wait."

Becky looked at me for approval. I gave her the "go ahead; you're doing fine" look. She and I had talked for hours about how the story was supposed to end. She knew as well as I did what Judas needed to do. Now she needed to close the deal. Judas would never suspect a woman was playing him. In his world, women weren't smart enough to do that to a man.

Good luck, Judas. I laughed to myself.

"What if you could use Caiaphas to help you start the revolution, Judas?" she asked, careful not to look Judas in the eyes. "What if Caiaphas knew where and when Jesus would be alone, away from the crowds? Perhaps with only the twelve of you and a few of the women. Surely he could put together a force large enough to arrest him quietly. You could have your remaining men hidden in the area, ready to attack. You don't have enough men to win but that was never the goal anyway, right? All you need to do is start the fight and get the Romans to fight back. If Jesus were ever going to use his power to protect us and stake his claim to the throne by force, that would be the time. He would never let us die at the hands of Caiaphas and the Romans. All you have to do is come up with a plan to get Caiaphas and his men ready to move. He may think he is getting a nice quiet arrest, but you can see he gets a lot more."

Judas thought about it for several minutes, "How do you know when this will be, woman?"

I watched the muscles in Becky's jaw moving as she grit her teeth. She had a hard time swallowing the lack of respect from Judas.

Hang in there just a little longer, Beck.

"I was with Jesus today when he told Peter and John to prepare a place to eat the Passover meal," Becky said. "We were there today cleaning and preparing the food. I heard Jesus say he plans to take a few of us to the olive grove in Gethsemane to pray after the meal. It will be well into the night by then and deserted except for his closest friends."

Judas listened intently now.

Becky turned to me. "I have passed that way several times with Mary and Joanna, Thomas. It is secluded, and there are plenty of places for the men to hide."

I nodded.

After a few moments, Judas approached me and put his hand on my shoulder. "Well done, Thomas. We may have a chance after all." Then he walked past me toward Jerusalem.

I looked back at Becky. She was kneeling on the ground with her head in her hands. "What's wrong, Beck? That was great! Judas is going to do what he's supposed to do."

"Not exactly, Tommy," she muttered, looking up at me. "He's going to show up alright. But how will we stop his men from attacking the Romans when they arrest Jesus? This could still turn into a giant mess. Judas could still get his war. I just couldn't think of any other way to get him to return".

I sat next to her and pulled her close. In my excitement, I hadn't thought it through like she had. "Okay, you're right. That's going to be a problem."

"Yeah. And we've got less than forty-eight hours to solve it."

CHAPTER 35
Barabbas

Two days before Passover, Jesus acted more cautious than ever. He stayed immersed in the large crowd accompanying him from Bethany to Jerusalem. He remained in the open as he taught in the temple during the day. The exchange that day between him and the Pharisees was the most bitter ever.

"Everyone who is tired and troubled can come to me, and I will give you rest," Jesus told the crowd. "My yoke is easy to bear, and my load is light. But beware of the scribes and the Pharisees." He pointed at a group of about twenty who had taken their customary places in the front. "They love the places of honor and the best seats. Their goal is to control you and place a heavy load on your back without offering so much as a finger to help you."

"Who are you to challenge us?" one of them defied.

"I grieve for you, all of you," Jesus continued, ignoring the man's question. "You are such hypocrites. Do you think because you appear so proper on the outside that I cannot see you are dead on the inside? You wash the outside to look righteous to the people, but you are full of filth inside. You tithe the smallest thing and practice your religion to be seen by people, but ignore the important things of the law like justice and mercy. You call people to follow you, but you are so blind you cannot even find your own way, much less a way for others." Jesus stood and addressed the crowd, "Beware of these hypocrites." Then he left the temple for the last time and walked back to Bethany.

We spent the next morning with Martha, Mary, Lazarus, and Jesus's inner circle of friends in Bethany. The twelve were there along with Jesus's mother, Mary, and the women who had been with Jesus from the beginning: Joanna, Mary Magdalene, Suzanna, and Salome. Becky and Nathaniel's wife, who stayed with him after the teams of two returned, were also there along with Clopas and Mary, who arrived from Nazareth the night before.

Near midday, Jesus asked the women and Clopas to return to

Jerusalem and make final preparations for Passover while he spent the afternoon teaching and preparing us for what awaited.

Finally, he spoke. "My brothers, I leave you with my peace. Do not let your hearts be troubled or become fearful. I have told you many times I must go away. If you love me, you will be happy because I am going to the father. I have told you this before it happens so that when it does happen, you will believe. I say this so the world may know I love the Father and do exactly as he commands me. Now come, let us go from here."

The walk into Jerusalem that afternoon was solemn and quiet. Each of us dealt with Jesus's words in our own way. I hadn't had an opportunity to speak with Judas privately and was about to come up beside him when the sound of horses' hooves and soldiers shouting rang out behind us.

"Out of the way! Out of the way, I say, or we will run you down!"

When I looked behind me, there were two Roman soldiers mounted on leather-clad horses barreling down on us. We jumped out of the way to one side of the road or the other to let them pass. One of the mounted soldiers had a thick rope secured to one of four posts on his saddle and pulled a group of six men behind him. Three foot soldiers ran alongside them on either side. At the end of the rope, a large circular link connected to six shorter chains leading to the iron shackles on each man's wrists. As they were passing, one of the men fell, causing the others to pile on top of him, slowing the horse to a stop after dragging the men through the coarse rocks on the road for several yards. The foot soldiers were on them instantly, roughly pulling them to their feet, beating them with their fists.

Even though he was bleeding badly from his knees and elbow, one of the men tried to help his fellow prisoners escape from the soldier beating him.

"Back in line, Barabbas," a second soldier shouted before driving the butt of his sword into Barabbas's face , sending blood and teeth flying.

Barabbas went down on one knee, spitting blood and vomit on the ground.

The foot soldiers wrestled the rest of the prisoners to their feet and were about to reach Barabbas when Jesus stepped in front and helped Barabbas to his feet. They moved toward Jesus, then stopped as if a silent voice commanded them to be still. They stared at Jesus as he wiped the blood from Barabbas's face with the sleeve of his robe. When Jesus took his hands away, Barabbas's wounds were healed.

"You are the prophet," Barabbas touched his restored face and jaw. "The one who has all of Jerusalem boiling over."

"I am."

"I saw you from the rooftop outside the temple." Barabbas laughed. "A Roman centurion knelt before you like a puppy. We would have rallied to you that day if you had wanted to fight. We were ready."

"That is not why I came," Jesus answered softly.

"I know," Barabbas shook his head. "Micah told me as much before he left. He said he did not think it possible but now claims he has forgiven them, these Romans." Barabbas gestured at the soldiers. "I cannot. I will not."

When Jesus didn't answer, Barabbas leaned closer and whispered, "I know you have the power. Can you free me?" He raised his arms so Jesus could see his shackles.

"I will but not today," Jesus replied, turning away from Barabbas to join us on the side of the road.

The mounted soldier gave an order and the group continued down the road, through the gate, and into the city.

CHAPTER 36
Passover

When we arrived at the room Peter and John arranged for us and where Becky and the other women prepared the meal, we found a table in the middle of the room set for Jesus and the twelve of us. The others sat along the outer wall.

"Come, my brothers," Jesus said, pointing to the table. "I very much want to share this Passover before I am taken from you."

We found our places at the table. Judas and I sat next to each other across from Jesus.

"This will be the last Passover we will share until everything is fulfilled in my Father's Kingdom," Jesus announced, motioning to his mother and Salome to begin serving the food.

Jesus seemed unusually moody during the meal, one minute laughing as we shared stories of our adventures and the next minute drifting off as lost in thought, no doubt anticipating the travail that would begin in a few hours.

My apprehension was having a similar effect on me, and my stomach threatened to reject the meal I'd eaten. I knew Becky and I had done our best, but we still didn't know if it was enough or even if we'd done the right thing. Had we done what God sent us to do, or had we followed our instincts and done more harm than good? Had Judas succeeded in making the arrangements that would lead to Jesus's arrest tonight, or had he abandoned those plans and would be returning to Carioth as intended? Had he found enough men to fight, and if so, how would we stop them? I looked at Judas, but his face revealed neither excitement about his plan for starting a revolution nor disappointment that he failed to get Caiaphas to move against Jesus, possibly provoking retribution from the Romans.

Jesus's familiar words brought me back from the edge, "This cup is the new covenant in my blood. Share this with each other." He passed the cup to John. Then he picked up a piece of bread and declared, "This is my body, given for you. Remember me when you do this." He tore the bread in half and handed one piece to John and one to Peter. "But I tell you this, the one who will betray me is at this table and will share my bread."

When Jesus got up to share bread with the others in the room, Philip leaned in and whispered, "What does he mean 'betray him?' Betray him to who? The Romans?"

"Who could do such a thing?" Nathaniel asked. "Why would anyone do such a thing? What purpose could they have?"

"Whoever it is, they will have James and me to deal with," John warned.

"And me," Peter agreed, looking at each of us.

I stared back at him, wondering if it would be me who would betray Jesus. Or had I already done it? Not directly, but I made so many decisions to motivate Judas to betrayal it might count. Maybe I should have let Jesus know who I was as soon as I arrived in Galilee. Did keeping my secret change anything? Should I have allowed Judas to make his own decision without getting involved? But, if that was true, then why was I here, in this time? I felt panic rising when Jesus put the final nail in my emotional coffin.

He returned to the table after sharing the wine and bread with Clopas and the women. Then he addressed us, "Do you remember when I sent you out and told you not to take a money belt or bag or sandals?"

"Yes, Lord, we remember," Matthew answered for all of us.

"Did you lack anything as you went?"

Everybody shook their heads.

"No, nothing, Lord," John declared.

"Nothing," James added.

"But now, I am telling you something different so the Scriptures can be fulfilled. If you have a money belt, take it. Also, take your bag if you have one. And if you have no sword, now is the time to sell what you have and buy one."

I couldn't believe my ears. I looked at Becky, who appeared even more shocked. I watched as huge tears began to roll down her cheeks. In the short time she had been with the disciples, she came to love and believe in Jesus sincerely. She was always sitting at his feet with Mary Magdalene, Mary of Bethany, or Joanna when Jesus taught. We both embraced Jesus's message of love, peace, and forgiveness. Unlike the men, the women never believed Jesus's Kingdom would be established on this earth by force. Now, doubt and fear were written all over their faces. They held hands solemnly. Becky turned away from me and buried her face in Mary's shoulder.

"So what is written can be fulfilled, and I will be numbered among the transgressors," Jesus finished.

I had no idea what he meant. All I knew was the man of peace I had followed wanted us armed with swords. Why? Was Jesus planning to finally fight? It made no sense. I looked at Judas, whose eyes sparkled with new hope. Maybe we hadn't played Judas. Perhaps Becky and I had fallen into his trap. If I'd let Judas walk away and go home, there would be no one in Gethsemane tonight to arrest Jesus. No armed Romans to fight. No men hidden in the bushes. No reason for Jesus to use his power to protect us and establish his kingdom through violence. I should have known better. All I succeeded in doing was messing everything up.

Peter threw back his robe to reveal two swords held to his waist with a leather belt. "Lord, look, here are two swords."

Jesus looked at Peter, then at the swords and nodded. "It is enough." Then he turned and walked out the door.

How had I gotten it so wrong? What was I even doing here in the first place, if only to ruin everything?

I nearly jumped out of my skin when Peter gripped my arm and shoved one of the swords into my hand. I examined it skeptically. It looked more like a machete. The sword was poorly made and better suited for chopping wood or cutting meat than fighting. A farmer's tool more than a soldier's weapon. Peter's other sword remained on his belt, tucked under the folds of his garments. I wondered if later, Peter would use his or if I was going to have to use mine.

We followed Jesus into the darkness, quiet conversations

occasionally arising as we walked toward the Mount of Olives. I found Becky walking among the women toward the back.

"Where's Judas?" I asked.

She slowed to allow a little space between us and the others, "I saw him break away and head into the city after leaving the room. Do you think we should follow him?"

"No, our best shot at helping is if we stay with Jesus."

"What's happening, Tommy? Why do you have a sword? Why did Jesus tell us to have them?"

"I don't know, Beck. I've been thinking hard about it. It doesn't make any sense. Even if every one of us had two swords or ten swords, a company of Roman soldiers like the ones at the temple would still cut us to shreds. There's no way a bunch of fishermen and an ex-tax collector with two rusty blades could stand a chance against trained soldiers. Jesus knows that as well as I do. Even if Judas found a hundred armed men to wait in the garden, it wouldn't be enough to defeat a trained regiment of Roman soldiers." I searched for any explanation I could find and began to panic. "There's got to be another reason we don't understand. There's got to be. Maybe once we start the fight with the swords, Jesus intends to call on the winds and his angels and—"

"Tommy, no!" Becky cried, pulling me to a stop and looking up at me. "That can't be right. It can't be. Is that the man you've been following? Is that who Jesus has been? Who he is really?"

I stood there, captured by Becky's questions. They were the right questions. They were the only questions that mattered. And they were the questions I should have already asked myself.

It only took a moment to see it. And once I did and realized what I'd nearly done, shame overwhelmed me. I dropped to my knees on the side of the road. Dozens of times since Becky first arrived, I thought I knew why God had sent her. I remembered her asking the question on our wedding night, *But Tommy, why am I here?* I didn't know the answer then, but I sure did now. She was here to speak the truth and save me from making a fool of myself.

"You're right, Becky. That's not who Jesus is. Not at all." I thought about it for a few more minutes. "I almost made a horrible mistake

Becky. Thank you for helping me see it."

Becky kept staring at me. She knew I needed to get the rest out.

"Pastor Nelson warned me about it before I came here," I relived the sermon the pastor preached.

"Tell me." she encouraged.

"We often make judgments without having any idea why or understanding what's really going on." I laughed at how crazy the situation was. "And I should know that better than anyone. People have been judging me for two thousand years for something I said. Well, ah… what Thomas said. And they have no clue why he said it. And I just did the same thing."

"What, Tommy? What did you do?"

"I tried to make sense out of something that doesn't make sense. That's what people do, Beck. We want everything to be black or white. We have to have answers even when there are none. I don't know why Jesus told us to buy swords. But I know one statement that I can't explain doesn't change who Jesus is. I know him, Beck. I've been with him around the campfire, in the boat, on the road, and in the cities. I've watched him give his life every day to some of the neediest and most helpless people I have ever seen. I held him upright when he couldn't stand on his own any longer because one more person needed to be healed. I watched him laugh and tumble on the ground with children and listened to him weep alone at night because those he cared about were just not getting it. I know him, Becky. I know who he is, and I know what he is like and what he would do and not do because I've heard him teach it, and more importantly, I've watched him live it." I paused to take a breath, realizing the most important changes happening right then were the ones happening inside me. "And tonight, when he told us to go buy a sword, I forgot everything. I let one sentence I didn't understand distort everything I knew to be true and real. I imagined Judas was right all along and Jesus intended to fight the Romans instead of giving his life for them. I let one comment redefine everything I knew about Jesus."

Becky reached out and touched my face. "It's okay, Tommy."

I shook my head. "It may be forgivable, Beck, but it's not okay.

People will be doing exactly what I did tonight for the next two thousand years. They'll take one verse here or one verse there from a book they don't even understand and decide what Jesus is like. They'll read what's written about him, what scholars say about him, or what preachers preach about him, but they never spend enough time being with him to discover who he really is."

"Like you have."

"Yeah, Beck. Like I have. Like we have. But you know what? If Jesus is who he says he is, I don't think you have to travel back in time to be with him to discover what he's really like. You can do that anywhere, in any time, and in any place. He's the real timeless apostle, Becky, not me."

I looked up the path to the garden and didn't see anyone. I still had no idea what would happen over the next couple of hours. Things might disintegrate into chaos at any minute. Judas may have found a thousand men to hide in the garden. But the one thing I knew was Jesus would not fight. That's not who he was or why he came. He came to give his life, not take life.

I got up and reached for Becky's hand. "Come on. In a little more than an hour, Judas will be back with a bunch of very bad men and who knows what could happen then. Maybe you should head back to camp. Try to get the other women to go with you."

Becky laughed. "Don't be silly, Tommy. None of us are going to leave him now. Whatever happens tonight happens to all of us."

I knew by her tone trying to talk Becky into changing her mind would be a waste of time. I also knew she was right. Everything we'd been through led us to this moment. Whatever happened tonight, we would face it together. Once we reached the garden, we might be able to persuade Judas's men to abandon their plans. Beyond that, I had no idea what to do.

When we entered the garden, Jesus spoke to the other disciples, "Stay here and wait. I'm going to pray. Peter, John, James, would you come with me?"

"Yes, Lord," Peter answered as the four walked toward a low stone wall about thirty yards away. There Jesus knelt to pray.

The rest of us found a place to sit on the soft ground under the olive trees to wait as Jesus asked. Becky sat next to me while the other women clustered together a few feet away.

"Why does he always prefer those three," Philip asked, obviously unhappy with Jesus's choice. "We have been with him nearly as long as they have."

"You forget, Phillip," Salome said, moving to sit next to him. "He has known my sons since they were boys growing up together in Nazareth. They are blood. And as for Peter? Well, Peter is about to have a very painful night. I am sure Jesus wants him close for as long as possible to give him strength."

I looked at Salome, wondering how she knew Peter was going to have a painful night. I was about to ask when she put her fingers to her lips, shushing me like a little boy. I turned to Becky, but she was leaning back on the trunk of a tree with her eyes closed. I glanced around at the others and saw each of them were sleeping. Some were curled up on the ground with their cloaks pulled tightly around their shoulders. Others, like Becky, found a tree trunk to lean against. I looked back at Philip and found him snoring peacefully next to Salome, the anger gone from his face. I glanced over to where Jesus had taken Peter, John, and James. Jesus knelt beside the wall, one hand on his face, the other on the stones as though he needed the support to keep from collapsing. Peter, John, and James sat with their backs against the wall, sound asleep. The last thing I remember as I sat there clutching Peter's sword was the tiny smile on Salome's lips and the slight nod of her head.

Knock, knock, knock.

"Tommy, it's time to get up, honey."

EPILOGUE

Something soft and warm caressed my face as I woke. A subtle flowery fragrance replaced my wool cloak's harsh, musty smell.

Is that fabric softener? I wondered.

Knock, knock, knock.

"Tommy?"

I bolted upright, taking in my surroundings through blurry eyes: no grass, no olive trees, no bundled forms of sleeping men and women on the ground near me. My TV came into focus, and my backpack sat next to the door where I'd left it last night.

Last night? I spun my head around. *Where was Jesus? The wall? Peter, John, James? Where was Becky?*

Knock, knock, knock.

"Tommy? Are you alright? Becky's downstairs. She needs to see you right away. She says it's important."

"Becky?!" I threw off the covers and jumped out of bed, banging my knee hard. "Ow!" I cried out in pain.

"Tommy?"

"I'm fine, Mom! Tell Becky I'll be right down."

I looked down at the ancient iron blade in my bed.

Incredible. No, more like impossible!

I pulled the blankets up to cover it and bent down to rub my knee, my fingers coming away with a small streak of blood. I listened for the squeak at the top of the stairs, then made my way down the hall to the bathroom.

"What's going on?" I asked the face of Tommy Evans, looking back at me in the mirror. I touched my bare chin and felt the day-old patches of whiskers barely beginning to appear. I ran some cold water and splashed it on my face feeling the shivers it sent down my spine. Yesterday I could have bathed in a cold stream without a care, but... that was yesterday, wasn't it? Or was it? "What's going on?" I repeated.

Three years' worth of memories danced in my head. People and places as real as the sink cabinet and towel rack I held in my hand to keep myself from falling to the floor. Still, the face in the mirror refused to answer. I ran back to my bedroom and pulled open my backpack. The sandwiches I packed were as fresh as they were... yesterday?

Think, Tommy, THINK!

It appeared whatever happened to me, whatever I did, or wherever I had been and however long I'd been there, only about six or seven hours passed here. But there was also no question in my mind, I'd spent the last three years with Jesus and his disciples.

I bent down and rubbed my knee again.

No! I thought. *It was all very, very real.*

I reached over and pulled back the covers on the bed.

Still there! Yep, it's real!

I sat down on the edge of the bed and put my head in my hands. Peter's sword lay beside me on the bed, though it was covered in more rust than when I'd held it moments ago in Gethsemane. I needed to think. The last thing I remembered after walking into the garden with Becky was Jesus going off to pray with James, Peter, and John. But what happened after that? Had our plan worked? Did Judas show up? Did he kiss Jesus? Was Jesus arrested? Did Judas's men hidden in the garden attack when they arrested Jesus or did we restore the timeline to its original state? I pulled on my pants, went back to the bathroom, combed my hair and brushed my teeth, and walked downstairs to face...my wife?

Oh man, this was getting crazier and crazier.

When I turned the corner at the bottom of the stairs into the living room, the blond girl sitting on the couch with her hands gripped tightly between her knees glanced up at me. Neither of us could keep the shocked looks off our faces. For nearly a year, the raven-haired Rebecca of Bethsaida and the bearded Thomas the apostle had been married and traveling with Jesus as he taught and healed throughout Galilee and Judea. But this wasn't Rebecca; this was Becky, and Becky's nearly panic-stricken eyes were staring back at me, screaming a thousand questions.

"Hey Beck, what's happening?" I asked, way louder than I intended, which only intensified the look of terror on her face. "Come on. Let's go out back." I grabbed her hand, pulled her off the couch, and led her quickly through the dining room, past my wide-eyed parents sitting at the table. We walked out the sliding doors and onto the stone patio.

As soon as I pulled the doors closed, Becky threw her arms around my neck and wept. Heavy, shaking sobs rolled through her trembling body in waves. I held her for a long time, steadying her until she finally began to calm down, then led her to the picnic table where we sat together.

As I held her, I tried to imagine all the absurd questions going through her mind and how I would answer them. Was it real? Were we actually in Galilee with Jesus? Was I truly friends with Mary Magdalene, and Joanna, and Salome? How did we get back? Do you even know what I'm talking about? Am I crazy? Oddly, I couldn't have been more wrong.

When she finally wiped her eyes on the sleeve of my T-shirt, she pulled away, took my hands, and looked into my eyes. "Do you still love me, Tommy? Me, not Rebecca?"

It was my turn to become choked up. If, after all we'd seen and been through together, this was her most important question? I knew she was the woman I wanted to spend the rest of my life with. "Yes, Of course I do, Becky. I would tell you I love you now more than ever, but it would be a lie, and I've given up lying forever. I could not possibly love you more today than I did yesterday. And I will never be able to love you more than I do this very second. I can promise I will always love you. I know you already said yes to me once, Becky, but will you marry me... again?"

Becky started to laugh. Then I began to laugh. Somewhere in the laughter, I think I heard her say "yes." I know I saw her nod, and then we laughed some more. We threw our arms around each other again, and I did what I said should never be done. I gave Becky one of those kisses strictly reserved for married people. Well, we were married... kind of.

"I need to take you to my bedroom," I said when we finally parted.

Becky's eyes grew as big as saucers. "Ah... Tommy, I know we were married in... well, before, but do you think—"

"No, no, I didn't mean...oh come on. It's important." I grabbed her hand and dragged her back into the house, where my parents were still sitting at the table. We walked past them, up the stairs, and into my room.

As I closed the door, I pointed to a spot on the floor in front of the bed, "Now stand right there." Then I grabbed the sheet and blanket on my bed and pulled them back.

Becky gasped.

Lying on the bed, a rusty, machete-style sword with a small drop of my blood on the blade sat on top of the sheet.

Becky took my arm, staring down at the ancient weapon. "It was real, wasn't it, Tommy? We were there. We were with Jesus! And each and every one of the others!"

"Yeah, we were Beck. That's the sword Peter gave me last night. I don't know how but we were definitely there."

I felt Becky tense before releasing my arm. She walked over to look out the window. "The world looks the same as it did when we left, Tommy. Does that mean we did good? That the story stayed the same? Was Jesus arrested and killed and then rose like he said he would?"

The answer to that question ate at me too. "Come on," I grabbed Becky's hand again. "There's only one way to find out." We ran down the stairs to the living room. There were at least a dozen copies of the Bible on the bookshelf left of the fireplace. I grabbed an NIV and headed for the picnic table again. A suspicious look crossed my parents' faces as we passed them this time. Or maybe they were shocked to see me with a Bible in my hand. Whatever the reason, I gave them my best "it's okay; don't worry, I'm fine" smile and slid the door closed behind us again.

We sat side by side at the picnic table as I leafed through the Bible as quickly as I could. I found the verse I was looking for and read out loud while Becky followed along.

"While Jesus was still speaking, Judas, one of the twelve arrived, guiding a detachment of soldiers and some officials from the chief priests and the Pharisees. They were carrying torches, lanterns, and weapons. Now the betrayer arranged a signal with them, 'The one I kiss is the man; arrest him.' Going at once to Jesus, Judas said, 'Greetings, Rabbi!' and kissed him.

"Then the men stepped forward, seized Jesus, and arrested him. With that, one of Jesus's companions reached for his sword, drew it out, and struck the servant of the high priest, cutting off his ear."

"Oh no!" Becky exclaimed, covering her mouth to keep from laughing. "It must be Peter."

"Yeah, it was Peter, alright, but it's okay, Beck. Jesus takes care of it." I flipped a few more pages and showed her where Jesus healed the man's ear.

"What happened after?" Becky asked.

I turned a few pages and scanned through to the end of the chapter. "It doesn't look like anything changed. Everything happened the way it was supposed to."

Becky shook her head. "No, something's wrong, Tommy. Why didn't they attack?"

"You mean Judas's men?"

"Yeah, wasn't that his plan all along? Even if he could only get a handful of men to be there, it would have been enough to change the story. What were they waiting for? They should have made their move as soon as they tried to arrest Jesus. They should have attacked the minute Judas kissed him or when Peter drew his sword. No, Tommy, something doesn't make sense. We didn't do anything to change Judas's mind, and we were gone before we could stop his men from attacking. What changed?"

"They were never there." I looked up to see my mother at the door. She turned back and said something to Dad, then closed the door behind her. She walked over and sat across from Becky and me.

"Who was never where?" I asked, chills running up and down my spine again. "What do you mean they were never there? Who, Mom? How do you—"

Becky put her fingers on my lips to silence me.

"Who were you?" Becky asked, her eyes sparkling with wonder. "Which one of the women were you?"

My mother smiled a familiar-looking smile but ignored Becky's question. "The men Judas counted on, the few remaining in Jerusalem he arranged to be there were gone by the time he got to the garden with the priests and soldiers to arrest Jesus. They left Jerusalem and went home."

"Wait! What? How do you know they—"

Becky raised her hand to silence me again. "What happened, Clair?" she urged again. "We were worried that persuading Judas to return to Jerusalem might have been the wrong choice because he was still trying to start a revolution. But getting him to return to Jerusalem needed to happen, right?"

I couldn't believe my ears. Just like in Bethsaida, as soon as Becky saw the puzzle laid out in front of her, she was able to put it together and move on. Meanwhile, I still struggled to accept the idea my mother may have been there with us the whole time.

Mom thought for a few moments, then nodded and began her story, "You were called to make sure Judas stayed in Jerusalem and followed through with his original plan. You gave him enough hope when you caught up with him on the road to get him to return and set up Jesus's arrest. Judas thought there were still enough men left to get the Romans to attack and cause Jesus to protect everyone with his power."

"There should have still been more than enough rebels in the city," I insisted. "What happened to them? Why weren't they in the garden?"

"Micah and Barabbas."

"Micah and Barabbas? How?"

Mom smiled that familiar smile again. "Well, after Jesus

encountered the centurion leaving the temple, many of the rebels left. Some left Jerusalem altogether, but most of them, especially Simon the Zealot's men, mingled with the crowds to hear Jesus teach in Lazarus's courtyard or in the temple that last week. By the end of the week, they were followers of Jesus".

"One of the men who left for home was your friend, Micah. But he returned the day before Passover and preached night and day, persuading everyone who would listen that Jesus's Kingdom could not be won through violence but only through love and forgiveness. He was very successful and won many to the Kingdom of God.

"The few rebels who remained in Jerusalem were followers of the outlaw Barabbas. When the story of Jesus healing Barabbas reached them, it was all Micah needed to persuade them to become disciples. By the time Judas arrived at the garden, the men he counted on to be there had either gone home to share the good news with their families or were gathered with Micah in the upper room praying."

"Amazing," I said.

"What happened to Judas, Clair?" Becky asked.

Mom reached across the table, picked up the Bible with one hand, and held Becky's hand with the other. When she found the place she was searching for she read, "When Judas, who had betrayed him, saw Jesus was condemned, he was seized with remorse and returned the thirty pieces of silver to the chief priests and the elders. He threw the money into the Temple and left. Then he went away and hanged himself."

We sat in silence for a long time.

I always knew how the story ended for Judas. But having known him personally, having served with him, having been the one responsible for convincing him to return to Jerusalem and follow through with his plan to entice Jesus to use his power to liberate Israel...it changed everything. Judas made a lot of mistakes. He misinterpreted almost all of Jesus's words and intentions, like so many others. He believed in a self-serving, temporary, earthly kingdom instead of the eternal Kingdom Jesus came to bring. Those mistakes, along with a bit of help from Becky and me, had cost him his life. And sadly like Doubting Thomas, those mistakes would be the defining moments in his forever story. No one would remember Thomas's statement of loyalty, "Let us go to Jerusalem and die beside him," nor would anyone wonder what great things Judas might have done in the three years he spent as one of Jesus's closest friends. Thomas would always be the doubter and Judas the betrayer. I listened to Becky cry quietly beside me and wondered if she was the first person in human history to weep over the death of the traitor Judas Iscariot.

I put my arm around her and pulled her close.

She looked at me with red, puffy eyes. "Was it worth it?" she asked, laying her head on my shoulder.

We both looked up when my mom began to quote from one of the gospels. I thought she read from the Bible again, but when I turned toward her, I realized she was actually reliving the story she'd been a part of. "It was very early on the first day of the week." she began. "Just after sunrise, and we were on our way to the tomb when Mary asked, 'Who will roll the stone away from the entrance of the tomb for us?' But when we looked up, we saw the stone had already been rolled away.

"When we entered the tomb, we were startled by a young man dressed in a white robe sitting on the right side. 'Don't be alarmed,' he said. 'You are looking for Jesus the Nazarene, who was crucified. He is not here. He has risen! Now go and tell his disciples and Peter, He has risen, and he is going ahead of you into Galilee. You will see him there, just as he told you.'" She squeezed Becky's hand. "Oh yes, Rebecca, it was very much worth it. For you, Thomas, me, and the whole wide world."

Mom got up from the table and headed for the door.

"Mom, wait. There are so many questions. Can you—"

"No, Tommy, I can't. You're going to need to be patient. Your answers will have to come from the same place you've been getting them the last three years." Then she smiled. "Besides, Becky and I, and her mom, have a wedding to plan."

Becky looked up at my mom's outstretched hand. She joined her, and they put their arms around one another.

Walking away, Mom added, "Oh, and in the meantime, you and your father have some serious work to do. There's a lot of forgiving and healing that needs to happen between you two before your next mission."

"Next mission?!" I gasped, jumping up from the table.

But they had already turned and gone inside.

www.ingramcontent.com/pod-product-compliance
Lightning Source LLC
Chambersburg PA
CBHW020758190726
48285CB00006B/2082

9 781953 263216